Neon Hemlock Press
www.neonhemlock.com
@neonhemlock

We're Here: The Best Queer Speculative Fiction 2023
Edited by Darcie Little Badger
and Series Editor Charles Payseur

Cover Illustration by Dan Rossi
Cover Design by dave ring
Interior Design and Layout by dave ring

Paperback ISBN-13: 978-1-952086-95-3
Ebook ISBN-13: 978-1-966503-03-3

WE'RE HERE
THE BEST QUEER SPECULATIVE FICTION 2023

Neon Hemlock Press

NEON HEMLOCK

We're Here 2023

EDITED BY DARCIE LITTLE BADGER
& CHARLES PAYSEUR

A Note From the Series Editor

I think the first story I read by Darcie Little Badger was "Nkást íí" from *Strange Horizons* in December 2014, not long after I started reviewing speculative fiction. And in short order she became one of my favorite authors, with amazing works like "Black, Their Regalia" from *People of Colo(u)r Destroy Science Fantasy* and "Owl vs. The Neighborhood Watch" (which won one of my short lived Sippy Awards). Her works highlight community and connections, featuring memorable (and often LGBTQIA+) characters who find hope pinned in on all sides by danger. Since then she's become a star novelist and comic book writer as well, with works like *Elatsoe* cementing her place as a powerful voice in speculative fiction. Which hasn't slowed her down a bit when it comes to short stories, luckily for me and fans of the form. In 2023 she was featured in a number of publications and anthologies, which sadly we couldn't consider for inclusion here because of her being the guest editor, but which were awesome all the same. Readers will definitely want to track those down, and be ready for more works in the future. And of course, we're incredibly honored to have her selecting the works to feature in this anthology!

2023 was a full year for queer short speculative fiction. And it was another where we received more submissions through our submission portal than any year previous, hitting almost 400. Added to that was my own reading, and it means we've considered over 750 works for this year's *We're Here*. Which is quite a statement, and a reason

we continue to champion queer stories, because for all that
we continue to face legislation and rhetoric that seeks to
push queerness back into the closet and out of public life,
these stories affirm that queerness is here and fantastic,
exploring the possibilities of storytelling in innovative and
exciting ways.

That said, 2023 wasn't without its setbacks or losses.
Fantasy Magazine, from which we featured two stories in
the 2022 *We're Here*, shuttered operations, while *Anathema*,
a publication dedicated to stories and poems by queer
people of color, has remained on hiatus the entire year.
On the brighter side, 2023 also saw *Prismatica* come
out of hiatus with new issues, and new publications
like *Small Wonders* have launched with an enthusiastic
inclusion of queer stories. *Baffling* Magazine, another
queer-specific publication, has continued to thrive. Add
to that LGBTQIA+ specific anthologies like *Bound in
Flesh: An Anthology of Trans Body Horror* edited by Lor
Gislaso, *Luminescent Machinations: Queer Tales of Monumental
Invention* edited by Rhiannon Rasmussen and dave
ring, *Kaleidoscope: A Queer Anthology 2023*, and the queer
speculative landscape is vibrant indeed.

I also made the concerted effort to read and consider
more work from anthology and print sources, of which
there were a number of great sources in 2023. Bogi Takács
edited the very queer *Rosalind's Siblings*, while *New Suns
2, Never Whistle at Night, Wilted Pages: An Anthology of Dark
Academia, Book of Witches,* and more each featured some
great LGBTQIA+ fiction. Indeed, four of the stories to
make it into *We're Here* this year come from anthologies,
which is the most we've had in a volume so far.

Digging further into the table of contents shows that
we've selected fourteen stories from twelve different
publications—*Lightspeed* and *Worlds of Possibility* both got
two stories each in. It's actually the first time that we've
featured a work from regular publications *Tales & Feathers,
Augur, Prismatica,* and *CatsCast.* At fourteen, this is the

shortest table of contents so far for *We're Here*, probably because there's a record five novelettes (stories between 7500 and 17500 words), much more than 2020's three and 2021 and 2022 which had only one each. On balance, there's also three stories under 2000 words, which is down a bit from last year's high water mark of six, but is still more than either 2021's one or 2020's zero. We do have one returning author to *We're Here*, Sharang Biswas, who was in the 2021 volume, amid thirteen new-to-us authors. It's also the first time we've featured a translation that I'm aware of, though some we've published might have been translated by their authors originally, as H. Pueyo's "A Study in Ugliness" in the 2021 volume appeared in translation in the author's 2022 collection of the same name.

After three years of writing these introductions, there's a part of me that wonders if I'll ever get to write something like "everything was awesome, and nothing hurt" and leave it at that. Until then, though, I like to use this space not only to reaffirm my own reasons and drive for being a part of this project, but to remind readers that for all our work proves that queer stories are being told across the genre and beyond, it's always work that feels fragile. Watching democracies around the world turn against freedoms of expression in favor of censorship, suppression, and prejudice is hardly a heartening thing, and while there are moments of joy and fortifying hope when this or that nation doesn't turn hard into fascism, there are plenty of reminders that when freedom of expression begins to slip, it's always queer voices that are silenced first.

And in the face of that, we're here. We're here in the stories we tell, that resonate long after the words are first put to paper, or first read out from there. These stories are histories. Are inspirations. Are warnings. Are whispers of comfort against a night that presses in cold and hard from all sides. These stories gain power and meaning in the sharing of them, and it is my honor and privilege to be able to do just that. To help them reach a little further, to find those that might need them. These are stories from writers from all over the world, to readers all over the world. Limited by the language in which we present them but part of a larger and multilingual conversation, preservation, and celebration. That dawn may come and we might find new and heartbreaking absences. But that the stories read on, as long as we can share them, with the promise that has kept us going since we started this project. Thank you all for being a part of it.

Charles Payseur
September 2024
Eau Claire, WI

A Note from the Editor

As a guest editor, I was delighted by the sheer breadth of stories to cross my desk. Turn the page. You'll find magic and science; heartbreak and joy; comedy, adventure, horror, and romance. Some characters live in our world (past, present, and future iterations). Or they're from distant galaxies. Or their homeland doesn't exist in our universe at all.

But despite the variety in genre, theme, tone and voice, each story shines a light on the human condition (even when the characters aren't technically human). That's the uniting power of this anthology. Within the lgbtqia+ community, there are innumerable experiences, all important. These stories reflect both our diversity and our shared humanity.

In *Mandy and Lulu Welcome Walter*, a cat makes waves in the lives of married vampires.

The young king of *Three Nights in Orissa* must defend his home from a powerful—and seductive—threat.

Lovesick Ada of *The Ng Yut Queen* makes a deal with the goddess of mercy.

The protagonist of *Sentience* wrestles with their grief on a planet-sized, sentient library.

While in *Eulogy for a Brother, Resurrected*, the characters outright defy death.

✂ *Braid Me a Howling Tongue* weaves a tale of survival in a prison with deadly hunts and other horrors.

✂ In a post-apocalyptic world, Temesghen of *Mama uat-ur* is enticed by a waterwoman of the sea.

✂ For the protagonist of *The Birds I Pull*, feelings take on a new life.

✂ Vani must coexist with an assertive ghost in *Please Mind the Poltergeist*.

✂ Astronauts juggle the complexities of love and scientific discovery in *Morning Star Blues*.

✂ Similarly, in *Promise in Bronze*, trust and affection grow between the trader Kalaa and a newcomer named Mishrakeshi.

✂ In *A Record of Lost Time*, a miraculous product called FastForward may come with unintended consequences.

✂ Monsters—both human and inhuman—exist within the pages of *Parásito*.

✂ While *Baobab Lover* is a gentle story of a dryad in America.

And now, I'll let the stories speak for themselves. But know this, dear reader: you're welcome here.

Darcie Little Badger
November 2024
California

We're Here 2023

Table of Contents

A Note From the Series Editor by Charles Payseur
A Note From the Editor by Darcie Little Badger

❖

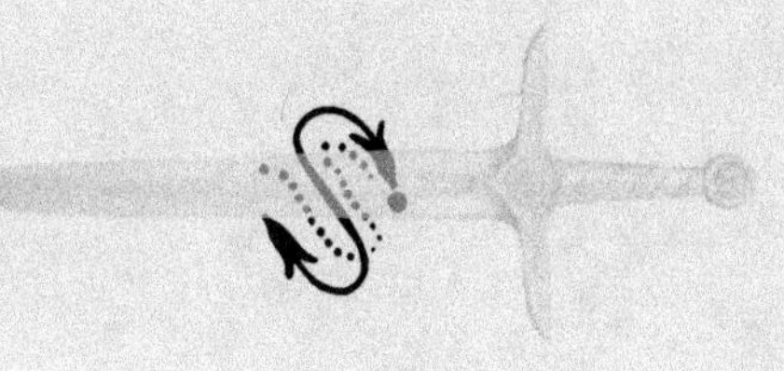

❖

About Our Contributors
Story Acknowledgements
About the Editors / About the Press

A Promise in Bronze

Ash Arya

*J*UST AS THE *wheel of Time neither stops nor slows down for anyone, so does the soul of Time neither melts nor is moved by individual events and actions. Time watches passively as civilizations come and go, letting Nature take over in the wake of one to clean house for the next. It's then up to those who inhabit this dominion of Time to leave their mark upon it.*

◆

KALAA APPRECIATED THE sight of the arcade, abuzz once more. The citadel walls were whole again, taller than before. The floodwaters that'd invaded the lower city were gone, the Sumerians who'd been asked to delay their monthly visit were back. It was time for business again.

"It's very hot, sweetling." Kalaa caught a petite claw reaching for her famed mango pudding, blowing on the earthen vessel to convey her point. "Why don't we wait for your Elder to pay for it while it cools down?"

She beamed as the boy ran and fetched an older woman, probably a mother. A merchant ought to know the speech of her customers and Kalaa deemed herself a *thorough trader.*

A thorough trader thriving in one of the largest urban centers of the Harappan world, at that.

At noon, panting between plating a loaf of venison and stirring the meat-and-herbs stew, Kalaa marveled at the seemingly endless influx of traders. *This* was the kind of deluge she appreciated.

Two more days of such footfall and I shall finally be able to commission some bangles...

"Excuse me. Please..." a rough voice, bordering on despair, cut through Kalaa's mental bookkeeping. She turned to see a broad-shouldered woman, a few years her senior, dressed in a knee-length wrap and a breastband that suited her curvaceous body all too well. She wore a new-looking pair of jute shoes but was entirely devoid of ornaments. Not even a headdress to cover those flowing locks, matted from travel. "I was told I could get some food here," stuttered she.

Kalaa assumed a smug look, "Even if you hadn't been *told*..." She pointed to the array of dishes, prepared and unprepared, then smiled awkwardly, loathing herself for her idiotic response.

But the stunning foreigner was unheeding of Kalaa's buffoonery, herself in the throes of hesitance. "I have nothing to trade. Gave my last quartz to secure passage on the ship."

An intrigued Kalaa immediately wanted to prod into the foreigner's story. But the thorough-trader-Kalaa only asked, "Didn't they give you any food along the way?"

"They did. I just," the foreigner tarried somewhat reluctantly, "ate it all."

Kalaa smiled to ease the sting of her embarrassed confession. "I enjoy food too."

The relief in the foreigner's round, brown eyes made Kalaa's heart skip a beat. For a second she considered offering the woman some food for free.

A thorough trader except when confronted by a dazzling woman, her own voice taunted.

Behind the woman, a queue was building up. Kalaa thought fast while scooping up some pudding and dolloping it on a circular vessel she'd made out of banyan leaves. "I can't just give you free food," she whispered, subtly indicating the prying ears. She couldn't risk the whole shipload of foreigners walking up to her with sob stories in exchange for free food.

"Of course not," the traveler flushed, announcing loudly, "I mean to pay you back."

Kalaa's brow puckered. Debts were something which the city traders only accepted of native citizens. It was unheard of to extend credit even to a fellow Harappan who came from outside the citadel. A *foreigner* then was a dubious gamble. "What, on your next visit?"

"No, I..." The traveler hesitated some more before sighing and declaring. "I'm here to stay."

"Stay?" Kalaa wondered if she'd gotten her word-meanings mixed up, only to realize that the words weren't spoken in the foreigners' language but *hers.* "Why?"

The traveler now addressed only her, in *her* Harappan dialect.

"The *priestess* said this is where I belong. That this is where I'll find a home."

"Priestess?" Kalaa echoed, unfamiliar with the lone foreign word the traveler had used amidst a rather fine flow of Harappan ones. Kalaa only now noticed that her skin too appeared darker than the other foreigners. Closer to her own...

"Important woman," explained the traveler, "Wise woman."

Despite her curt words, Kalaa caught the vulnerability in her eyes. She nodded, whispering in Harappan,

"Well, if a wise woman sent you." Then, squaring her shoulders, she spoke loudly in Sumerian, "Even though you're *staying*, I still can't give you free food. I *can* give you however, a chance to earn your keep. You can help me and get yourself a meal of your choosing."

A slight smile appeared on the traveler's drawn face. "I can pick anything?"

Kalaa nodded, amused. "Know that the duration of your service will be weighed against your purchases." As the woman eagerly accepted her terms and asked for some mango pudding, Kalaa felt a strange sense of pride in herself and her work. Trying to keep her tone light, she taunted, "Quite the taste you have. I should inform you this is my priciest dish and alone will cost you the entirety of an hour's service."

"That's fine," the woman laughed, her first, "I shall pay for it with unmatched assistance."

She did. By sundown, not only had Kalaa taken full advantage of the foreigners' influx, rather she'd done so with novel precision. One that took her a step closer to her beautiful bronze bangles. She told the foreigner— *Mishrakeshi*—as much when she closed shop.

◈

MISHRAKESHI GLEEFULLY ACCEPTED her day's last earnings, barley cakes and chicken soup.

The slim Harappan girl watched intently as she bagged her dinner, twirling a lock of curly hair on a long finger as she asked, "Where will you stay? I don't suppose you have lodgings?"

Her hands froze on her jute satchel. She panicked, until she saw a gleam in Kalaa's eyes. "I'm petrified of incurring more debt from you," she jested, bones aching from the day's work.

Not that Kalaa looked any less fatigued. "Yet, it's inevitable. You won't find work right away, outsider that you are. But you *will* need food tomorrow..." she trailed off, probably having noticed her wince. Yet, she boldly asked, "You didn't think this through, did you?"

Mishrakeshi sighed, mumbling only, "They didn't want me there," before pursing her lips anew.

She couldn't bear to speak of it, even to a near-stranger. The priestess had told her to forget her otherness and talking about it was certainly not the way to do so.

It was then somewhat relieving to hear Kalaa say, "You can stay at my house."

Equal parts surprised and fatigued, Mishrakeshi accepted the offer at once.

Soon they were immersed in the crowd exiting the arcade in the upper-city and fanning out into the many rectilinear lanes leading into the residential lower-city. Rows and columns of double-storied houses organized in straight lines, each street a systematic replica of the other.

Trees lined the sidewalks which were separated from the middle path with a...very narrow tunnel with dark water flowing through it.

"What are these tunnels...these cracks?" Mishrakeshi was unsure if these were the right words.

Kalaa though easily articulated her confusion. "Drains. They often surprise the foreigners."

"*Drains*? What are they for?"

"They carry away the sewage from the houses. Wastewater, human refuse, and such."

The very idea produced galling images in Mishrakeshi's head. "You defecate in your homes?"

"Not just anywhere!" Kalaa exclaimed back. "We have a room for it. A very small room with a very small hole in it and that's the *only* place we relieve ourselves in."

Mishrakeshi felt both stupid and confused as she mumbled, "Oh."

Kalaa scoffed, "Never ask this to anyone else or you won't be *belonging* here anytime soon."

Despite Kalaa's lack of malice, her words hurt and Mishrakeshi couldn't hide her sorrow.

Kalaa hurriedly changed the subject. "My house is just in the next street. Luckily for you, I've just moved out of my parental home and in with my sisters. Or else you'd be answering a dozen questions from each one of my six parents."

Mishrakeshi tripped over her own feet. "How many—"

"Err...six. Two Mas, four Pitas." Kalaa answered, steadying her by the elbow. "It's called a family," she pressed. "They aren't all always there—"

"How do you tell who your real Ma and Pita are? I'm just curious." Mishrakeshi asked after due consideration. *It isn't rude if it's coming from a place of genuine curiosity,* she told herself. *And if there's no place for my curiosity here then it's doubtful there'd be a place for me.*

Kalaa, thankfully, was unperturbed. "They all are."

"But—biologically?" she let the question hang, giving Kalaa the option to ignore her enquiry.

At length, the dark-eyed girl shrugged. "What does it matter?"

That meagre but earnest reply reduced Mishrakeshi's apprehensions a great deal.

So, matching Kalaa's smile as they resumed their walk, she prodded, "How many sisters?"

"Two," Kalaa chirped. "Ameeyati and Sabrivalla."

"Just two?" Mishrakeshi smirked, "I was preparing myself to greet a house full of gorgeous Harappan belles like yourself." She felt the embarrassment from those words only when a blush travelled over Kalaa's round face and colored her high cheekbones.

Yet, Kalaa sounded unfazed, "You still should. For, between Amee Didi's sworn partners and Sabri's lover visiting, we do have a full house. I hope you won't mind?"

Mishrakeshi instantly shook her head. "I've lived in crammed spaces all my life. I'm just so grateful you'd let me intrude upon your space..." Ever mediocre with words, she took Kalaa's hand and clasped it between both of hers, hoping to convey how she valued her kindness.

The girl only jested, "I need not your gratitude, Mishri ji, for I have your impeccable assistantship. I shall like to avail of it as long as I can. It's been a pleasure to meet you."

Mishrakeshi suspected, or hoped, those last words to be more than a jest.

She, on her part, replied earnestly, "Likewise."

◈

KALAA ADMIRED MISHRAKESHI's unending surprise over the city's workings. In the last six days, she'd used her leisure hours to show Mishrakeshi most of their metropolis. From the Great Granary to the cattle farms and foundries in the upper city, to the Gathering Circles where the elders convened, and the fields on the periphery of the lower city. Mishrakeshi loved it all.

So, last night, Kalaa took her along on her jaunt to the bronzesmith—having finally collected enough bronze to have herself made a small set of bangles. Four, was what she ultimately obtained. They felt like forty. Moreover, the place gladdened Mishrakeshi beyond expectations.

The only place Kalaa had left to show her was the one she was taking her to now.

The ceremony to thank Mother Nature for giving them enough strength to cope with the flood. The celebratory ritual at the Great Bath.

"So many people. Everyone looks so enthusiastic," Mishrakeshi murmured.

Seeing her glee, Kalaa refrained from saying that there were actually *fewer* people than usual. This month's flood, the third this year, had made three whole families migrate to the relative security of Lothal. It petrified Kalaa to see people she'd known all her life leaving so abruptly.

"So what do we do in this ceremony—" Mishrakeshi's question was cut off by a gasp, just as they rounded the high wall encompassing the Great Bath. She gaped wide-eyed at the rectangular stepwell, slowly taking in the people descending into the freshwaters.

"Come along," Kalaa nudged her when she remained frozen, removing her jewels, and placing the ensemble among a heap on one of the dry, top slabs. "We're to join them."

"Join them?" the alarm in Mishrakeshi's voice made Kalaa halt. "Like so?" she demanded, indicating Kalaa's tiny form, naked save the cowry-string around her neck and the wrap around her waist.

Kalaa perceived discomfort on her new friend's part. "That's the ritual," she cautiously drawled, adding quickly, "You don't have to—"

"Good," Mishrakeshi inserted, "Because I shan't."

Kalaa cocked her head to a side, "Might I ask why?"

"Why?" Mishri echoed wide-eyed, "They'll all *look*. That's why!"

Kalaa couldn't contain the ensuing scoff. "You are pretty, Mishri ji. But not that much. They're here for Ma Nature, not you. Even if they needed diversion, they each have their own," she indicated the paired off youths and adults who comprised the majority of the gathering.

Mishrakeshi, though, was unmoved. "I shall wait for you here to finish your ritual," she declared, fisted hands crossed over her chest.

Kalaa laughed. "Very well. Maybe next time."

"Not unless Ma Nature herself drags me by the scruff of my neck and shoves me into that pool."

Kalaa winced. "Oh, careful what you wish for. There are just too many stairs there. Maybe we could ask Ma Nature to give you enough courage and inclination to come voluntarily."

"Sounds unlikely."

"So does a wanderer finding a home. You managed that well enough."

A startled Mishrakeshi frowned incredulously. "Have I?"

Kalaa simply took her hand and placed her bangles on it. "Take care of my hard-earned treasure until I return, won't you?" She dashed away without giving Mishrakeshi a chance to respond.

❖

MISHRAKESHI GAWKED AFTER Kalaa as she carefully descended the wet steps and joined five youths sporting on a deep end of the pool.

She couldn't fathom how they felt no apprehensions, no fear of prying eyes, frolicking like that.

However, she soon realized that true to Kalaa's claims, there was no disconcerting ogling.

But they'd look at me, for I'm different, Mishrakeshi's brain prompted, recalling the sad sight of the villagers bidding her adieu. They'd grieved her departure but deemed it inevitable. For she had a wanderer's blood. Gritting her teeth, she recalled the Priestess' words:

Forget you are different and different you no longer will be. Craft your belonging and all the universe shall aid you in becoming worthy.

Mishrakeshi wondered if the old woman had only said those words to ease her pain, to give her hope long enough to get her out of their village. But then her gaze fell on the bangles in her hand. Seeing them, she understood. Whether by fate or by sheer stupidity, this was where she now was. These were the people who'd taken her into their city, the girl who'd fed her and given her shelter, the youths who now waved to her from the pool. Waving back, she smiled down at the bangles.

Perhaps she could make the Priestess' words come true.

❖

KALAA PESTLED THE lapis lazuli in the noon's silence, admiring the blue stone being pulverized while Amee Didi prepared the resin and the beeswax to make the dye for her shop.

The foreign traders never tired of the blue brilliance. Nor did Kalaa.

"What's going on with that foreigner-not-foreigner of yours? A quaint creature, that one." Amee Didi broke the silence.

"She *is*," Kalaa gleefully agreed, recalling all she'd seen and heard from the aspiring Harappan in the last two weeks, ending with, "Do you know what she did yesterday?"

Didi theatrically shoved away her equipment and placed her chin on one hand.

Kalaa laughed and began. "You heard of the travelers from the far-off country, yes? Tall, broad shouldered, males all," she squeezed her nose. "The arcade was awash with them, but none could understand what they wanted. For an entire hour, trade was sluggish. I was losing all hope of business when, lo and behold, Mishri ji begins yelling at the top of her lungs. Gibberish that means nothing to me. But it meant something to the foreigners who began ambling towards my stall. In no time, I was running to prepare more pudding, more stew, more *everything*. Other vendors came to borrow *Mishri*—"

"Quite the wonder," Amee Didi cut in, smiling crookedly, "So, you gave her the day off?"

"She quite deserves it." Kalaa felt compelled to add, "I don't always need assistance. Actually, I never needed it before she showed up. Besides, she needs time, to secure herself the apprenticeship she's been eyeing. Leena, the bronzesmith, is a tough nut to crack."

"Right, and how'd she do that between working with you until late noon and loitering around the city with you until sunset."

Kalaa frowned, "I'm just showing her around."

"And dragging her to community rituals. Baths and dances and whatnot."

"Someone must. She's new here."

"And bringing her to family dinners."

"Well, the woman wants so badly to belong—" Kalaa bit her lip, mortified. "I've said nothing."

"Yes, you have. Explain?" Amee Didi raised a brow. "Either you tell me, and we pestle this down with the blue or I ask her—"

"Don't you dare," Kalaa pointed the pestle threateningly at Didi, then sighed, "It's just something she said. *Refusing* vehemently to say more." It was the truth, for despite her unsubtle prodding, Mishrakeshi persistently shot down all her enquiries about her life in Sumer.

As if reading her disappointment, Didi threw a piece of resin at her, saying, "Best not to prod. She'll share it with you if she sees you as worthy."

Those words made a nest in Kalaa's mind. "You're actually right," she mumbled. She didn't know what'd be *worthy* in Mishrakeshi's eyes, but she dearly hoped she'd be it, someday.

◆

MISHRAKESHI WOKE ONE morning, three months into her stay at the apprentices' residence, with a dreadful realization.

She'd spent an entire month living under Kalaa's roof, often eating a meal beyond her daily earnings. She'd used Sabri's cinnabar to paint her face and Amee's lapis lazuli to dye her skirt.

And she'd never repaid the pudding-girl or her sisters for any of it! That had to be remedied.

She had to give Kalaa something. And she wanted it to be something special, at least for her if not for her sisters. Her best piece of work perhaps?

But artistic grandeur isn't something to be coerced into existence by agitated minds.

Which is why, when she went to meet Kalaa the next day at one of the Gathering Circles in the lower city, Mishrakeshi brought her, not a seminal work of art but just some two dozen varieties of that "bangle" ornament that she admired so much, clumsily bundled up in her spare garment.

Unable to come up with anything truly ingenious, she'd simply melted her practice bronze, collected over months, to make those bangles, engraved with commonplace motifs.

She hadn't expected them to make Kalaa squeal until passersby began to eye them askance.

"But these are just brilliant! All the bangles I could want! And how finely you've engraved all these motifs onto them."

"It's really rather amateurish," Mishrakeshi stuttered, looking around in embarrassment.

"Rubbish! I've never seen such craftsmanship. I would've said so the other day itself when you brought me those *bowls* to use for my pudding. Mishri," she grasped her hand when she was done putting all the twenty-four bangles on. "How're you so good at this?"

Seeing Kalaa eyeing her in amazement and keen to know the story of her being, Mishrakeshi felt a rush of warmth. First time in years, she didn't fear judgement, and so gladly shared her tale.

"My mother was a sculptor from hereabouts. A wanderer in Sumer. She travelled far and wide. Until she had me and settled down in one of the small villages. They loved her, almost like family. She taught their children the art of sculpting from metal and from clay. These motifs you like so much came like breath to her. Sadly, at the time she died of a fever, the village had a new headwoman. One who wasn't very keen on our family, especially me, for I was past twenty and unclaimed. Not to mention my *foreign* appearance. Plus, Ma had created enough sculptors among the villagers. There was no need for me, only to get rid of me. There were those who opposed but the headwoman was so...hostile. By the end, I myself chose to leave."

Kalaa, sitting across from her on a stone, listened patiently all along. Mishrakeshi, at one point, had risen to walk around, hard pressed to continue when she saw her words sadden Kalaa. She was then, facing the opening of the woods ahead, when Kalaa turned her by the elbow and took her in her arms. "I'm sorry you had to endure that. But I must tell you one thing. The loss is all theirs." She said emphatically, cupping Mishrakeshi's face, holding her gaze.

A surprised laugh escaped her, and she leaned in. "And the gain is all mine, I suppose? To have found this land and this home?"

"Indeed," Kalaa ran a thumb over her jaw. "Yours. *And mine*," she whispered, a moment before drawing her lips in a lingering kiss. A kiss deep enough to fulfill the Priestess' prophecy.

◈

KALAA COULDN'T FATHOM the force of nature that was Mishrakeshi.

Courting her was proving to be an intrigue like none other. One day she'd deem herself a slave to Kalaa's whims while on others she'd decline every proposition she made.

It took her months to realize that Mishri's temperament was linked intrinsically to her artistic success and failure. There was something she wanted to make, she'd told Kalaa, something that'd both survive her and immortalize her, but she knew not what it was to be. Kalaa barely even knew what those words meant.

They weren't however as perplexing as seeing Mishrakeshi walking up to her...

At the Great Baths. On a ritual evening. Removing her necklace...

"Are you...really doing this?" she asked when Mishri came to a halt in front of her, placing her necklace and amulet beside Kalaa's. Mishrakeshi's response was a coy smile. Kalaa's own turned teasing, "They'll look at you, you know?" she quoted her mad words.

Never expecting a grin in return. Mishrakeshi bent her lips to Kalaa's ears and whispered, "As long as you're one of them, I really don't mind."

◈

MISHRAKESHI HADN'T EXPECTED to find her home and her inspiration in a single, lithe girl.

Yet ultimately, she did.

The realization dawned suddenly as she sat on the porch in the wee hours of morning, musing how she'd gone from being a guest in Kalaa's home, fawned on and treated with formality, to a part of the family, casually handed out chores at feasts and dinners. All in a few months...

"You didn't wake me," Kalaa's voice rang in the doorway behind her.

Mishri recalled she was supposed to awaken Kalaa before dawn so she could make the mango pudding for Amee Didi's journey. Wincing, she turned to apologize.

But the sight that greeted her took her breath away.

In that space between their home and the world, stood her Kalaa, clad only in her bangles—the four bought by her and the twenty-four of Mishri's making—and the cowry necklace that was Mother Nature's insignia. With her hair in a hurried bun and a hand on her hip, she looked ethereal. Her head tilted backwards ever so slightly and the miniscule bent in her knee, rendered her indignation madly endearing.

It was watching her, like this, that Mishrakeshi concluded, "You really are."

Kalaa frowned, "What?"

"Kalaa," Mishrakeshi whispered, "Craft-manifest. My craft," she murmured, pulling Kalaa onto her lap and kissing her heartily.

"Well," Kalaa pecked her cheek before leaving, "Now I *must* see you put *your Kalaa* to use."

◆

KALAA DID. A year later.

The occasion was a solemn one, frighteningly so, for Kalaa. They were leaving for Lothal.

The floods had become an incessantly recurring phenomena in the last few months. The city could no longer recuperate at its earlier rate. It was losing its brilliant sheen.

It was among such tumultuous circumstances that Mishrakeshi gave Kalaa a piece of her Kalaa.

She uttered no vows, made no grand claims, but simply promised to stay by Kalaa's side in times good and bad, and placed on her hand a tiny piece of metal.

Kalaa herself, cast in bronze, no bigger than the palm of her hand.

The belonging Mishri had crafted for herself. The promise that assuaged all of Kalaa's fears.

Mishrakeshi called it a memory captured by her heart, a testament to her Kalaa, her home.

The world—unaware of the lovers in the lost metropolis—would call her *The Dancing Girl of Mohenjo Daro.*

Mama uat-ur

Z. K. Abraham

P RESSING HER FOREARMS against the first-floor
window's metal frame, Temesghen watched aegean-
blue waves splash against the concrete walls,
searching for another flash of the being's presence in the
sea below. The stars were partially shrouded by the clouds;
the sky was a milky greenish swirl like rotting leaves and
tree sap, while the taste of sour algae and salt hung in
the air. In the distance, several tall, concrete structures
loomed: the Stacks, all that was left in a now-drowned
world. Every Stack was the same inside as hers—at least,
that's what the overseers assured them. No way to tell for
sure, since they weren't allowed to sail or swim to the other
buildings.

A flicker in the sea below: she perked up, but it was only
a silverfish. The yellow beam of a flashlight danced over
the waves. Temesghen dove to the ground, cursing herself
for losing track of the time between patrols. The guards
opened the windows above, searching for any illicit activity

in the water, their torches passing over the windows of the lower level where she now hid, hoping she'd left no trace of her presence. A bloom of sweat drenched her chest under a loose tunic. Pushing down gurgling nausea, she leaned back against the gritty stone wall and crouched as still as possible. Wandering alone at night on the upper floors was considered trespassing, punishable by only a few months malnutrition and some light torture in the barracks, but those who went down to the forbidden lower floors were often never seen again. Her elderly parents were hard of hearing; she was able to sneak out without disturbing them. As long as she wasn't caught by the patrols now, no one would ever find out about her desperate desires.

Before the world ended, Temesghen had travelled everywhere she could, visited the remaining green lands and diminished icebergs, taught herself to swim in the Red Sea. Freedom was a cacophonous sunrise, all bright oranges and flagrant pinks. No splintered guilt guiding her, no rumbling, bilious fear; none of the shades of trauma her parents carried everywhere, always. She'd once been a traveler, a nomadic researcher. No one to tell her "no." As the water had further encroached on the land, she'd worried about the changing shape of the world, but had also been enthralled by the ever-present shimmer on the horizon, the tumult and texture of rising waves. Since being brought to the Stacks years ago, she took solace in watching those waves when she could. Weeks ago, she'd come to her familiar spot to observe the waters and seen a glimpse of pale eyes in the dark. Many people did not believe that ocean dwellers even existed; the overseers firmly denied the possibility that anyone could survive outside the Stacks. But she knew what she'd seen. The spotlight swept across the water, back and forth, then it was gone. She counted a full minute before she finally rose and continued her search.

There—a flash of copper in the waves.

A flat sound, like a fin slapping against the surface. An arm. Something, *someone*, was breaking the surface.

Toes pressing into the rough concrete, Temesghen held her breath as the being emerged from the water. The moon was nearly full. Its pale light burst through the clouds, stabbing like a dagger, to illuminate the scene. The object of her interest had long, matted, dark hair. Brown skin, stretched taut over high cheekbones. Unnaturally pale irises. The being cocked her head when she noticed Temesghen. Tonight, she did not swim away like a startled shoal, but ebbed closer. She trod waters coated in a film of overripe algae like the rotting blooms of spring, waters sometimes lit by hordes of luminescent jellyfish, waters that had seemed endless, impossible, until now. Closer still, until she was right below the window. The rumors were true. Temesghen raised a shaky hand to wave. Her knees wobbled. Through a daze, heart hammering, she remembered the traditional sign her grandmother had taught her as a child, the way to greet a water dweller. Hands pressed together, like a prayer, she motioned as if diving.

The being watched the motion with curiosity, yet did not return the salute. She bobbed up and down in the waves, the webbing between her fingers translucent as she trod the water with muscular arms. Puffing out her chest, she dove backwards into the depths; her head, torso, and breasts were covered in serpentine, coppery scales, followed by thick legs and webbed feet. The waves churned, picking up in height and speed, as if stirred by an angry god.

Transfixed, Temesghen stared out at the waters, waiting. A thud from above. Her bones thrummed, her whole body trembling with a fine, tense anticipation. Another thud, then the clomp of footsteps down the stairs. Guards in this staircase, at this time? They had changed their patrols. A bitterness on her tongue, her breath tight in her throat, she searched for an escape from the guards. She ran up one floor and pushed against the door.

It was unlocked. She ran down the hall, landing light on the balls of her feet. Guards' voices echoed down a perpendicular corridor ahead. Stopping, she gently pushed open a door, hiding out in a closet full of brooms and dust. Suppressing a cough, she waited as the guards passed. After they turned a corner, she ran to the opposite staircase, barrelling up to the twentieth floor, gasping by the time she arrived in her family suite. Gripping her knees, her pulse was palpable in her temples.

Temesghen had started late tonight. In fact, it was already morning. Sunrise's fingers of warm peach and tender pink were already slipping through the window. As the crests of waves sparkled with light, she caught her breath.

It was too late to get any sleep. Her father's mildew-induced coughs, like the morning rooster, were already broadcasting from the bathroom. She dressed as she heard her mother rummage in the bedroom, preparing her and her father's uniforms. Her mother emerged from the room and avoided Temesghen's gaze. Usually, she couldn't dodge her mother's stream of mumbling, seemingly meaningless gossip about so-and-so's pregnant daughter or lazy neighbors. Something was wrong.

"What is it?"

Her mother ignored the question, continuing to brush the living room floor with her graying head bowed. Her parents' once buoyant brown faces were now shriveled by a lifetime of upheaval and long-buried sorrow.

"What's wrong?!"

"Don't speak to me in that tone." Her mother's head snapped up from her broom, as if awakening from sleep. "Where were you?"

"What do you mean?"

"I'm not stupid. What were you doing?"

Temesghen's face grew hot. "I was just on one of my walks."

"You went down too far again!" Her mother's voice grew shrill. "I know you did. I know—" She abruptly stopped.

The sound of heavy footsteps could be heard passing by in the hall.

"Relax," Temesghen whispered. Occupied with tidying the dining table, she avoided her mother's gaze. "I don't go down that far anymore. But wouldn't you want to see them?" She turned to her mother, unable to keep the pleading note from her voice. "If there were people surviving out there?"

Her mother started muttering something in their native language. Temesghen recognized a few words: *bless, demon, protect.* Her mother closed her eyes, pressing her fingers to her face. Small scars, parallel lines cut into the flesh below her eyebrows, were like talismans; she used to claim all kinds of reasons for these scars—a cure for poor eyesight, an aesthetic preference. One night, after Temesghen had come back too late, her mother had pointed to those scars and announced that they were for protection from the angry old gods, the ones before Jesus.

The demons in the water.

Communal breakfast was eaten in the cafeteria, where the barred windows let in an orange-hued light. Temesghen picked at the dry, flaking skin along her thumb, a consequence of the eczema they all suffered within these walls. Two other teachers sat nearby, bemoaning dissidents through open mouths and teeth caked in reddish bean sauce, but she soon ignored their chatter, devising a new method for returning to the lower floors. An overseer, his dark-blue jumpsuit zipped to the collar, glared at Temesghen as he passed their table. She tried to smooth the errant curls escaping from her bun. Her head ached. This might be her last chance.

Smoothing the wrinkled front of her baggy gray jumpsuit, savoring the last dregs of her bitter coffee, she rose from the table. Her father mumbled goodbye, while her mother remained silent.

Last night's revelation pulsed through her. She failed to redirect the rowdy children in their small, moldy-cornered classroom, while trying to teach them the day's lessons. The overseers set the curriculum: math, a narrow range of biological sciences mostly confined to botany and farming, and a few prescribed fairy tales designed to promote adherence to benevolent authority. When she had the energy, she injected resistance where she could. A story of a boy's unsanctioned journey through a forest, little breaks for art. The kids were boisterous today, requiring her full attention.

Over dinner, her parents made no mention of the previous night. Her father blathered on about manufacturing new parts for the unreliable generators, which were prone to shorting and causing power outages, while her mother remained quiet. That evening, like always, they sat together and listened to the radio broadcasts, the propaganda plays and jangling showtunes. Bedtime was heralded by the clomp of guards' rubber shoes down the halls. Supposedly, the guards kept them safe from dissenters, or the invaders on hijacked ships that navigated the ocean, climbing up walls and taking what they could.

As she prepared her cot, buzzing with plans for reaching the lower floors that night, her mother emerged from the bedroom. "I need to talk to you."

Gritting her teeth, Temesghen shook out her sheet. "I'm pretty tired."

"You must be. Going where you shouldn't." Her mother marched to the cot and sat down, triggering a series of high-pitched squeals from the cot's springs.

She considered simply leaving at that very moment. A simmering canary-yellow rage, bright and simmering, bubbled underneath her skin. Using all of her patience, she pushed down the rebellious feelings and sat.

Her mother took her time, a monarch letting her subject stew before the royal lecture. "I nearly died as a child.

First trip to the sea. I can remember it now. My mother held onto me this tightly." She raised a fist. "But I didn't listen. I only wanted to feel the water. The sea was something I could not understand." Her mother wiped her face, her shoulders suddenly drooping. "I thought it was like God: too deep to reach the bottom, stretching around the world with big arms. My little brother and I ran away from my mom into the water. It was warm and full of salt. And then a big wave, something *powerful* underneath us, like hands pulling so hard. And he was gone like that. I woke up on the sand and my chest hurt and my mother was crying." Her mother paused, jaw-slacked.

"But Uncle, he was found later?" A small and curled-up part of herself was afraid her mother would cry. Her cheeks were hot with shame. She had the urge to leave the room.

"No, this was before your Uncle. My first brother died. My mother would cry all day, wake up at night and kiss our faces so hard it hurt. 'Stay away from the water. The ones of the water took him. Stay close to me', she said. When I was sixteen, I had a secret boyfriend. But he was arrogant, from the wrong family. She told me no love is worth danger. 'Stay close to me, listen.'"

"Grandma told me about the sea." A pressure bubbled in Temesghen's chest. "She loved it."

"Oh, you knew her when she was an old woman. Soft by then." Her mother sighed, the long rattle of a kettle about to wail. "I thought I did everything right. Left home for America. Big brick houses, streets paved with gold. But this land was so lonely. Eventually, the water took everything anyway. Maybe I should have never left home. At least then..." Her mother turned, a spotlight reflecting at various angles to shine through the window, catching flecks of hazel in her dark-brown irises, the twisting blood vessels snaking along her sclera. "Stop chasing what will destroy you. It is not worth it. Just listen to me."

Her mother's shoulders rose again, her chest raised, as if she had regained a certain solidity. She nodded to herself, agreeing with a group of invisible listeners. Her eyes were wet, but she did not cry.

Temesghen turned over this story, trying to shake off the spiky intimacy of her mother's warning. She didn't know what to say.

After several silent minutes, her mother went to bed.

Her mother's pain had always been a long arrow, twisted and bent toward her daughter, so she too was pierced by it. Or perhaps that fear was a buoy, tight around Temesghen's middle. It was the same, always; she tried to escape their fear, they tried to pull her in tighter. A glossy rage foamed and crackled within her. Gathering the hem of her tunic, she crept barefoot over the threadbare carpet, past her parents' bedroom, and out the front door of the apartment. The lock on the back stairwell remained broken, the door swinging open with delicious ease. She still could avoid the guards if she timed it right; they still needed a certain amount of time to patrol each floor. Sneaking down the ghostly stairs, navigating by touch, she quickly reached the first floor. Her legs were strong from her nightly trips. The air tasted sour and metallic, like wet clothes and old spoons. She slid the window open. Moonlight swam in the air as if she were already underwater. Closing her eyes, the wind dragged its calloused fingers along her cheeks as she tasted brine on the breeze.

When she opened her eyes, her water dweller was right below. There was a bright alertness in her expression, irises such a light gray that they merged with the whites of her eyes. The waves were quiet tonight, so quiet the ocean appeared to be a turgid, vast lake.

"Hello?" Temesghen leaned out the window.

"You've returned." The water dweller's voice was startling: raspy and low, the timbre of rumbling violets and indigos.

Perhaps Temesghen had not expected her to speak. She glanced up at the outer, blackened gray walls overgrown with purple lichen. No lights in the windows, no faces peeking out. Her limbs were tremulous. She resisted the urge to leap out the window. "I'm Temesghen. I've been looking for you for so long. I've seen you here before. And in my dreams."

The water dweller raised her hands. Palms pressed together, a swift diving motion.

"You remembered?"

"Of course. I remember everything about you." The waves swelled and retreated around her. "I have seen your face many times. Although you did not realize. Every bright moon. And your face, too, returns to my mind." She bobbed in the water, dark nipples just above the waves, her webbed fingers barely disturbing the surface. An oak tree, swaying in a breeze.

Temesghen clutched the window's metal frame, skin pimpling in the cool evening air, or perhaps the thrill of the moment. An exquisite pain echoed through her chest, the high note of a brass instrument. The small holes along the water dweller's neck opened and closed. She still had mammalian lungs.

The being jerked her head upwards, then refocused on Temesghen. "I hear them coming."

Temesghen's throat tightened. She couldn't yet hear the approach of the guards, but knew they would return soon. "Can you come in? You can climb in through the lowest windows. I can help, I can—"

"I don't go inside. Behind bars and cement, in these prisons...I can't." The being dove beneath the water.

"I've been so lonely." Temesghen's eyes watered. The salt in the air was burning them. Aware of the seconds ticking by, she waited, waited, until the water dweller emerged again, eyes wide and unblinking.

The water dweller's mouth opened as if trying to form the right words. Night stretched out in its smoky green, the hazy half-light nuzzling against the distant Stacks, settling over the horizon. Flicking her head up, she gurgled. "They're coming!"

"They'll never go to the ground floor, please!" Temesghen cried.

The water dweller thrust her broad shoulders back. Gasping for air through her mouth and the holes in her neck, she sent out a low whistling sound before diving into the water.

Footsteps thundered behind Temesghen. Lights already bounced down the stairs, ready to sear. Instead of going up, she followed the swell rising within her, rising to a round and clear amber that overtook her, encased her, and drove her down to the lowest, ground floor.

No one went to the ground floor. It was all foundations, rough concrete, and invading seawater. They were told the water was toxic. Jumping over a barrier, stuck with the bits of cloth of those who had tried to escape in the past, she began to smell a slick, ancient green. The darkness was dense, undisturbed. Ahead, she saw the faintest shimmer of the water, seawater she had not touched in years. She submerged one foot, then the other. They were shouting right above her. The water lapped around her face, bitter malt in her mouth, splashing up her nose, but she remained still. Her skin did not burn. She was not overcome with toxic fumes. After several minutes like this, she felt the sting of the salt in her cracked skin, then felt her fingers prune, sucking in the moisture. The guards argued and stomped above, but soon began to rise again. They were unwilling to go farther, unwilling to believe someone would risk a swim.

Their voices faded. Her eyes had adjusted to the darkness, making out the smudged borders of concrete columns, the edges of a window caked in fungus. Squinting in the darkness, she made out another window on the opposite wall. She could see clear through it, catching a portion of the pulsing moon. It was open. A splash behind her.

She turned in the water, her body confused by the lightness of her limbs, and was face to face with the waterwoman.

"You made it." Her voice cracked.

This close, even in the darkness, she could better make out the waterwoman's features. The faint moonlight grazed her nose, painted her jaw. Her skin was smooth, then a mosaic of sharp angles below her collarbone; her scales emerged like a revelation, catching the light in proud coppers and delicate reds. They stood at the same height. She glanced at the window, twitched her arms closer to her sides, her movements flighty.

"It's okay. They're gone."

"We never go inside these walls." The waterwoman raised her head to the ceiling, breath threaded with feathery, low whistles. "I'm Helena." She reached out a webbed hand to Temesghen's face.

Shivering, Temesghen lay a hand on top of Helena's. They stood like this, feet adjusting for grip against the slick floor, which was covered in a layer of underwater growth.

"I had to reach you."

"Can you tell me about yourself? While we have time. I want to know everything."

Helena ran her hand down Temesghen's arm, speaking in a low, layered voice. She told a story of a life far from here, a life that started before the Stacks, in watery caves and rocky beaches. Her people had always lived between the land and the sea. When the land receded to the water, it was a natural conclusion, an inevitable second coming. But the land dwellers blamed them. She had always stuck to the waters, migrated with her clan from beach to beach, cave to cave. As she spoke, Temesghen was transfixed by her rising and falling cadence. Their fingers brushed underwater, sending shivers like the brush of electric eels. They moved around the water, closer to the window where they were better illuminated. She breathed in Helena's metallic musk through the brine. She shared too, details emerging in bursts. Helena listened, her lips parting as she searched Temesghen's face.

Finally, Helena stepped back. "I have to go. Tomorrow, we are migrating. I've been wandering too far as it is. We aren't supposed to go so close to the Stacks. My dreams drew me here, but I have to leave."

"Migrating? Will you return?"

"I don't know. We follow the old routes. Maybe in a year, we'll be in this region again."

"Please, don't. Maybe…" Temesghen gripped the waterwoman's hands, velvet-soft in her own. She didn't know what to say, how to make the moment last. Instead, without thinking, she leaned over and kissed Helena. The waterwoman stiffened, then kissed her back. Helena's lips were full and tart, her breath hot and bitter. They wrapped their arms around each other, scales impressing themselves into Temesghen's skin. Helena pulled away, blinking slowly. A second later, she was gliding to the window, grasping its edge and launching herself through it, into the night.

It was some time before Temesghen emerged from the water, dripping wet, coughing up seawater and steadying herself from the rush of adrenaline. Pulling off her tunic and squeezing out the water with trembling hands, she climbed the stairs, naked and cold, entering her family rooms as quietly as she could.

She awoke confused. She'd been dreaming of shadowed figures and glistening waves. Bleary-eyed, she made out a face above her. Heart pounding, she rubbed her eyes.

Sitting up, Temesghen grabbed at the sheets, remembering she was naked underneath and covered in a layer of sweat and grime. It was a dark morning, little light coming in through their window.

"I didn't realize the time."

Her mother shuffled closer, fiddling with the head scarf tied below her chin, tears streaming down her face.

The tunic she'd stuffed under her bed last night was now washed and drying on the clothes line along the hallway.

Her mother grabbed Temesghen, shaking her by her shoulders. "Why are you doing this?" Her voice was strained, a too-taut violin string. "Don't bring us any more shame! Don't fall to her!"

"What? Who?"

"My own mother warned me about her. I should have never left, that's why this is happening. Why has she chosen to curse us now?" Her mother's grip tightened. "I can help." Before she could react, her mother was pressing the point of their smallest kitchen knife into Temesghen's left eyebrow.

Jumping up, she pressed her hand to the small cut. "Stay away!" Warm blood was already trickling into her eye and down her cheek.

"Just let me finish, let me help you." Her mother's voice grew higher, ready to snap. "It releases her power over you."

"No one has power over me." Jaw tightening, she ran to the bathroom and locked the door. She had to get ready for work. In the shower, she quickly washed the blood from her face with trembling fingers, pulling her hair into a wet, misshapen bun. Peeking out of the bathroom, she saw her mother was gone.

At work she could hardly pay attention to her lessons. Blood soaked through her bandage, which she hastily replaced during a short break. Halfway through teaching the students a calculation, the numbers began to confuse her. Wiping the chalkboard clean, she started again. Helena kept flashing into her mind: her glistening skin, the slope of her neck, her graceful dives, the sharp pressure of her scales. She ached to hold her, to swim beside her.

There was life adapting to this world, transformed by it, free of the Stack's narrow, stale rooms and its constant, violent gaze.

At dinner, Temesghen watched the sallow faces along the tables. The chatter mixed together into a familiar static, never too loud, unspoken rules restraining the volume. The tart smells of vinegar, onion, and sweating bodies swam around her. The fluorescent lights shuddered. She ate mechanically, until acid bubbled into her chest. As she stood to deposit her half-cleared tray, one of two guards stationed near the exit looked right at her. Five years back, before the windows had been barred, someone had flung themselves out of a cafeteria window, desperate to swim, to be free. Their escape had led to a clamoring panic. She had been in the canteen then, pushing through screaming people to get to the exit. Guards had been stationed at the doors ever since. One of them, a man she didn't recognize from the day shifts, pointed in her direction.

Head down, she veered through the aisles. The guard called her name. Avoiding their eyes, she pretended not to hear. As she passed by them, one stepped forward and grabbed her arm. "You there! Stop when you're called!"

An impulse, like a long-rising wave, seized her. She yanked her hand back. "Let me go."

The first guard stood, slack-jawed and mouth agape. The other guard began to pull a club from her waist. Temesghen ran through the doors. She was crashing, no longer able to hold, erupting into foam. Everything before had led to this point. Her footsteps rebounded down the empty halls. The guards were catching up.

She ran faster, turning right, then left, diving down a staircase to the floor below. The lights continued to shudder. She lost the guards around one corner, then hid in a utility closet, crouching beneath dusty shelves. Her jumpsuit was drenched in sweat, her breath jagged in her throat. The guards passed by the door, unable to find her. Settling in, she waited.

When she'd first arrived here years ago, she'd imagined the Stacks to be a temporary measure. All that sea could be navigated, unsubmerged land to be mapped. After a while, she'd lost hope that she would ever leave. Then she'd learned of those impossible people, those who lived in the water and on distant, hidden shores. Her dreams had become suffused with long limbs, scaled bodies, salty musk. A clock ticked on the opposite wall. She waited. Several hours passed. The lights flickered on and off. Her knees ached. Guards passed by the door but didn't open it. It was past 10 p.m. The lights shuddered and went off. Another outage. Now was her chance. Without power, she could take the electronically locked western stairs. The guards would be changing shifts now. In the dark, they wouldn't catch her in time. She still remembered how to swim; whenever she was alone, she practiced the strokes.

Leaving her shoes in the closet, she ran down the hall and jiggled the door to the western staircase. It caught, then unlocked. A thrill, tangerine-sharp, pierced her. As she ran down the stairs, she heard guards shouting along each floor. Finally, she arrived at the first level. She turned the corner and came face to face with a guard. A young face, half-illuminated by the moon.

Trembling hands raised a club. "Free—freeze!"

"I saw one of them. In the water. Please, let me look." She had nothing to lose, and this one was young. Perhaps still accessible, before intimidation and doctrine had taken his ability to empathize. "Two minutes. If she doesn't come, then take me away. I saw someone out there!" She'd let a long-repressed desperation slip through. Tears fell down her face, along with a warm trickle of blood from her cut. She tasted salt and iron. "Please."

He stepped back, eyes searching her face, as if recognizing something familiar. "I see." He pulled back his club. "I saw one when I was little. They told me I was crazy. Two minutes."

Temesghen yanked open the unbarred window. They waited. Ten seconds, thirty seconds, one minute. Her pulse drummed through her ears. An eager wave, rising and falling. A flash of copper.

Helena burst out of the dark waters. "You've returned. Are you safe?" Those small holes along her neck opened, gasping little mouths.

"No. Neither are you. I want to come with you."

The guard was breathing down her neck, a whine in his throat.

"Temesghen. I'm meant for the water, I always was. But..." Helena's voice echoed like the old singers on the radio, "...what of you? Others have left, but not everyone survives away from here."

"I'm strong, I can swim. Take me to where you live, the place you rest on land."

Helena's dark hair fell in many small, tight curls around her face and down her back. "Are you sure?"

"I have to go."

She smiled. "I think I knew you would come with me. I dreamt it. Come down. We'll go east. To our islands."

"They're coming." The guard whispered.

Temesghen peeled the bandage off her face. Maneuvering her body through the opening, thighs pressing into the iron windowsill, Temesghen watched Helena, felt the pulse of the waves crashing against the walls, and jumped. She soared, feet pointed down in a ballet dive. Then she was submerged. Everything was darkness, water, granules on her tongue. Flailing, she forgot her strokes, until a pair of strong hands reached underneath her arms and pulled her up. Choking, she emerged face to face with Helena. By instinct, Temesghen began to paddle. The water embraced her. She'd missed it so much, this lightness, this freedom. Leaning in, she kissed Helena, fingers combing through the water as she kept herself upright by instinct now.

She glanced backwards, paddling her arms through the water. Through the lower windows, she spotted the flashlights bouncing down the stairs. Her gaze wandered to her floor, her family's small window. The moonlight was brittle-clear tonight, illuminating the outline of a face. Squinting, her heart rate accelerated. A shadow of a figure in the frame, blocking out the light. They did not move. She held her breath, imagining her mother's face, eyes shining, light tracing her jaw. Was that a hand, lifted to the glass? Then the shadow disappeared, like an apparition, replaced by the wash of light on the glass.

Temesghen turned to Helena's gold-brushed cheeks, long eyelashes, pale eyes, hair splaying out in every direction.

"My darling. Let's swim."

The Birds I Pull

SHARANG BISWAS

WHEN I TOLD my grandmother I wanted to wear a cross around my neck like that hot guy in that one action movie we'd watched together, she told me that only Christians wore them. Instead, she got me a bronze pendant in the shape of the sun to better reflect our Hindu sensibilities—only, the sun's rays were poky and uncomfortable, and I wore the thing exactly twice. The second time only after my mother hassled me to show gratitude for the gift.

Okay, that wasn't *entirely* true. I never mentioned the "hot guy" part to my grandmother.

When she died, I was oceans away in a dormitory, thinking about a Physics exam. I only found out because a crow tore its way out of my chest, feathers the colour of a chalkboard that had been licked clean, eyes glistening with beady malice.

My roommate tried to shoo it away with his paper copy of the *Undergraduate Student Handbook*, but it hopped away from surface to surface with supreme unconcern. I opened a window and let the cruel winter yank it outside.

◆

WHEN I TOLD my best straight friend—

No, that sounds like I had a best *gay* friend and a best *bisexual* friend and a best *asexual* friend.

When I told my straight best friend—

No, that defines him by his heterosexuality, which is, I dunno, unfair and reductive?

When I told my best friend who was straight—

No, that just sounds ridiculous.

When I told *Jason* that I'd been madly in love with him for the last few months and that it was extremely cringey of me and would he please punch some sense into me—not in a homophobic way, but in a "why do I always fall for straight dudes? BLARGH!!" kind of way—he turned to me in the middle of the snow-slathered cemetery and hugged me so hard, a parrot the colour of an overly-manicured suburban lawn popped out of my chest.

It squawked clumsily. I buried my face in my mother-knitted scarf, because of all the birds, it had to be a shitty parrot, the most awkward of all avians. Once, back in New Delhi, a prophetic parrot had selected a card to determine my future. The fortune-teller claimed the card meant I would have a "healthily-built" wife with "skin the colour of milk-toffee" who would bear me ten children (I don't think he suspected that "wife" wasn't exactly an ideal option for me. Though in all fairness, I had only *just* begun to notice that footballers tearing off their jerseys during the World Cup elicited somewhat different reactions from me than in most other boys).

Even penguins are less awkward than parrots, and they can't even fly!

Jason tried to catch the bird for me, but it cawed obscenely at him and vanished into the sepulchral verdure, which was actually pretty awesome, because I could just imagine it learning some random English words and scaring the daylights out of some hapless, drunk freshman who stumbled into the graveyard to pee on a poor college president's tombstone or something.

Jason laughed about the whole thing that night over hot chocolate and then asked me what my jerk-off fantasies about him were like and then laughed again when I threw a pillow at him.

◆

When the random guy on the subway yelled at me that I should take the train all the way to the airport and then "get the hell out of the country," my chest pounded so hard I thought I was having a panic-induced heart-attack, but it was just a Northern cardinal bursting out of me, red as a bloody sunset, domino-masked like a fucking comic-book vigilante.

I only knew it was a cardinal because I'd seen what a cardinal looked like in the copy of Audubon's *Bird of America* that my ex-boyfriend had proudly shown me in the Special Collections Library at my college a few years back. He'd been a library intern at that time.

The bird pecked at the man's face, and I ran out of the subway car with my friends at the next station. I don't know what happened to the cardinal, but I like to think it joined the pigeon community in the city as one of their hot, out-of-town lesbian cousins who's friends with sex workers and underground abortion doctors.

◆

When my parents announced they were getting divorced, I expected a honking great goose painted with tear-stain streaks of moonlight or something equally dramatic to galumph out of my body. But nothing like that happened. I just sipped my glass of milk (I'd recently switched to low fat). I nodded somberly even though they obviously couldn't see me over the phone.

I ordered pizza that night. I only remember because I never order pizza. It had irregular chunks of unseasoned chicken on it, which I remember thinking was weird.

◈

THE DAY AFTER you asked me if we were dating, and I answered "Yes!" faster than I'd answered any question in my life—and let me tell you, I'd been THAT kind of nerd in high school—I reached between the buttons of my shirt and the bird I pulled out was brilliant, *brilliant* blue, like powdered gemstones caked onto canvas in tongue-thick streaks of vivid paint.

I have pulled out a bird like that every day since. I could repaint a slate-grey sky into glorious daylight with the sheer number of blue birds that have blossomed out of me.

I've never looked up what kind of bird it is.

I'll stop there. I don't need to dwell on the bird that resulted from the last kiss you ever gave me, or the one that grew out of the last tear you shed for me. Let's stick with the birds the colour of the pristine seascape where we honeymooned, the birds the colour of your favourite fruit freshly picked from your family farm, birds the colour of icicles clinging to granite cliffs the morning of a solstice hike, birds the colour of glory, the colour of frozen, joyful possibility...

Sentience

NKONE CHAKA

T HE LIBRARY'S RINGS pulsed in greeting. It welcomed the waiting ships with three flashes of bright blue light, calming once all its visitors responded. Storm clouds swirled on its surface, a blue-green spinning top glistening in the surrounding blackness of space. Salmik watched it from the standing observation deck with awe.

They shuddered. Gooseflesh dotted their arms at the unbidden memories of alien ecosystems, little monsters alive and thriving in that thicket. The ships were trapped in its orbit like unfortunate flies caught in a web. Though they'd seen it before, the planet-sized archive never failed to fascinate them into a stupor. In all their years, they'd only visited twice.

The first time was on a desperate research mission aimed at countering the spread of a nasty, flesh-eating fungus on the fringes of their solar system. The plague hurtled toward them at alarming speeds, rousing every habitable planet in the system to the peak of panic.

The second of the visits was to bear witness to the best and rarest performance of their life. *What a way*, they had thought, *to usher one's ailing mother into the arms of death.*

On both occasions, the library left them feverish and overwhelmed. It was like dipping a toe into a completely different universe. More accurately, it was akin to entering an amalgamation of every place, a piece of every single world in existence pressed, folded, and on display, held down by the library's gravity. They'd touched down on its surface and been blessed with the chance to see some of it with their own two eyes. Before that, Salmik, like everyone else who hadn't yet been there, believed most accounts to be exaggerations. Butter made stories smoother, after all.

When the library's message began disseminating over a decade ago, communication channels buzzing with whispers of what it planned to do, they dismissed it as a hoax. An entire planet, an infinite repository of knowledge thousands of years old set to blow itself to bits? It was simply unimaginable. Nobody who hadn't flown within its atmosphere could understand the depth of Salmik's heartbreak.

And who in their right mind would allow it? Millenia worth of botanical and ecological archives, ancient texts and works of film, tapestries, memories, histories, records of civilizations that no longer existed, all lost to an end of the library's own choosing? It was too ridiculous to even consider.

It only started to feel real when the invitation reached them personally. They had it tracked and traced. Messages could be faked, and the universe was a large place. Somewhere out there, Salmik was certain, on some cold isolated rock with nothing in the way of entertainment, a little cretin thought it would be funny to play a practical joke on every serious scholar with access to a communication device.

The longer the tests continued, the harder it was to deny where the message had come from. Soon, there were teams of data analysts, and before Salmik knew it, an official one was sent to the compendium Zattina itself to determine the invitation's legitimacy.

In their studio on Sunar, Mika had tried and failed to hide his obvious glee. Their assistant bit what was left of his fingernails, long torso unfurling as he sat up straight in his chair. "You're busy."

"Not busy enough for this," Salmik had muttered, releasing their tower of dreadlocks to ease the tension headache that threatened to spread from the base of their skull down their neck and shoulders.

"Don't worry, boss. I'll tell you everything."

"Everything means nothing without footage."

Salmik stood up with a start, trying to think of ways to end their current project. At any other time, the chance to raise their planet's first fully mycelial building would have taken precedence. It paled in comparison to Mika's new position as assistant liaison between the compendium and the rest of the universe.

"You know," he said, laughing, "If you didn't speak so highly of me to your peers, you'd probably be doing this instead."

Salmik heaved a resigned sigh.

"I can't *lie* to them. This is the first time I've ever found myself wishing you were less competent."

The library's confirmation had sent ripples of chaos reverberating through the cosmos. Ambassadorial commissions were formed, beings of every species imaginable tasked with preparing and delivering a plea to the library.

Keep your doors open. Stay alive, for at least one thousand more years. Five hundred, two hundred—it couldn't possibly expect all of the valuable information housed within it to be preserved elsewhere on such short notice. The library, to Salmik's horror, revealed that not only was it set to self-destruct in the next decade, it planned to keep everything it had acquired so far in its possession. Nothing about its imminent death changed the operating rules. No object or life form left its surface without the library's consent, and no foreign body was allowed to leave anything else behind unless an archival request was approved. And there was Mika in the thick of it all, first a representative of Zattina's patrons then later an ambassador of the compendium itself. A betrayal for the ages.

"We can't let it do this," Salmik said, pacing the length of their studio. The schematics for the new building lay abandoned on their drafting table, the mushroom specimens meant for the building's cladding neglected. Mika sat watching them with a frown on his face.

"I thought you loved that it was sentient."

"That's not the point," Salmik said, stopping to dig their fingers into the thicket of their dreadlocks. The cold of their skin against their scalp provided no relief from the heat in their head.

"Well, I mean, it kind of is, isn't it? All sentient creatures get to choose how and when they die. *You* get to make that decision. If the library is alive, then surely it deserves to be treated like it."

"This is not about ethics," Salmik hissed.

"Then what *is* it about?"

"Fucking history! No one who genuinely cares about scholarship, about preservation, about *information*, can be fine with this."

"Well," Mika said, standing to leave Salmik stewing in anger, "It's not your choice to make. You can be bitter about this, or you can accept the invitation." Salmik decided to do both. They seethed, entertaining the thought of stealing a shuttle and descending to confront the library, person to planet. A decade had done little to temper their rage.

◆

"YOU SHOULD JOIN the celebration," Mika said, coming up behind them. Even in the relative solitude of the observation deck, Salmik didn't hear his approach. He remained young, stuck in that immortal, uncanny valley that happiness tended to trap people inside. His skin was waxen.

"I don't see any cause for celebration."

"It's happening, old friend. Whether you like it or not. Come down with me. At least meet my children."

Children? Salmik's eyes widened—it really had been a decade hadn't it? It was only just a few years ago when Mika's entanglement with the library began, just yesterday when it took over their relationship, the young man abandoning Salmik for the thrill of a lifetime project.

In the months following the end of his employment, Salmik recalled a sense of betrayal that showed no sign of abating. They felt full with it, the edges of their skin threatening to tear open when news of Mika's position as the library's new advocate spread through all systems faster than light.

"What would you have done?" Their therapist had posed the question gently, as if approaching a rabid dog.

I would have fallen in love with it too, they thought. Rage became under standing and then pity as they imagined what a toll the library's decision had taken on the universe at large, especially on the people it chose as ambassadors. Though they were still jealous, envy was tapered by the reassurance that the job which stole their assistant was not only one they desperately wanted, but also one to which they were the least suited. Whose very existence they protested.

It stung now to think that this consolation may have been a lie. Mika appeared content, the trajectory of his choices having led him to family despite all the ways in which Salmik believed them to be an atrocity.

Still, the mention of children knocked the anger from their chest. It was the way of Sunari to bow at the altar of parenthood. Salmik had no children of their own and no desire to procreate, but just the mention of young ones was soothing, like cold ointment on burnt flesh.

"Congratulations," they said, trying and failing not to sound defeated. They wished their mother was here.

"There's nothing wrong with you, Sal," she had said from the garden, pulling weeds out with her bare hands as her android sat staring at a small hive of bees dangling precariously from a tree, its metal head stuffed to the brim with bright, fragrant flowers.

"Children aren't for the weak. I know your siblings are all giving it a go, but if I could do it over again, I might have chosen something different." When Salmik laughed, she rushed to explain.

"I love you all, of course, I just meant...It's not easy. You have to really be sure you want it, and even then, there's no real way to prepare for it, you know?"

"I know, Ma."

"I realized after your sister that what I really wanted out of life was brevity. To be here for a short time, to be beautiful, and then to rest. Raising you has been such a pleasure, but—"

"You don't have to keep defending yourself. I'm not Pearl. This kind of thing doesn't hurt me much," Salmik said, leaning over to kiss their mother's dirt-covered cheeks.

They understood each other. Where the rest of their family remained intent on continuing with Sunari custom, Salmik chose to medically terminate their ability to give birth. There was so much out there to be done—mycelial buildings yet to be designed, solar sail cladding and intergalactic botanic gardens, algae desalination plants to build and deadly fungi to eradicate.

They knew from early on that child rearing was not the right route for them. Still, it warmed their heart to see Mika's young ones. Spry and energetic, the twins ran between all three of their parents' legs, sliding from parent to parent in a hyperactive storm that exhausted Salmik just to watch. They darted through the crowd like mice on stimulants, garnering annoyed looks and free candied gifts alike, returning to their parents to share the spoils. Salmik popped the sticky sweet proffered by one of the twins into their mouth. Mika beamed with pride as his former employer greeted his partners, and then bent down to his children.

"Maybe you can show Salmik your new nano-fabric," one of his partners said. Salmik had to crane their neck upward just to maintain eye contact with her.

"This is a *festival*," the other whined.

A short, portly man of about thirty-five with a long, braided beard and an explosion of thick, tree-like hair reached out to shake Salmik's hand, motioning at their surroundings with his free arm.

"There's so much to do, and this one wants to bore you to death with a seminar on nano-fabric."

The ship burgeoned with stalls. A small walk away were throngs of people, all personally invited by the library to witness its final moments. Parents and children, lovers, friends, and families, congregated around organic stalls either selling decadent foods or aromatic teas.

Closest to them was a stall covered in the Basha mushroom, one based on their very own design. The mushroom's blue tops lit up the stall, facilitating the growth of different species of edible lichen and moss. Every once in a while, an apron wearing cook emerged from the back with a giant pair of shears and snipped off both mushroom and moss, digging into the carpet of flowering goods to flavor their wares.

The people passing by wore smiles, sipping cool drinks from recyclable containers. They strolled leisurely through the ship, as if one of the universe's most valuable artifacts wasn't about to go up in flames.

Anger rushed back into Salmik's body, lighting the tips of their ears on fire. How could everyone be so nonchalant? Did they not understand the gravity of what was happening?

Mika, recognizing the rage as it re-entered them, placed a hand on their shoulder. It was madness. Music streamed from invisible speakers in the domed ceiling, the sound of the crowd like little complacent rats scurrying from one stall to the next, willfully ignorant as they ate and sang and laughed.

"Come," Mika pulled Salmik away from his family. "Let's get you some thing to eat."

The Basha sandwich was divine. When cooked, the mushrooms lost their coloring, changing from a deep blue to a light brown. Salmik resisted the urge to sigh in pleasure. Spiced with the varying species of moss and flowers, the bread baked from Basha wheat flour, Salmik allowed the flavors to dance on their tongue. It was almost as good as their mother's cooking.

A pang of guilt hit them at the thought of her. She, like Mika, seemed content to leave the library to its own devices. Her attempts at consolation were futile. During one of Salmik's visits, which had become less frequent as she insisted on sitting them down to offer well-intentioned but useless platitudes, she'd said, "You have no control over this, Sal."

Zattina was open to requests for visits from all over the cosmos. As a result of their last interaction, or perhaps some other factor known to the library alone, Salmik's application, though personal, was approved.

It was well crafted, detailing the pain and desolation of losing an entire species of native flower to blight. When their mother described the extent of her loss, it made Salmik want to weep. The knowledge that she would never again hear the Sunari singing plant bloom, give the only performance of its life before its death and propagation, was to them a tragedy of epic proportions.

They'd seen the plant before, but only within the confines of a national park or conservation center, and even those were now gone.

"You must see them in the wild. Sometimes, a group of them would bloom together. Every song is different, but when they came of age at once, it was almost as if they were part of a symphony, each flower playing its part to create a singular song. It's the only time I feel like I should have birthed you all earlier. That type of thing doesn't happen anymore."

The blight had torn through Sunar like an invading army on a rampage. Attempts to bioengineer a cure failed, sometimes even making things worse, damaging the singing plant until a request was made to store the remaining population on the library.

Salmik and their Ma landed in time to hear the chorus unfold. To this day, it remained the most beautiful, frightening, and heart-breaking moment of their life.

This sorry excuse for a celebration was an insult. Though anger still consumed them, they realized just how exhausted they were. They allowed themselves to be pulled by Mika through the maze of stalls and people, stopping every few minutes for a one-of-a-kind fruit pie here or to run their hands along Iulien paper, as rare as it was forbidden, displayed without fear and going for a ridiculous price.

They spotted a swath of several people wearing strange, iridescent body suits that blinked in and out of the environment, blending into their surroundings with slick ease.

"So that's what you've been doing. Ambassadorial duties aside, of course." Mika grinned sheepishly.

"I guess I'm just as brilliant as you always insisted."

For what felt like the first time in years, Salmik laughed.

"I'm sorry," Mika said. His grin was gone, and he held out a piece of fresh fruit cake, the smell of caramelized sugar wafting from it in waves. Salmik shook their head.

"I might have done the same in your place," they said.

Leaning against a curved metal rail, they looked down into the chasm below to avoid Mika's gaze. Though they were not ready to admit it, not even to themselves, Salmik was both proud and ashamed to see their assistant progressing so quickly, and with such ease. Both science and scholarship were about forward motion, yet as hard as they tried, they could not move on, could not accept what this gathering represented.

They remained firmly anchored in the past, refusing to accept the library's autonomy and need for change. To their mounting frustration, it seemed like they were the only one who couldn't let go. The rest of the universe appeared to have made its peace.

Below them was an amphitheater that also doubled as an observation deck, the stage swallowed by the expanse of space behind it, the library's blue green surface in the background.

Dancers flitted about on the stage like little birds. They threw each other up into the air, leaping and catching, flipping and collapsing as the audience gasped and held its collective breath. A cycle of *oohs* and *wows* rose and fell in a regular rhythm. It was a while before Salmik noticed that they were all clad in Mika's nano fabric, its surface morphing to mimic the vacuum of space in the background, and then the library in its quiet splendor.

On the far edges of the stage were two gigantic harps, each one made of an alloy that Salmik couldn't identify from where they stood. The androids playing them were also dressed in Mika's nano fabric, and if Salmik squinted, they could almost believe that the harps were playing themselves.

"A thoughtful homage," Mika said beside them.

"Come on," they sighed, feeling even more drained than before. The food in their stomach was leaden, the weight of it moving slowly downwards to rest like steel weights around their ankles. "This is a fucking joke."

"This is life, Salmik," Mika said. "Things end. That's how it goes." Their old boss stayed silent. Mika rushed to fill the quiet like a man spurred by guilt.

"Imagine," he said, "living for millions of years. No friends, no companions, nothing but yourself and the passage of the eons to keep you company."

"You're telling me it's doing all this because its fucking *lonely?*" They tried to imagine how old the library must be, how tired. How, after years of allowing space-faring peoples on its surface, it eventually insisted on contracts for any species requesting either visits or wanting to add to its archive. It was an ancient animal, a thing that would continue living far beyond Salmik's capacity to truly comprehend unless it took action on its own. They felt a twinge of sympathy. It was easier to revel in bitterness and anger if they did not think too closely about the library as a creature with its own autonomy, with emotions similar to their own, with a history it could recall and a life it retained the right to end. Still, no amount of sympathy was enough to dampen their wrath.

"Whose idea was this?" Salmik spat, motioning with an arm at the crowd. "Yours or Zattina's? You wanted to rub our faces in it, eh?" Their voice rose an octave, cracking with the effort it took to restrain their fury.

"Salmik—"

"I don't have to do this," they said.

Shoulders slumped as low as they could go, back hunched like a curved claw, they left their former colleague to watch the dancers, foolish in their tribute.

❖

THE SHEETS BIT every surface of their skin despite being freshly laundered. In their cabin, Salmik tossed and turned, waking every few minutes to wipe the sweat from their forehead. They adjusted the temperature controls to no avail, changing their night shirt several times until they gave up and allowed the fabric to plaster itself to their skin.

It took them more than an hour to reach their quarters. The dancers concluded their performance by leaving the amphitheater, floating on the magnetic levitation stage and landing on the upper decks smack in the center of all the celebratory activities.

The crowd parted to let them through. If the whole thing wasn't so ridiculous, Salmik might have found it beautiful. Dancers of all physiques turned in unison, leaning backwards with long, languid fingers pointing up to the ceiling. They rolled their necks in slow, fluid motions, black and brown skin radiating warmth among the plant covered stalls in the ship. The nano-fabric glistened like oil on water.

Salmik wondered how long they'd rehearsed. Did they even grasp what they were performing for?

◈

Their first visit to the library was an act of desperation. As disease tore their system to shreds, Salmik bid their mother goodbye with a pained grimace at the conditions they were leaving behind and a rush of excitement at the journey ahead. Still, there was a fundamental misunderstanding of what it even meant to have Zattina accept their request. Sure, the library was a thing of scholarly wet dreams, but it was one of many in a large universe. At this point, they'd spent more than half their life exploring as their work required. It was a wonder, a fascinating phenomenon. But it wasn't the be all and end all of research. This was just a stop on the route to helping their solar system. It would either have a solution for them, or it wouldn't.

They received a notification confirming permission to be in the area before they even came into the library's orbit.

"A bit of an exaggeration," they said to their colleague Frank, who'd made the trip once before.

"You laugh now, but you're going to shit yourself when we get there. I swear Sally, I've never seen anything like it."

"It's a sentient planet. It's not like there aren't hundreds of those in this galaxy alone. How is this one any different?"

Frank paused, running a hand over faer bald head.

"I can't explain it," fae said finally after minutes of staring blankly ahead. When Salmik's eyebrows rose and they pretended to choke, trying to suppress a bout of laughter, Frank said, "It has full control of all its systems, like some fucking supercomputer."

"Most sentient planets do."

"No, Sally, not like that. It's..." fae paused again, rubbing faer thumb and forefinger together. "It's *alive*. Genuinely alive, like it has thoughts and feelings."

"That's what the word sentient means, Frank."

Salmik was amused, not just because it was a welcome reprieve from the havoc wreaked by the fungus so close to home, but because their colleague was obviously full of shit.

Every single library they'd ever been to worked the same. There were variations, of course, peoples whose history was stored a little differently, but ultimately, archives were shaped a certain way. It was about keeping records, preserving information. Sometimes it was music or spoken word, and sometimes it was blocks of data housed in gargantuan buildings, towering centers constructed away from civilization, ranging from austere in architectural design to biophilic.

Same structure, different cladding. Frank was like a teenager who'd taken faer first hallucinogen, sure beyond all doubt that this was the most breathtaking experience of faer life.

When they were in the library's close orbit, they received a welcome message and a set of coordinates telling them where best to land in order to find what they were looking for.

"You don't need suits," a voice said through the communication channel. The library hijacked their artificial intelligence with ease. "The air is breathable, and there are no contaminants in that area. None that would make you ill. The atmosphere and gravity are safe for you."

The descent onto the library's surface was as odd as it was striking. Life on habitable planets, sentient or otherwise, tended to follow similar patterns—the bright green of photosynthetic life on planets orbiting warmer stars and the vast blue of wide, open oceans. From their ship, this seemed to be true for Zattina as well. But when their small shuttle lowered, Salmik was met by a forest of what they could only tangentially describe as trees. Their bark was blood red, rising like the broken teeth of some sub-planet demon to eat all who dared to walk upon the library uninvited. They were three times as high as any building or station they'd ever seen.

When their feet were on solid ground, they dared to touch the trees, whose bark felt less like wood and more like stone. Up close, it hid layer upon layer of white, milk-like swirls. A long moment passed before they saw the patterns *moving*.

Salmik blinked, rubbing their eyes several times to confirm what they were seeing. The movement itself was unnoteworthy—plenty of other species of vegetation, if this could even be called that, behaved in similar ways. But...something about this particular one caused unease. An alien combination of blood and milk superimposed onto large pillars, the trees were a fleshy yet solid kind of presence that made them gag.

They traversed an animal turned inside out. Salmik shuddered and looked back at Frank, whose turn it was to be amused.

"We've both seen stranger things," Salmik scoffed.

Though fae found their discomfort funny, they saw a combination of eagerness and hurry in Frank's eyes.

To those who'd been there, the library held an inexplicable allure, leaving them with the ache to return. But it was so unknowable, so alien, that it left some of the lucky visitors afraid.

Salmik drew back their hand against the cold trees as, in response to their touch, spikes made from an equally hard material shot out from the bark. At their tips were large mounds of glassy balls that resembled eyes. Marble white and bulbous, Salmik thought they might explode with the pressure, releasing a stream of pungent puss or poisonous gas.

"I thought you said we'd be safe." They scowled at the empty air. It was then that they noticed the deep silence of this place. There were no chirps that indicated some species of bird or flying creatures above, no scurrying underfoot, nothing but the sound of the wind as it snaked between the pillars, and the two feckless idiots who'd trusted the library enough to land on a foreign, potentially toxic environment unprotected.

"Frank," they began, heart hammering in their chest, but their partner was otherwise occupied. Faer mouth was wide open, staring at the strange protrusions on the closest tree and shaking faer head in wonder. "We should fucking *leave*," they said, but Frank was not listening. When Salmik approached fae, they understood why. From the white balls of stone-flesh, pushing up from its surface in a slimy squelch, were teeth. White as ivory, the teeth were covered in a yellow mucus that reeked of death and decomposition.

They retched. Salmik's small chunks of digested food landed on the tree's glossy surface. Through their watery tears, they watched as the tree opened, revealing a row of similar teeth-like structures within it that swallowed the mush whole.

"Get your shit together," Frank whispered. They heard fae as if through a thick wall. Frank was already taking specimens of the little teeth by the time Salmik found their footing, placing them into tiny test tubes that fae slotted safely into a carrier once the job was done.

"Where is this thing even from?" they wondered five hours into the sample collection, their now gloved fingers painful with the effort of extracting the teeth from their cocoon. Though no other element appeared immediately harmful, the mucous housing them burned to the touch. A mild acid, strong enough to hurt, but not enough to cause lacerations to the skin. Even so, neither scientist wanted to take any chances. "And why would the library suggest that we didn't need protective gear?"

"Because the fungus is not harmful to most species unless ingested," a disembodied voice replied.

Frank and Salmik stopped. The answer echoed in their heads as if it was an extension of their thoughts, but a glance at each other confirmed that they both heard the explanation. For a few seconds, Salmik lost control of their bladder. Splotches of urine dampened their underwear, and they had to take a deep, steadying breath to regain a semblance of control.

"Shit."

"I told you," said Frank, shrugging, "that it would be like nothing you'd ever seen before."

"The samples you sent in your request have been genetically modified, fused with something else that I have never encountered," the voice continued. "This forest is a biological graveyard. The species that inhabit this environment can communicate with it and use it to dispose of their dead."

"Where exactly can we find this species? It would help our cause to establish communication," Salmik asked, trying and failing to keep the tremble from their voice, to ward off the sense that, by taking residence in their mind without permission, the library had performed a great violation.

There was no understanding the extent of this capability—if it could force itself inside their brain, could it then extract information, read their thoughts, decode their memories? It was an invasion of privacy that made their skin crawl.

"I cannot disclose that information," the library said.

"Millions of lives are at stake—"

Frank shook faer head.

"Don't argue with it. Just be grateful we have these."

"But—"

"This is more information than we ever would have found on our own. Be happy we've been granted access and get back to work."

Salmik began to protest, but a thought stopped them short. How powerful was the library? It was certainly more evolved than they'd originally estimated. The swift nature with which it infiltrated their ship's artificial intelligence, and now this penetration of their mind—what else was it capable of? They tried to reassure themselves, to confirm that there was no cause for alarm, but Frank's caution, faer insistence on obeying the library's every order, sent an involuntary shiver down their spine. It took all their strength to keep their bones inside their body, hands shaking as they stowed away specimen after specimen, glancing up at Frank to ensure that their partner was still whole.

The end of their visit couldn't come soon enough. By the time they mounted the shuttle leading back up to their research vessel, Salmik's legs and thighs shook with the effort of controlling their panic. It was not until the shuttle was off the ground that they dared to look back down at the library.

Below them as they ascended, the landscape began to evolve. It appeared at first as a blur in the periphery, a melting of the world that temporarily shook things out of focus. And just like that, the ground appeared to be flipping itself inside out. The strange trees inverted to reveal rows upon rows of sharp teeth that splayed outward like the tentacles of an angry sea beast.

The pillars ejected shards of broken bone upwards to land against the shuttle's hull in a clatter that Salmik might have mistaken for rainfall had their eyes not been wide open. The ground split apart with a crack, the earth beneath a dry, bloody red. Plumes of dust enveloped the planet's surface. Before it could settle, the compendium was already rearranging itself with frightening efficiency.

The flesh on Salmik's arms pimpled. Even from this distance, through the destruction and clouds of crimson dust, they spotted the unsettling arrangement of beehive-like holes as the very fabric of the planet's surface altered its composition. They suppressed revulsion as the library morphed, the array of strange holes causing them to clench their fists and curl their toes in an unsuccessful attempt to still their mind.

Only when the nausea dissipated did Salmik piece together the final transformation in their mind. It was a field of Sunari singing plants. They could almost feel their mother's fingertips brushing against their cheeks as the blobs of violet solidified themselves. Salmik's mouth hung open.

Was the library mocking them? Had it extracted this specific piece of information from their mind to torture them with it, as if to taunt them for ever doubting its superiority?

Days passed before Salmik returned to themselves, crawling back into their skin like a scared snail finding its abandoned home once again.

❖

THE FESTIVAL WAS well and truly underway.

Insomnia chased Salmik from their quarters, the celebration reaching them through the walls of the cabin even though it was supposed to be soundproof. They suspected that the ship's crew had done this on purpose to get the heavy sleepers out of bed, bulking up attendance at the site of the main celebration. It was an unnecessary strategy—scores of people poured from the ship's every orifice.

In the center of the great hall, a multi-headed monster danced, its many arms reaching to brush the tops of heads, its numerous feet stomping on the ground below. The hologram blinked and shimmered, a rainbow array of lights streaming from its body and exploding from its extremities. All around it, dancers with painted faces and skillfully designed holographic masks threw each other up into the air. Spectators hooted and clapped with each safe landing, allowing themselves to forget the magnetic levitation technology just visible in the dancers' ankle jewelry.

It was the truest representation of the library Salmik had ever seen. Its designer had to have taken the trip down more than once. Compendium Zattina was not a single entity, but a many-faced being with layer upon layer, everting itself, to its visitors' absolute horror, at will. It was an ancient beast, deceptive in its willingness to be communicated with, unknowable in both beauty and danger.

Mika's nano-fabric costumes ebbed and flowed in their mimicry of the holographs, dancers morphing mid-air to the delight of children and adults alike. The giant timer displayed above the monster's head counted down from seven hours. Salmik tried to hurry. The thought of Mika made them wince. They could almost imagine his face frowning with disapproval at the level of their immaturity. Or even worse, they saw his face become a sad mix of concern and pity as Salmik, stalking through the halls like a scorned child brimming with vengeance, planned to steal a shuttle.

Music oozed from the ship's walls, heavy drums played by unseen musicians beating in time to all of the monster's feet as they hit the floors. The creature's masked faces— oblong things with multiple large eyes like alien larvae— moved out of time with the rest of its body.

They tried to maneuver themselves away, but the throng pressed in against their body from all angles. Drinks sloshed around and landed on bare skin, wet and sticky sweet as it mixed with people's sweat and spit, mouths open as they cheered.

Beneath these layers of sound were the hisses and sizzles of food stalls still going, savory sandwiches and replicated meats seasoned with natural spices to mask the metallic aftertaste of synthesized protein products.

When they looked around, Salmik felt themselves to be the only one drowning. In the technicolor sea of costumes, they spotted Mika with his partners, children presumably asleep despite the din, head thrown back in delight as they both wrapped their arms around him.

Salmik dipped their head into the thick of the crowd, pushing against it to the outskirts, heaving once they'd reached the path that opened toward the shuttle bay. The ship's bioluminescent algae walls lit up the dim corridors the farther away they moved from the heart of the festival.

Text flashed across the space ahead intermittently in a different language each time. *A celebration of a life well lived,* it read, mirroring the myriad of the algae's natural colors.

Death was a thing to be mourned, especially if it was senseless. Though the crowd had thinned, it was still busy as the children who'd defied sleep wove between the stalls, parents losing all pretenses of control as their kids disappeared into the recesses of the ship. Even as far back as the entrance to the shuttle bay, guards were lax, allowing people to slide through the doors, at least making sure that the younger, more rambunctious of the children steered clear of the aircraft.

Intoxicated pilots leaned against the shuttles, trying and succeeding to impress groups of bystanders who laughed loudly and wrapped their arms around each other, collapsing into silly, drunken giggles as the ship's crew soaked in the attention. Salmik crept up the ramp of an abandoned shuttle close to the entrance. They felt ridiculous, like a child who thought they were getting one over on a pair of vigilant parents. Pausing each time the cool metal creaked, they scanned the hanger to make sure nobody noticed the silly adult sneaking onto a shuttle like the protagonist of an ancient spy movie. They yelped as a meaty hand landed on their shoulder.

"And where might you be going?" the guard said, slurring as he clamped down into their neck. He stood beside an equally drunk pilot with glassy eyes.

"My partner's on the neighboring ship. We want to watch the library's end together," Salmik lied.

"No one leaves the fucking ship!" the guard bellowed, staggering back and bumping his head against the pilot's, who screamed and pushed him aside. They then began laughing, the force of their amusement causing them both to sway unsteadily on the ramp. A few people in the shuttle bay glanced at them, but they soon turned away, enthralled by the other pilots' demonstrations.

"I won't be long," they said conspiratorially, leaning in close to steady the clumsy pair with their arms. "We haven't seen each other in *months*."

"No," the guard said, wagging an unsteady finger in their face. "You stay here! Here!" He sounded out the words as clearly as he could manage, leaning forward to blow hot, foul breath right into their nostrils.

"Listen," Salmik snapped, losing their patience. The countdown swam in front of their eyes. They had to make it down to the planet's surface and back in less than seven hours, and these fools were wasting their time.

"I'm a very important guest. Dr. Salmik Motebang. If you just look me up in the ship's guest list, you'll see."

They'd never used this line before, so their heart hammered in their chest as realization slowly dawned on the pilot's face. It was all they could do not to sigh in relief as she stammered, "Shit! It's the fucking doctor!"

"What?" her companion asked, confused.

"The one who made a cure for the necro-virus."

Salmik bit their tongue in an effort to prevent themselves from correcting her. *It was a fungus,* they wanted to say, *not a virus. And I didn't find a remedy on my own. We worked as a team.*

Brief visions of Frank flashed before their eyes.

"What? Be serious."

"I swear man, this is them!" The pilot pulled out a pocket computer and slurred into it, then shoved it in the guard's face. His eyes swiveled between the screen and Salmik's face, rocking forward and back like a lone tree in the middle of a hurricane.

"Shit! You're right!" he said finally, stomping his feet together and performing a sloppy salute. "Thank you for your sacrifice."

"Sorry," the pilot said, moving aside sheepishly.

"The ships are set to leave four hours after the show, so make sure to be back by then."

Salmik recoiled at the audacity. They were not here for exotic entertainment, but to observe a murder. And what would that even look like? There were several ways a celestial body of this mass could die. The star around which it orbited—out of necessity or arbitrarily, Salmik didn't know—was nowhere near its own end. It was among the first things that scientists checked when the library made its announcement. The ships invited to witness its death were too close for any manner of explosion, unless Zattina planned to take all of them, crew and passengers alike, along for the ride.

The pilot pulled her colleague off the ramp. They were too drunk to notice Salmik's forehead, dripping with sweat. Had they both been even remotely sober, they would have spotted the lies before Salmik had even managed to open their mouth.

With a curt nod, they boarded the shuttle and strapped themselves in. In the midst of what the ship's crew and passengers were insisting on calling a celebration, they hoped a single missing shuttle would go unnoticed, at least long enough for them to land safely on the library's surface.

They held their breath as the shuttle descended, waiting to hear an alert either from their own ship or the other vessels invited by the library itself to bear witness to its end.

None came. There was no warning, as in previous times, when the shuttle neared the planet's rings, sliding in between them to lower itself into the library's atmosphere.

◆

SALMIK RECALLED THE sense of trepidation as they led their mother into the thicket. Her bones were like frail spiderwebs, loose skin hanging between each finger as if she were slowly evolving into something aquatic. They'd left a note in their request asking for the library not to apparate inside their mother's mind as it had done on their last visit with Frank. They worded their request carefully, trying to ensure that it understood the severity of their mother's condition.

Despite her exhaustion, she insisted on walking, acquiescing at regular intervals to Salmik's help as she leaned against them, allowing them to shoulder her weight.

The singing plants were the largest either one had ever seen. It was more forest than field, floppy violet petals turned inward as they awaited their bloom. They towered over them both, stems pregnant with sap. Salmik was sure the plants would burst if their bulbous surfaces were so much as pricked with a needle.

Smaller singing plants without petals grew up to their shoulders, the heavy, slightly medicinal scent so thick, Salmik felt they only had to reach out in front of them to grab it in their hands. Though the forest seemed to spread eternal, a glance up at the canopy revealed that most of the plants were on the verge of song. The petals were full, as if pumped with gallons of water, and there was a slight quiver at their pointed tips, a vibration like the purr of a beloved house pet.

Sunlight streamed through the foliage, the underbrush dappled with it, as their mother's hands gripped their forearm with surprising strength, curved shoulders clenched in both anticipation and fear. This was nothing like the singing plants of her childhood.

"Have you sent word to Pearl and them?" she croaked.

"Of course I have!" Salmik snapped, swallowing a surge of anger. "Sorry Ma. You know how busy they all are."

Pearl and their other siblings abandoned their mother. Her care, they argued, should be the responsibility of the childless one. Salmik, Pearl insisted, had less duties, more free time to devote to their Ma's recovery.

Besides, weren't they the scientist? Couldn't they do something about Ma's illness, cook up a cure in a lab somewhere to slow the alarming speed of her decline?

The fungus that Salmik had spent years fighting made its way to Sunar faster than their team could find a long-lasting solution.

Nothing could repair the damage it caused. When she began to refuse treatment, Salmik was heartbroken but sympathetic. She deserved rest. Visions of their first trip, of the library's wild, unprecedented metamorphosis, bloomed in their mind's eye. They'd always imagined, as they watched the change from the shuttle with Frank, that the library was laughing at them. Cacophonous cackles echoed in their skull. Fear settled in their stomach as memories of the library's forced entry into their mind returned unbidden. In her state, Salmik wasn't sure their mother could withstand it.

But as they sat in a small, grassy clearing beside her, singing plants rising to the heavens, they wondered if they'd been wrong, if the planet's transformation was simply a fragment of their own being left behind involuntarily for the library to absorb.

They resisted the urge to close their eyes as the singing plants finally unfurled. The first one was a singular chime in the silence. Sharp and clear, it brought to mind a metal rod hitting a bowl fashioned of some alloy or the other, ringing in the ears long after the sound itself had faded. Its siblings joined slowly, more sounds like pieces of enormous, polished metal clanging against each other in the wind.

And then several erupted at once, their song sliding seamlessly into each other, coalescing to form something resembling a string section in some alien, hitherto unforeseen orchestra. It burgeoned from the damp ground, the call stimulating the bloom of other plants in the forest.

The sound dislocated their insides, sending vibrations so strong that their body began to shake. Or at least they felt like it was shaking. Panic overtook Salmik as the rattle of their bones against each other grew, as the song swelled like the roiling waves of a tempestuous ocean. It spilled from their ears and mouth, from their nostrils, every bit of it overflowing from inside them as their internal organs vied for space in the song's presence.

Impossibly, the song continued, reaching a place inside their mind that inexplicably felt like the middle. A ball whose presence they never noticed in their brain shattered, and they seemed, for the remainder of the sound, to be observing their own body from above. Among the howls of unfolding plants, Salmik saw that their mother was going through something similar.

But there was no space inside them to feel horror, or anything, as a sound like a million organ pipes and harps continued, growing even louder with the addition of each unwinding set of petals. They tried to sort through their mind, but it was like trying to gather sand with a sieve. The song was an onslaught, ringing in their brain, screaming through their body, holding their lungs hostage. It filled the cracks inside them where terror ought to have been and replaced all feeling with itself. Like a river rushing downhill, it swept every part of Salmik into its roiling heart with a force so brutal, a colonization so hostile and unforgiving, they saw no choice but to grant it passage.

Their mother cried. She couldn't say anything, but tears fell down her cheeks, and Salmik felt the tension in her shoulders dissipate, felt the pain leave her body as the chorus swelled.

"Thank you," she whispered to no one in particular when the song ended and the plant's spores burst into the air. Flecks of purple and white floated before them, and with a contented smile on her face, Salmik's mother closed her eyes for the last time.

It was with great shame that they left her body behind, crawling to their shuttle as the song reverberated inside them, destabilizing them, still tearing them apart. But even as the guilt gnawed on them, Salmik knew they still would have turned tail. They were weak. For years, that sonic entry into their person, the manner in which it displaced them, orphaned them, and pushed them out of their own body, remained a powerful deterrent.

❖

SALMIK HADN'T FELT a thing as Pearl slapped them across the face. They sat in the garden watching her yell, hands waving about as if swatting away springtime insects. They looked at her without hearing a word that came out of her mouth, noting only that the veins in her neck bulged as if ready to burst. She requested visits to Zattina until she was blue in the face.

"Bitch!" she screamed at the memorial service, digging her nails into Salmik's neck and face. They allowed her to hit and kick and scream until an attendee saw fit to intervene, grabbing her by the waist and dragging her away as the rest of their siblings sneered down at them with a vitriol that made them want to die.

Now, as they entered the library's atmosphere for a third time, Salmik was ready to beg. They folded their pride neatly and stowed it in the compartment beneath their seat. At the very least, this wretched place could give them back their mother's bones.

The library did not provide coordinates this time, so they chose a place to land at random. It was painfully silent.

The quiet was chimeric, shifting and twisting, taking dark, ominous shape in their mind. They resisted the urge to wait for the planet to instruct them as it previously had, the countdown looming over them like a fat winter cloud.

The ground resembled polished concrete with occasional ridges that indicated some kind of foreign stone. An expanse of nothing stretched ahead, dotted with a single gray pillar made of the same material in the distance.

Salmik walked toward it, the timer on the ship still counting down in their head. On the pillar, perched upon a cylindrical mound of dirt, was an unremarkable Sunari singing plant. A ways from blooming, its petals were coiled tightly enough to know that its end was not imminent. Nothing else existed in the vastness of this place.

"Where is she?" they ventured, voice low at first, then louder as their head turned to their shuttle, then the empty, cloudless sky.

"Give me something," they pleaded. "Her skull. Her ribs. I'll even take a fucking toe! Anything."

They were met with a deep, deliberate quiet.

How much longer did they have to stand here, screaming into the void? Would the library wait for them to depart before its suicide, or would it kill itself regardless?

They lifted the singing plant off its pillar and trudged back to the shuttle. What were they even supposed to do with it? No singing plant had been successfully reintroduced to any Sunari eco-system. They almost laughed at how pitiful, how utterly useless this offering was. Salmik considered discarding it as one last fuck you to the compendium. If it was truly sentient, let it know spite. Resentment. Hate. But...this delicate thing would have brought their mother joy. They bit down on their tongue, drawing blood only to swallow it, the dull, coppery taste spreading in their mouth like ancient paint dissolving in water.

Would it be foolish to wait, to test the library, to see if it would indeed kill itself with Salmik still on its surface?

They hovered beside the ship in their shuttle, watching the library's rings as they began to pulsate again. A final goodbye. The singing plant sat wrapped in a dirty uniform they pulled from the shuttle's small storage compartments.

Compendium Zattina's end was quiet and uneventful. In less time than it took for Salmik to take a breath, it blinked out of existence. They imagined the shock on people's faces aboard the ship, the scramble as Mika and all the scientists on board tried to figure out how a thing of that size could simply vanish.

All they could feel was a profound sense of emptiness inside them. They were lost. The shame of leaving their mother's body to the mercy and whims of this *thing* bore down on their conscious, leaden, dry, and violent. Before them was a path steeped in an all-encompassing darkness. As Salmik sunk into the pilot seat of the shuttle, they saw in their mind's eye a single flower, thirsty and wilting in a flat expanse of desert. It was a nothingness so immense, so infinite, Salmik began to sob.

The Ng Yut Queen (The 五月 Queen)

Eliza Chan

ADA LEUNG HAD been looking forward to three things when she got home. Devouring the takeaway she had ordered—currently oozing grease into a paper bag. Taking off the stupidly tight shoes that were crafting perfect blisters on her toes. And sitting down to binge-watch the rest of *Pompey Peepers*, the Blitz era detective romance series that everyone was talking about. But opening the door to her flat, she realised her plans would have to be adjusted.

A smell like the perfume counter gauntlet at a department store hit her first, then the overwhelming feeling she had walked into a florist's. Flowers, everywhere. The floor was strewn with waxy banana leaves like a beach holiday. Dripping pastel bouquets filled every jar, mug, abandoned glass of wine and dirty saucepan in the tiny space. Orchids spilled from the opened cutlery drawer and peonies with heads like powder puffs poked through the wire lampshades that hung from the ceiling.

"What the actual—?" she said, kicking off her shoes.

Some sort of joke? Ada waited for friends to jump out at her from behind doorways, for a camera crew to appear at her shoulder. Instead, she felt her eyes start to water and her nose tickle. Hay fever. Great.

Opening all the windows and shifting enough flowers so she could actually sit down on her sofa took the best part of an hour. Now her takeaway was congealed, she'd lost her appetite and it felt like her nose had swollen up like an overripe strawberry. Ada snapped a photo to send to her best friend.

OMG, secret admirer?
Like something u see on
insta! So cute!

Not cute. I have to
breathe through my
mouth. If it's a secret
admirer then they're doin
a shit job. I h8 flowers

Yeah, yeah, u hate
flowers + romance.

I have hayfever

That's what
antihistamines are 4.

OMG u could go viral?
Post it online!

❖

ADA DID HAVE to admit, although not to Lou, that with the camera filters, her apartment took on a shoujo anime blush. Still, cherry blossom petals in her toilet bowl was a step too far. In the morning, Ada swiped her phone alarm without looking and tried to roll back over, but tug as she might, something was pinning down her duvet. A goddess was lying on one side of her bed, propped up on one arm. "Do you realise you snore?"

Ada fell off the bed with a yell, grabbing one of her flip-flops as defence against the intruder. The goddess had perfectly styled black hair in intricate loops and a red dot on her forehead. But it was the ethereal glow from her skin and the fact her white robes floated like they were being held by tiny invisible birds, that really gave the game away.

"Also, some joss sticks or fruit would have been nice. You know, to say thank you."

"I—what? Also, who?"

The goddess sighed as she stood up. Or rather, straightened like a bamboo stem in a serene forest. What? Where were these ridiculous images coming from? Ada felt her mind being assailed by soft-lit TV drama cut scenes. She had to rub her eyes to clear them away. Her unexpected visitor spoke with the patience of someone explaining a simple fact to a child. "The flowers. You prayed for them."

"I...did?" Ada had prayed to many gods for a number of things. The winning lottery numbers, a date who didn't turn out to be a douchebag, a self-cleaning flat. Only two days ago she had prayed for her mum to hang up after a one-sided conversation about how her biological clock was ticking, but she had serious doubts the gods were listening. She certainly had *not* prayed for flowers.

"Are you sure you've got the right person? Wrong number vibe going on here," Ada said, backing up to put more distance between herself and the ethereal screwball in her bed.

"At Qingming, with a whole packet of joss sticks."

"Qingming? I haven't celebrated Qingming since— oh." Ada remembered. Being about ten years old and living in a rural Yorkshire. Desperately wanting to fit in with her classmates, desperately wanting to be crowned May Queen to sit atop the annual float at the parade. They had given it to Louise Fowler with her beautiful blonde curls and parents in the PTA. Not to the Chinese kid with the single mom who burnt paper gold in a trash can. And Ada couldn't really fault them for that: Louise was the nicest girl in the year. Pretty and funny and never saying some of the ignorant things the others did.

Ada had indeed pilfered a whole thick bundle of joss sticks and lit them all at once. She remembered wafting them up and down. The smell had lingered in her hair for days after. *Someone, anyone, please please just make me the May Queen.*

The queen of flowers. Then she'll ask me to sit with her at lunch. She hadn't needed it in the end. A chance meeting over the tombola stall was enough. Swapping their dubious prizes of blonde shampoo and a pack of broken biscuits with rueful grins.

"Guanyin?" she ventured. The goddess of mercy nodded in confirmation. Nobody warned her that praying to a Chinese goddess about a British tradition might get a little lost in translation. "That was over a decade ago."

"Every single time—*you're late. I don't want it anymore.* Well, you aren't the only one praying. There's a bit of a back log. And then when we do get to your request, you've moved! Not just to the next village—all over the world. Changed your names or genders. Do you bother to pray with a forwarding address? No."

"Sounds like you need the internet." The words were utterly mundane, as if she was talking to her por por about installing broadband rather than an actual goddess sat cross-legged on a cloud floating above her overfilled laundry basket. Ada decided a coffee might help her get through this most unexpected of conversations. She padded through to the kitchenette and popped a pod in the machine. The reassuring chug followed by the velvety smell of the blend did much to calm her. When she turned from unloading the dishwasher, Guanyin was sipping at her brew. "Hey," Ada said reflexively. "That was for me."

"I thought you were finally making me an offering. What is this delicious elixir anyway? It's not tea."

"It's coffee," Ada said, resigning herself to making a second cup. "So, um, about the flowers. Thank you? I appreciate the sentiment. But I'm sure you have places to be, prayers to answer so..." Ada's eyes drifted towards the front door. She had plans for this weekend. Plans that involved a long hot shower, quality time with her TV and some online shopping.

"Actually, we're trying something new." The goddess's eyes shone and her smile widened. Looking at her teeth was like staring into the sun. Ada could sense a salesperson if ever she'd seen one. She girded herself to say no.

"New?"

"Well, there hasn't been a lot of youth engagement, especially in the overseas communities. It's a bit of a trial. An outreach programme."

"And what does this programme entail?"

"I answer all your prayers. And in return you show me around."

"Like a tourist?"

"Oh yes." Guanyin pulled out a rice paper scroll from her long sleeves and started to read from it. Chinese calligraphy in highly structured seal script filled the page. "I have a list. Westminster Abbey, the Houses of Parliament, Buckingham Palace, Tower Bridge, afternoon tea."

Ada groaned aloud. She'd already been tour guide for dozens of friends from home, not to mention their parents, aunties and uncles. Everyone and anyone found it oh so convenient that she lived in London now. Except her. She tapped her finger, wondering how you could politely refuse a goddess. But before she could answer, Guanyin started blinking rapidly and a hand clutched to her chest. "I...think there's something wrong with your coffee. It's making my heart go funny."

That gave Ada an idea.

❖

INSTANT RAMEN FOR breakfast was a hit. Guanyin fluttered around the polystyrene bowl, steam escaping from the sides of the lid until Ada said the five minutes were up. Given that every usable bowl in the house happened to be filled with the stems of wilting flowers, it was a win-win. But Chinatown was where Ada truly found her stride.

Cheese foam brown sugar boba in one hand, matcha bubble wrap in the other, Guanyin craned her neck every which way to look inside shop windows, at the K-pop stans and gossiping aunties. The tourists in their matching visors following a jaunty flag-waving guide. The influencers pouting under the two-tiered gate. It was perfect. Ada kept Lou updated with sneaky photos throughout.

What's she doing now?
Updates!

Watching buskers doin K18 moves

I can c her foot tapping LOL

🙂 U should join in

What? No.

Go on A! Let your hair down. Bet she'll be up 4 it

A?

Ada?

There, happy?

YES ☺

🩶 Look at the two of you! Ur laughing. I wish I was there

This message was deleted.

It was fun. For a minute.

◆

ADA BLEARY BRUSHED her teeth at the sink. Her head hurt from all the sugar of the day before, but the memories made her smile to herself. Guanyin had taken to karaoke like it was her natural form. Soft 70s Chinese pop ballads, 80s power ballads and 90s Disney princess songs were her favourites.

A flash of something light caught the corner of Ada's eye and she looked up at the mirror for the first time.

Her shriek brought Guanyin from the sofa bed. "What-what? What did Sun Wukong do this time?" she asked, cheek flushed and imprinted with soft lines from the cushions she had been sleeping on.

"My hair!" Ada said. Her easy to manage short black hair had somehow been replaced by cascading blonde locks. Curls that wouldn't look out of place on a Barbie doll. It was heavy and when she touched her head, it felt tacky against her fingers.

"Your second prayer," Guanyin said beaming. "Aiya I didn't realise there would be such a lag for this one too. Honey blonde hair."

As soon as she said it, Ada knew that's why the hair was sticky. Actual honey. "When did I wish for that?"

"The year after you wanted all the flowers."

"I was a kid! I didn't know what I wanted."

Guanyin raised an eyebrow. "I think it was quite clear what you wanted. More than now."

It was true, Ada thought. When she was a kid everything had seemed so clear and simple. If she could just be May Queen, everything would fall into place. In the years since she'd made those desperate wishes, she'd learned that life was a lot more complicated than that, though. Ada had been drifting ever since she had moved to London. Certain that she would find herself in The Big Smoke, she had instead fallen into the anonymity that came with being one of millions of ants in a city that never stopped. Constantly on the go; constantly feeling like she was missing out. She would flick through friends' photos and videos, envious of the parties, the galleries and theatres, the drinks out and dinners in. Even when she had been at the events, she was anxious she wasn't enjoying herself as much as she could be. Something was always missing.

They went to Brick Lane for market food. The heat of the Tube sent dribbles of honey down Ada's neck and she couldn't enjoy her tacos because of the bees congregating around her head. Guanyin had paired down her white robes, wearing a more kaftan-esque outfit today. Big gold hoop earrings swung from her ears. They looked familiar. A gift from Lou years ago that Ada had never felt flamboyant enough to wear.

My hair is made of honey.

Is this... a Chinese thing?

No. It's literally honey.

Bloody heck Ada

Bite me

I would.

◆

GUANYIN RAN OVER, her face flushed. "Why haven't you taken me to watch a show?" She was brandishing a flyer from a half-price ticket booth.

"It's never as cheap as they say. By the time you get to the front of the queue you feel obliged to buy something."

"But the man said I'd like this one..." Guanyin pointed with her delicate porcelain fingers to the iconic red poster. *Miss Saigon.* Ada raised an eyebrow, wondering if she should warn her. Wondering also if there was enough money in her account to pay for two tickets just to see her reaction. She bit her bottom lip and decided. Yes. Even if she had to put it on her credit card.

Guanyin's impassioned rage outside the theatre was not just filmed by Ada. It went viral. Videos of the goddess, semi-obscured by camera phones and bobbing heads, filled her feed. Ada scrolled through them, seeing her own gawkish face watching from the sidelines as Guanyin paced the pavement. Scattered applause and cheers responded to her points.

"I thought this was an enlightened era. Tornado potatoes and sushi tacos! But you've fallen short. Tantalised by distress, using it for entertainment. A little cathartic cry and get on with your day. Compassion? You know nothing about compassion!"

She went on, her robe loosely floating around her like a billowing jellyfish. Even the modern update to her clothing could not hide Guanyin's glow, a spotlight trained on her face wherever she went.

100,000 likes. OMG
she's a meme!

My phone hasn't stopped
pinging. The counter
keeps going up. It's wild

People can't figure out
her angle. Chinese
beauty products, herbal
medicine, yoga classes.
Lol

No-one believes she's
just an actual goddess

Nope. Just u + me

Lots of DMs as well. Freebies! Hair and makeup collabs. I'm like her agent now

Ah yes, the girl who once tried to bleach her hair with toilet cleaner so ud look like moi. How far uv come.

Shut it.

◆

NABIL LOITERED AT the side of Ada's desk, prodding at one of the orchids growing from her pencil pot. "Didn't the cleaners throw these out last week?"

"They keep coming back," Ada said, not raising her eyes from her monitor. Her hair was wrapped in a silk headscarf. She had to rinse out and replace it every few hours as the thick honey slowly oozed through. It was manageable though. Sort of. Washing her hair every morning made the honey runny enough that it didn't bother her until at least lunch. And her colleagues complimented her on her sweet smelling perfume.

The clothing was a new one though. She had put on her usual trousers and shirt but when she turned around, it had become a white wedding dress. Puff-sleeved, lacey and voluminous. Ada had immediately taken it off, kicking it into the corner of her room like a rat on the Tube. She eyed it suspiciously as she grabbed another outfit. Stared at herself in the mirror. Navy shirt dress. It was still a navy shirt dress. She just had to grab the belt and—she only glanced away for a second. When she looked back, she was wearing a wedding dress with a plunging V. Figure hugging satin. Ada swore.

"I'm late for work as it is!" she yelled as she prodded Guanyin awake. The goddess snorted once, wiping the drool from the corner of her mouth as she opened bleary eyes. A smile curved across her face. "You look good!"

"This is a wedding dress, you numpty, I can't go to work in this!"

"I mean, I wouldn't choose that one, unless you used some tape around your...you know," Guanyin said helpfully, gesturing at Ada's chest.

"I can't wear any wedding dress to work! When did I want this?"

"When didn't you? Every other month at least, if not more frequently for years."

Ada groaned. She tried to sit on the carpet, but the tight fit of the dress meant she could barely bend over without the seams splitting. "Every little girl wishes that. A white dress, a handsome prince...it doesn't mean anything."

Guanyin sat up and shrugged. "Your prayers, not mine."

Ada had changed several times. She tried outstaring her reflection, but the furthest she got was to the front door with a hand mirror and then she had blinked. The abandoned wedding dresses piled up in the corner, a mountain of chiffon and lace. Ada was running out of actual clothes, considered calling in sick until jeans and a T-shirt became a tea length white dress. It would have to do.

Nabil was still there, clearly after something. Ada finally looked up at him, impatiently drumming her fingers. His stammered question took a while to sink in. It was only after the longest pause that Ada responded.

"You're asking me out?"

"Um...yes."

"Aren't you gay?"

"Yes."

Ada waited for a follow-up but there was none. Nabil didn't seem to see the clear and insurmountable impediment to his proposal. She politely declined. After her other colleagues, the man who came to service the vending machine and one of the building security guards also asked the same question, Ada saw where this was going. She would have to use that sick day after all.

❖

AT THE KAITEN sushi place, Ada had to stop Guanyin from taking yet another plate from the conveyor belt. The number of cucumber maki rolls she had already taken were far more than the two of them could eat. Ada picked a plate of inari sushi for her instead, insisting that no, there really was no fox in it, it was just a name.

Someone tripped over her train and Ada hitched the dress further up, sitting on a lumpy pile of tulle. The thing is, after all her clothes were magically transformed into wedding dresses, she couldn't really afford to buy a new wardrobe. And even the more wearable dresses needed to be washed. Wedding dresses weren't exactly easy to launder at home. So Ada had to wear the bouffant dresses. After all, with honey dripping hair and flowers anywhere she lingered for too long, what was an extravagant dress or two?

"I don't see the problem. You look pretty," Guanyin said.

"The dresses by themselves are bearable, but the men..." They were interrupted by one of the waiters asking Ada out. She didn't even pause for a breath as she politely rejected him, waving her chopsticks at Guanyin. "They aren't my type."

"None of them?" The goddess's tone was one of curiosity rather than outrage. Not the horror her mother had shown. Guanyin refilled her green tea, marvelling at the boiled water tap on the table. She pushed it once, twice, three times, giggle hidden under her hand. Ada cleared her throat to remind the goddess they were mid-conversation.

"Well then what *do* you want?" Guanyin asked. "You're the only one who can decide."

Ada was flustered by the question, a sliver of ice dropping down her throat. She swallowed hard, doubling down on her annoyance. "What does that even mean? You're fulfilling wishes that are a decade old! Are you telling me I could wish for a million pounds and you'd give me it?"

"I'm here, amn't I? Providing a personalised service. But you've got to truly want it."

Ada snorted, the lingering sharpness of the wasabi prickling her nose. It sounded too good to be true. Which meant it probably was. But if figuring out what she really wanted was how to get rid of the goddess, she was willing to give it a go.

U rly think she's telling u
to wish for money???

Would be nice to have
sum

No arguments here. But I
suspect that's not what
she's talking about. More
sumthin from the heart?

Have a think A, might b staring u in the face

A mirror?

Har har. BTW b4 I forget, u free on 15th? My birthday dinner

In Aldborough?

No, on the moon. Where else? How long since u came back? Saw ur mum?

Maybe two Christmases ago. U know it's complicated w mum.

Would be nice to see u IRL

I would love

This message was deleted.

I'm definitely

This message was deleted.

I'll think about it

◆

GUANYIN ROLLED ONTO Ada's bed, bouncing with glee. Ada pretended she was asleep for as long as she could but the glow from the goddess's body made it difficult to keep her eyes closed, as much as she pulled the covers over her head. Like standing in front of a wind tunnel.

"It's like six in the morning."

"It's seven already. Also, I got a ticket."

"Ticket?"

"Yes, I normally prefer a bowl of oranges and some good quality joss sticks but I got a complimentary ticket."

Ada finally turned. The goddess was making less sense than usual. She grabbed the cracked handset from her hands, squinting at the blue screen to make out what she was being shown. Ada had given Guanyin the old phone a few days ago. Shown her how to create social media accounts and use the camera. Set up @genZgoddess for her and linked it to a 4Tea donations account for virtual offerings. It had a trickle of success. People posted prayers and thanks on her page. A few that had seen the previous photos and videos. Guanyin had a field day. Selfies in Camden market trying on neon goggles. Getting a shiatsu massage in a pop-up bell tent. Face painted and dancing at the front of the crowd in an open air concert.

And someone in K18's publicity team had left an offering of a backstage ticket to their concert. Ada sat bolt upright in bed. The tickets were like gold dust. Sold out in minutes.

"Are they any good?" Guanyin's eyes were wide as saucers.

"K18? The biggest selling boy band in the world? Yes."

Guanyin rolled this information around like a hard-boiled sweet in her mouth, nodding emphatically. "A good offering then."

"In the grand scheme of offerings, this beats all your fruit baskets and lotus flowers."

Guanyin raised an eyebrow. "Nothing beats a lotus flower in full bloom. But I take your point. A *very* good offering."

❖

No longer her tour guide, Ada finally had time to round up the wilting flowers for the bin. Scrubbed the green scum line from her glass tumblers and mugs. Her flat felt cold and sanitised without the colourful stems everywhere. Like no-one actually lived there. She washed her hair for an hour until the honey thinned out, sat in her comfiest wedding dress (winter wedding dress replete with a hooded cloak) and reached for the TV remote. But there was nothing on. Nothing that interested her the way Guanyin had. Nothing that had the naivete of the goddess and her enthusiasm for every little thing. All of those things that Ada said she would do when she moved to London. She never actually did them. Too busy, too expensive, too many people to talk to. There was always an excuse. But she was glad for Guanyin. The goddess was living her best life. Reminding people that she existed. If anything, Ada could live vicariously through her. Her phone pinged.

u decided yet? Bout the 15th?

Ada started composing a response. Deleted it. Tried again. Deleted. Her fingers lingered over the keyboard. Searched through the gifs for a cute puppy. Maybe an otter clapping. But what the heck sort of response was that?

She threw her phone onto the sofa. A lump had formed in her chest. Like all of the honey had dripped down through her skin and hardened, amber resin around her lungs. Like she had inhaled thorns in her sleep and they had twined between her ribs. Like an embroidered wedding veil swaddling her heart, stopping it from beating the strong pulses of its desire. She just wished...

Guanyin was there, backstage pass around her neck. She said nothing, offering an arm and the softest of smiles. This time Ada leaned right in, letting the goddess's glow encompass her. It felt like that first dip into a hot bath. She was tired. Exhausted by a city that did not want her, by a life that did not feel like hers.

"I wanted to be her. The pretty blonde girl who got to be May Queen. The friend who was always certain of her place in life." Her voice sounded reedy. Drawn out.

"What did you pray for? Really?" Guanyin pushed.

"I wanted to be her," Ada repeated. Guanyin shook her head tenderly. Waiting. Ada took a deep breath—like she was plunging her head underwater—summoning words she'd never said aloud. "I wanted her."

The relief spread like ripples across her surface. Tentative joy that the world had not crumbled. She had not broken in two.

"And now?" Guanyin continued. The goddess's brown eyes were liquid patience.

"I still want her." Like a toothache that pulsed against her gum, concealed behind a fake smile. It had always been there and would continue to hurt until she finally dealt with the root. Guanyin's face was a full moon on a clear night. She took Ada's hands and press something into her palm, curling her fingers around it.

A voucher for 10% off bubble tea. Ada looked up perplexed until Guanyin noticed. "Whoops, wrong pocket!" She took the voucher back, rummaging in her long sleeves for the right thing. An open return train ticket to Aldborough.

"I could've bought this myself," Ada said, wiping her eyes with the back of her hands.

"But you didn't."

Ada couldn't argue with that. Let a small laugh escape her lips. Her body was lighter now she had shed her baggage. It wouldn't be easy. Sketching an image she could only dimly see in her mind. But she had an outline. "Aren't you missing your concert?"

Guanyin reached into the air with a finger and thumb, pulling down a K18 thunderstick from nowhere. Winked, "I'm in all places at once. You'll rate me, right, on the app?"

"What?"

"Good luck, Ada," the goddess said, standing up. She pulled down another thunderstick, testing them on each other like a drummer readying a set.

"So we're done? I don't mean to sound ungrateful but about the hair and the dresses..." Ada said.

"Should return to normal after a while." Guanyin looked at her cracked phone, smacking her lips together as she clocked the time. Checked left and right as if crossing a road.

Ada struggled to her feet, ignoring the pins and needles prickling at her legs. "How long exactly is a while? Guanyin? How long?" But the goddess had gone. Slipped between spaces in the blink of an eye. Ada stood for a long moment, staring at the empty coffee cups on her counter. If she stared hard enough, she could imagine them once more filled with brightly coloured flowers. The same flowers which adorned Lou's hair as May Queen. Ada picked up her phone. Looked at the last message.

u decided yet? Bout the 15th?

Ada is typing...

Baobab Lover

Kwame Sound Daniels

I.

You and your sisters left your bodies where they were standing, in a grove in Zimbabwe, some fifty years ago. You left the dead buried among your roots, but still remember the way their bones nestled against your bark. Corporate development hadn't really reached you yet, but you could tell it would eventually. As the years wore on, the droughts became longer and drier. It was time. So, you and your sisters each took a piece of your bodies with you as you left. You wear a seed around your neck in a tiny glass bottle. When the wind blows and you hold the seed in your hand, you can feel the thoughts of your sisters brush against your skin—you have skin now, a deep, burnished brown that drinks in sunlight. You've let hair grow in a kinky halo around your head, emphasizing your height—a height that echoed the height of the body you left back in Africa. It's still standing. When you sleep, that is where you are. Letting your leaves rustle in the wind and sinking your roots down, down, down.

II.

You weren't sure what you wanted to do when you came to America. There aren't many marketable skills that dryads have outside of craft and gardening—but you weren't ready to miss the earth of your home that much, not yet. You weren't ready for this new soil. You're not used to soil without flesh mingled among the minerals—it was so much more lonely without it. So, with the assistance of various assimilation programs, you bounced from job to job, never quite finding something real that you could hold onto. Nowhere to put your roots.

You are on the east coast now, where the rains come and stay, until they don't. You work in a diner late into the night. Your boss likes you—which is good (he's quite intimidating when he's angry; smoke drifts from his nostrils, and his skin takes on a metallic sheen)—because you can stand for long hours without getting tired and only really need water breaks. You were offered longer breaks, and they are in fact mandatory, but you don't want to stop and think about what you're doing, here, in America, far from home, with your sisters scattered across the globe. So, you stay active, and you smile at customers and display a saintly amount of patience. There's a sort of ongoing bet among your coworkers to see how much you can carry in your wiry-strong arms. You've never lost. You get excellent tips in addition to the decent minimum wage. You start to think you could make a place for yourself. Maybe. Even if that place will never be the grove in Zimbabwe where you would drink water and blood from the soil with your sisters.

III.

You have a studio apartment, where you stay. There isn't much room, but you don't really need it. You only sleep a little bit. You spend most of your days reading books, taken

from the university library, and tending to houseplants—
those bratty little distant cousins of yours with ancestry in
other lands. They're finicky things and very particular about
where they are placed, but you can usually coax them into
behaving. They remind you of your younger sisters, the way
they were delicate before they grew strong. You invite your
coworker Celia over sometimes to share space or partake
in one another's bodies. Like you, Celia isn't quite used to
having flesh. Ae were a sylph, a thing of air and thought. Ae
were a suggestion of a breeze. You both feel adrift, though the
feeling pricks at your heart more than aers. After all, you lived
hundreds of years with roots. Ae were nomadic in nature.
With the directness of the earth under your feet, you meet aer.

IV.

THERE'S A PARK you and Celia go to visit, though ae only
accompany you rarely and when your days off coincide and
only if ae're in the mood. You like to sit and absorb the sun
and whisper to the local trees. You hum sometimes—your
voice is an alto, and you sink easily into a low register. Celia
thinks you should join aer band, but you don't see a reason
for that when the band already has a washerwoman with an
incredible wail and who cries tears of blood. You don't have
a flair for theatrics, and only barely tolerate crowds. Celia
accuses you of being boring. You are inclined to agree. At
least, sometimes. Celia is flighty and impulsive and doesn't
have the breadth for long hours of contemplation. When ae
get excited, ae shimmer. Ae talk fast, and you have a low,
measured tone. You think the two of you just live at different
speeds.

V.

THERE'S A CUSTOMER that you've started to notice as frequent.
She always comes in after midnight, orders a coffee, black,

and scarfs down the biggest breakfast on the menu. She's as thin as a rake, and you wonder if she eats at any other time in the day. She's pretty quiet. Her name on the ticket is Sofia Saar. She unerringly wears black clothes with something floral as an accent. She looks as though she is perpetually attending a funeral. She's dainty in all ways, with the exception of these big black boots she constantly wears—often tracking mud in with them. (She's one of Celia's least favorite customers because of this, but you don't mind. You like the dirt.) You don't really get to talk much, but one day, while you're giving her the check, you murmur her last name. She looks up. She says, "It's Estonian."

You wonder how long her family has been here.

She says, "I'm first gen. We came over when I was ten." She sighs. "I'm more American now than I am Estonian, but some things you never shake. You know?"

You *do* know. You can relate.

Sofia tilts her head to the side. "Do you have family here?"

You have family all over the world. But mostly in the lower hemisphere. A lot of cousins in Australia. Some of your sisters have drifted to Europe, some to the Americas. But when you stick your hands in the dirt at night, you can hear the sounds of their roots drinking water from the earth. You feel happy knowing that they live.

"That's evasive."

You shake your head. It's the truth. It's just that your kind don't have immediate family the way humans do. Family is different. Family is interconnectedness. Family is abstract and specific. There is a knowing in entwining roots. But you and your sisters talked through the air and through touch, much the way humans do. The words were slow but they were received.

Sofia nods slowly, making the same face she does when she's considering the taste of something she finds particularly...particular. (You watch her sometimes, the way her face shifts with her changeable moods, how her fingers dance over her books as she works). She slides a twenty toward you and hops off the bar stool. "Thanks for the food."

You nod.

She walks away.

VI.

WHEN SHE COMES in now, she asks you questions. You respond, as best you can in between attending to other customers, but you like having time before you answer. You like to sit with your words. You get the feeling that Sofia is exercising a possibly uncharacteristic restraint while listening. She is, after all, so quick with everything else. You learn a lot about her too. Tonight, the topic is education. You've told her that you're self-taught on most things, that you get all of your skills from books or trial-and-error. You tell her that your patience with yourself and with things outside yourself help with how you learn.

"I wish I had patience in general."

You shrug. That is something that must be cultivated over time, like many other things.

She wrinkles her nose. "You use the word 'cultivate' a lot."

Well, it *is* integral to your process. All plants do is cultivate. You suggest that Sofia cultivate patience with herself.

She rolls her eyes and shoves a forkful of omelet in her mouth.

VII.

YOU FIND OUT a few nights later a little of what Sofia's family must be like. She claims she is the family disappointment. You don't know if you could have ever been a disappointment to your sisters. That's not how the quietude of existence alongside family was.

There was a sacredness to your silences. It is easy to honor the dead with quiet.

She smiles wryly, "The look on my mother's face when, instead of restoring our family's crow-friend, I reanimated it, like, five minutes after it died. My birth father was appalled. My other dad was—he had an expression that I hadn't seen before. He was the one who suggested I go to college for it. It's not like the family carries any books on necromancy when our entire heritage is healers and birth doulas. I suppose I'm carrying on the doula work. Just, with death. There aren't enough death doulas, and there's always more grief."

You wonder if Sofia wishes it were any other way.

She grins and shakes her head, closing her eyes for a moment. "I like what I'm doing. Human anatomy is so interesting. I've always liked *that* aspect of my family's magic: the rate of decomp, the pull of a fresh spirit. There's a lot more spirituality to necromancy than I first realized." She drags a bit of pancake through the swirl of melted butter and syrup that's coagulated on her plate. "I'm minoring in psychometry rather than mediumship, though. I think having an understanding of a person before they died—the life they've lived, their connections to personal objects—will help my necromantic practice. Especially if I want to get into law. Which I do."

You raise an eyebrow.

"What? People pay good money to settle will disputes. And I'm hoping to get a side practice going where family members can get closure with sudden deaths. Doula work, you know."

You think that's a good thing to do.

"Well, let's not get into the ethics of making money on grief."

You won't, if it bothers her, but you make a point of reminding Sofia that everyone makes money off of *something.*

VIII.

It's nearing 2 a.m. and you and your coworkers are trying to close the place up as fast as you can. Sofia has been hovering for the past half hour, lingering instead of inhaling her meal and leaving as soon as she is done. You look at her levelly and let her know it's about closing time.

She bites her lip and looks everywhere but you. Then she says, "What are you doing after this?"

You think for a moment. Celia's off at a show so you don't really have anything planned. You suppose you might read for a bit. There's a compendium of North American Coniferous trees you've been enjoying really digging into.

"Would you like some company?"

You guess there could be some merit to sharing tree knowledge, and invite Sofia back to your place. So long as she leaves so your coworker can mop the floor.

Sofia nods and slides off her barstool. "I'll be waiting outside."

IX.

The walk home is quiet. There's a tension between the two of you as you walk, but it isn't unpleasant.

When the two of you are sitting on your futon and you're talking about how the boreal forests of Canada and Russia are the lungs of the earth, she kisses you. You're surprised. You ask if she's passionate about plant respiration, too. She rolls her eyes and says "For fuck's sake" before grabbing your face and kissing you further. You shut up.

X.

You and Sofia are hanging out in the graveyard on one of your free days. She was going over her notes and examining the quality of the dirt in this graveyard in relation to the one near the college. She has been saying that this one was a lot older and had melded more with the bodies due to its porous quality. She's been grumbling all night, worried about her practicum. You've been watching her work, jot down notes, and mutter to herself. You like how prickly Sofia is, like a *Pachycereus marginatus.* Tall, retains a lot. You tell her she could have been a dryad.

She snorts. "I doubt it."

You ask if perhaps a garden gnome would be more appropriate considering how similar her temperament is to theirs.

She slaps your hand lightly. Then something catches her eye. She points at your necklace. "What's that?"

Adansonia kilima. You carry a part of your body with you. It is your seed. It's part of your home. It was grown of bone and soil.

She asks, tentatively, "Can I see it?"

You hesitate, then nod, carefully uncorking the little bottle and letting the seed slide into her open palm, and it's like the world stops. She is holding your heart in her hand. Gently.

You watch, stock still, as her eyes cloud over with white and her breathing slows. You realize this is how she must look when she practices her psychometry. Her mouth opens and shuts. Then her eyes return to how they usually are and she says, "You have known so many years. You've lived so long. You carry death. I hadn't thought—"

You ask for your seed back. You think about what it means for you to have let her hold it. You've never let anyone hold it before. You tell her this.

She looks a little nervous. "Thank you," she says quietly.

You nod. You aren't sure if she understands the gravity of what just happened, if she knows that she holds your beginning and others' ends. But you lean over and kiss her and walk her back to your place. You let your body talk.

XI.

IT'S ACTUALLY SOFIA who gathers the courage to ask The Question. She's eating apple pie á la mode. She takes a deep breath and asks, "Would you like to be my girlfriend?"

You don't really know that you could be termed as a girl. Gender is abstract for a tree.

She groans. "Fine. A tree-friend. Dryad-friend. Partner."

You don't know what that would entail and politely ask for details. You've never been in an official relationship before. (Celia most emphatically does not count.) The way you and your sisters took lovers was in passing moments. It was learning to breathe alongside one another. It was learning companionable aloneness.

Sofia narrows her eyes at you. "Yes or no."

You say yes. You can figure out everything else as you go along.

"Good," she says, before leaning over the bar and pecking you on the lips, tasting like vanilla and cinnamon sugar. "I'll be outside."

You smile and collect her plate, wiping the counter with a rag. You think of your sisters and entangled roots, of the way breathing comes easier to lungs when you don't think about it. You think of the skeletons in your soil, the way your fruit was fragrant because of their burial. How would your fruit taste now? You think of all the lands you could have been in and you are glad you are here.

Braid Me a Howling Tongue

Maria Dong

WHEN I WAS young, I used to fray apart my mother's tales, seeking the threads of their structure. They were journeys, always, and marked by transition-places: doorway, gate, river. On the other side, someone offered the rules of this new environment. I liked the stories where these interpreters were animals or hags, though in my least favorite, it was a child with ragged clothes that admonished, *that's not the way things work here.*

I understand. Understand that people bore easily, that stories must be pragmatic. No time to waste on the heroine, bumbling her way through years of figuring out the rules.

But this isn't a story. There's no interpreter for me when I arrive, and no quest to speak of.

1

I'M THROWN THROUGH a doorway into a room full of girls.

I use this word loosely. Most are past bleeding age, some with bellies that round like rising moons. They sit at a large table in the middle of the room, dressed in matching gray smocks, identical white sashes tied around their waists. To my people, white is for funerals; the color seems fitting.

They watch as I hit the ground. Like me, they wear hobbles of strong, light chain.

The squat man that brought me stinks of poppy-smoke. He gestures to a woman in the back, twice as old as anyone here. She doesn't wear a hobble, and I hate her already.

Besides the door, there are no exits, just a number of square windows too small to crawl out. Each wall is lined with identical beds, all topped with lumpy mattresses.

The woman nods at a spinning wheel near the right wall. The man pushes me forward, saying something I don't understand, and again I'm struck by the flow of their language, the way it rises and falls like a raptor gliding on currents.

He pinches his fingers in front of him, miming. He wants me to make thread.

The girls have already turned back to their work— carding, weaving, sewing—as if bored by my presence. I almost refuse, but I'm afraid, sure that in another room there are women performing other, less desirable jobs.

I examine the wheel. It's different from the ones I know, but the pieces are all there—treadle, wheel, maidens, a horseshoe-shaped flyer that holds the bobbin. I test the treadle with my foot, get a sense of the drive wheel's rhythm, and start to spin.

❖

I SPIN WOOL until the backs of my legs go numb from the chair. Until my ankle aches and my fingers cramp from holding the same pinched positions for hours. The man has long left. The woman never looks directly at me, which means she's watching me closely. I do the same when I hunt deer.

I count the girls as I weave. There are twenty-nine, their complexions all like mine. I can't tell which are from here and which are stolen like me.

I wave at the girl carding wool and ask to trade via gestures. Her brown eyes flash amber as they widen. She glances at my waist and turns away so violently the length of her braid whips over her shoulder.

Maybe she didn't understand, I think, but I know this isn't the case.

◆

I APPROACH A girl to indicate I need to relieve myself. She, too, glances at my waist before addressing the woman instead.

I conspire to get a sash. I could steal it, maybe, but I think the sashes are just symbols of something else.

I go back to weaving. *Any color but white*, I think, as the wool runs harsh between my fingers. With so many of my people dead, maybe I should get used to the color.

◆

SOME HOURS AFTER night falls, everyone finally puts up their handicrafts. The woman approaches me and touches herself on the chest twice while enunciating slowly: *Alena, Aaaaa-leeee-naaa.*

I nod.

Alena taps my chest, her finger as imperious as a woodpecker's beak. I knew this was coming, but I shake my head. Her expression turns sour, and she repeats her ritual: *tap-tap, Alena, tap-tap.*

I open my mouth. Alena's gapes in response.

Three months ago, my closest kin fled a plague that ravaged our summer grounds. Asleep in the back of the wagon, I didn't see the raiders until I woke to a blade at my throat. Their leader cut out my tongue before I could weave a defensive spell—perhaps as punishment for spitting at him.

I will forever feel his knife. It cuts me as Alena studies his work, so sharp I taste copper where words should be.

My people are steppes herders, but I was a word-worker, the strongest of the tribes. Now, I'm left with only two spells. Calming a terrified animal is woven from a combination of *ah* and *bah* and *mah*. The spell that energizes an exhausted horse is mouthed silently.

I would give up either to say my own name.

Alena recovers, finally. She gestures at a bed near the back-right corner. The straw-tick shifts under my thighs as I sit. She pulls a wooden box from underneath and flips the lid. Its contents are cloth, stacked and folded like layers of the earth—two gray dresses, one white, an extra blanket. She shoves them at me, and I understand this is my place now, everything I own represented by this box.

I'm used to traveling light—but that is our freedom. This, here, is deprivation. I long for the howl of the fresh wind over the steppes. Since my capture, everything has been cages, each smaller than the last.

Alena leaves me and calls out. The girls hush and sit on their beds. None are empty. I wonder whose bed I've just taken, and what happened to its previous occupant.

◈

Despite my exhaustion, I can't sleep. I'm torn between crying and not crying, unshed tears twitching at my eyelids like ants.

I lie facing the room and trace shadows in the dark. The girls sleep in all positions, and the varying curves of their hips and heads and shoulders, feels like bedding down beside the sheep. Their combined breath rushes like wind through long grass.

A few snore, but I close my eyes and pretend I'm with my herd.

My mind drifts. I wonder if they'll be allies or enemies. If they were born into this life, or if some were captured like me. A rabbit claws in my throat.

I open my eyes and turn over.

Now, there's only the carding girl's bed between me and the back wall. She faces away, lying so still my skin prickles—but then her side drops and raises, too quickly for sleep. She was holding her breath. Her elbows twitch—slight movements, but fast and regular. She keeps her arms tight to her sides, her forearms in front. I can't see her hands.

I blush, but then I'm angry. My mother often lectured that my tragedies don't affect the world around me—and still, I reject the idea that this girl is pleasuring herself in front of me when I've just been dragged to this room as a captive.

She stills and slides closer to the wall, before looking over her shoulder. I feign sleep until I hear her move again, and then I open my eyes just enough to sense her form through my lashes.

She pushes her fist under the corner of her mattress. When she pulls her hand back out, it's open, as if she's stowed something away.

2

THE FIRST THREE days are the same. We wake early and eat. We wash our faces, our teeth, our hands. We clean the room, our bedding, our clothes, the chamber-pots.

Then, we're led single-file to a kitchen that accommodates us all at once. The grounds here aren't open like the steppes. There's just a small clearing for the buildings, ringed by a thick forest of trees unlike any I've ever seen.

The trees are massive, their leaves bright yellow and shaped like flower petals, their branches heavy with fist-sized golden fruits. Nobody ever tries to eat one.

I imagine sprinting for the tree-line. Were I not hobbled, I'd take my chances—but there's always a guard, leaning against a wall, a bow slung over his shoulder.

We spend our mornings cooking horrendous volumes of bland food. I crave my herd's meat and milk, but here, the diet is starches—tubers, flour, nuts. Filling, but not satisfying. At midday, women with hoods take away the food we've made. There are at least twenty buildings, and my group of girls is the only one ever in the kitchen, so it must go to feed the encampment.

Then, we return and switch to our handicrafts. My mother's ancestral home was not the steppes, but a sea village to the south. Like us, the women there weave with spinning wheels, instead of the hand spindles of my tribe.

Our work here is frantic. We produce cloth, cord, and rope until our evening meal. Only then are we allowed a few short hours to do as we wish.

I am in awe of their craft. It has all the components of good spell-work: intention, repetition, beauty that elicits emotion. Every time the carding girl outpaces me and switches to weaving rope instead, I imagine it thrumming under my hand—but thread-work is so rare, I've only met two practitioners. They crafted garments that allowed the wearer simple illusions. Our best hunter once paid thirty sheep for a jacket that temporarily banished the wrinkles around her eyes.

The girls ignore me, gossiping in that sweet, light language. As the days go by, fragments emerge, like bits of flotsam washed ashore. I comb for these words, eager to feel less alone. So far, I have three names, the word for relieving myself, a word I think means *do*, and an exclamation; I don't know if it's good or bad.

I am proud of my vocabulary, because nobody speaks

to me, or at a speed I could hope to follow. The only exception is Alena, who gives me the same word over and over.

Do, she says, pointing to the weaving, the cooking, the cleaning. *Do, do, do.*

◆

THE MORNING OF the fifth day, she points at the white dress in the box. *Do.*

I swallow hard. The funereal dress makes my skin crawl.

Do, she says, the pitch of her voice dropping, and I'm forced to comply.

We complete the morning chores and the cooking, but that is all—no handicrafts. When we get back, the girls all sit on their beds. There's an electricity to their whispers, an odd energy in the way their gazes connect across the room.

Alena locks the door. She removes our hobbles, one by one, and tears come to my eyes. A few of the girls rub their ankles, but they don't seem to share my relief.

Someone knocks at the door. Alena clears her throat and adjusts her smock before opening it.

A man stands on the other side, a slip of paper in hand. She takes it, and he steps away.

She steps inside. "Marali." Her eyes search the room. "Awen. Terzanne." She pauses between each word. "Ronata. Kalen. Mea." When she finishes, the named girls walk to the front of the room. It is strange, seeing them take long strides. They stand, single-file, like a slim line of cat-tails edging the bank of a river. The man says something, and they all leave.

Alena locks the door. It feels like the moments before a loosed arrow, one kind of nervous hush converted to another. Some of the girls look relieved. Others, disappointed.

The girls open the boxes under their beds and pull out belongings while making conversation—a deck of colored wooden squares, a drawing, a small comb. The girl with the bed on the other side of the carding girl pulls out a wooden hook with a small bit of weaving on it. I don't know how she could choose to weave after being forced to all day, but I say nothing.

◆

THE SUN SETS. Alena lights a lantern that spills a golden glow over our faces.

Finally, there's another knock at the door. Alena opens it, and girls tiptoe in like a line of deer. They go straight for their beds without looking up.

I catch a whiff as a girl passes—sweat, and something more acrid, but I could be imagining it.

I don't think I'm imagining it.

A short time goes by—a quarter-hour at most. My stomach gurgles, for we haven't eaten yet, but the girls all perch on the edge of their beds and whisper. I realize all their little bits and bobs have been put away.

Even in the dim light, I can see it. They're afraid. None cry, although some have wet eyes. And there's a cloying miasma in the room, one that makes my skin prickle and all the hair on my body stand on end. *Something's going to happen.*

And then we hear it: a long, drawn out note, like the baying of a wolf, and that's when a few of the girls start openly weeping.

◆

THIS NEXT PART, I'm not sure if I am telling right. I worry fear has re-written my memories. But I will try.

◆

ALENA FLOATS TO the door and opens it. There's nobody there, save the dark.

A piercing horn blast fills the air, and the girls all jump up at once. They fly out of the room, a great school of fish that swirls around and past me, streaming like bats into the dark.

I don't move. I don't know what's happening—but Alena comes running. She points at the door and shouts things I can't understand, but then she says, *do, do,* and her voice is so frantic, I catch her fear like a disease. I sprint out the door, not sure if I am running to or from something—but I hear the thunder of feet, and when my eyes adapt to the dark, I'm shocked by what I see.

There are hundreds of girls, running in all directions, fighting and snarling and pushing and shoving, their shadows shifting like a herd. A few climb into trees, as nimble as squirrels. One girl kicks another in the face, trying to keep her down. Most, though, just run.

Less than a minute passes while I watch the chaos—and then I realize I can't see any of them anymore. The sound of their steps has faded.

The air fills with a low, keening howl, like the baying from earlier, but throatier and louder.

An enticing shiver climbs down my back. I was one of three word-workers in my village, the strongest for a hundred miles in any direction. During wolf-hunts, I often laid in wait for hours, spinning the spell of confusion under my breath. I'd loose it when the wolf appeared, and the animal would stumble to its belly as our hunters rushed in to slit its throat.

But I have no tongue anymore. No magic at my disposal.

My breath catches as I sprint away from the sound. My body stirs awake after a week of being confined, the terror pumping through my arteries somehow glorious. Dangerous or not, this is far better than endlessly spinning thread in a room made stuffy with the fear of thirty girls.

My legs eat up the distance. Clouds roll over the moon. I can barely see, but I sprint through the trees, trusting my heart to guide me in the dark.

❖

I DON'T HIDE. This is my mistake.

One moment, I run with a vicious joy in my heart. In the next, the thing is upon me, so fast that by the time I catch the sound of its paws, it has reached out and thrown me to the ground.

I land on my belly and roll to face it. Fear fills me, so complete that my bladder voids and piss runs down my legs. I try to scream, but it's as if there's a nightmare sitting on my chest, crushing any sound. This, this *creature*—it's not a wolf. It's at least as big as a bear, and although it has a long muzzle and pointed ears, its eyes and paws are feline, and it has whiskers.

It approaches with that languid, yet focused way all cats have, its maw open and the end of its nose twitching. I lie still as it sniffs me—my feet, my legs, my stomach, my neck. Its breath is hot on my belly and smells like rot.

I remember my mother's smile. My father's soft voice. The way the light looks when the sunset catches on the woolly backs of our herd.

But the monster lifts its head and scents the air. It springs into motion and melts into the trees with a bay like the rumbling of an avalanche.

I let out a long, shaking breath. I think the creature spared me because I have no sash, but I'm not sure, so I climb to my hands and knees, to my feet. My leg is wet, and swiftly turning cold, but I don't care. I run, even faster than I did before, because I now know what I'm running from.

❖

TOO SOON, I sense something looming before me—a sharpness to the black, as if the trees have pressed together so tight, they've cut off all hope of escape. There's a flat plane that makes my vision dance in the dark, the shape too straight to be natural.

A wall. It's three times taller than me, the sheer face slick and vaguely reflective in the moonlight, but I don't care. I will claw my way to the top.

The moment my hands touch its surface, they burn as if they're on fire. It hurts so much that despite my fear, I scream—but the sound is lost again, in the long blast of another horn.

I fall backwards, but the pain barely fades. My palms are covered in a sticky substance that smells like fat and burning twine. My eyes sting from the vapors.

Three blasts of a whistle echoes through the forest— *heeeee, heeeee, heeeee.* The trees around me burst into light, the globes of fruit all turning into small yellow suns, bright as day. I blink until I can make out the wooden wall. A dark-green pitch coats its lower half.

My hands look ruined: bloody, as if I've skinned them.

The air fills with the thumping of hooves. I sprint away, seeking some place to hide, my hands held out in front so I don't accidentally touch myself with the poisoned pitch.

Before the wall leaves my sight, I am brought down by a heavy net.

❖

A MAN BRINGS me back to the room. Alena rubs a salve on my hands that snuffs out the sting. There is no meal, but I don't care. I couldn't force myself to eat.

We all lie in our beds, me in my piss-soaked dress. Alena blows out the candle.

I fight sleep, but once the fear leaves my body, I'm dragged underneath its surface. In my dreams, the hunt continues, the creature baying behind.

Once, it seems like I hear someone scuffling in the box under my bed. I surface, but I don't stay. Soon, they're gone, leaving only the silence that swallows me.

In the morning, when I open the box for a clean dress, I find a white sash-belt inside.

3

I WAKE SHORTLY before dawn, the sky barely graying, my hands burning. It feels like I'll suffocate if I lie flat any longer. I quietly sit up.

In the chaos of being dragged back to the room, I didn't notice that the bed on the other side of the corner from the carding girl's is empty. Did someone slip out during the night? Or was it empty all along, my mind playing tricks on me?

But I remember the wan face of its former occupant.

I look out a window and imagine crushing my body through its small surface, extruding out like milk through an udder, and running for the wall. I should be screaming, we should all be screaming—but it's like this body isn't mine, like this place isn't real.

I turn at a rustle behind me. The carding girl is awake. She reaches her fingers for the empty bed and strokes them through the air, as if searching for a warmth that has long faded.

I remember, then, that first night, the way her elbows twitched in the dark. I wonder what it was that she pushed under the mattress.

◈

I WASH AND change, but I can't shake the long fingers of the night. Before we start our morning chores, the door swings open, and the man that brought the slip with the girls' names steps in. He holds a box, a twin to the ones under our beds.

He gives an impassioned speech. There is something

primal about the resolute set of his jaw, his commanding voice, something that tries to claw its way into my head. I can tell from the faces of the girls that his words have an effect—jawlines tightening, cheeks reddening. It makes me grateful that I don't understand, but my reprieve is like a candle, already burning lower, the wax dripping onto my flesh.

After a few minutes, he opens the box and pulls out a thin scarf of undyed wool, crocheted so finely it looks like lace. There's an odd ripple to the weave, one that makes me feel like I'm bouncing on the back of a fast horse when I look at it.

He takes out a match.

Once, a girl from our tribe fell asleep while sitting in front of the fire. She leaned forward, and her pigtail caught—*crack-whoomph*—before it disappeared, right down to her scalp. It's that same sound I hear now.

When it's over, nothing remains of the scarf but a sulfur-smell. He intones a final sentence that can only be a warning, and then he is gone.

◈

MY HANDS ARE too burned to weave thread. I'm moved to carding. When the girl gives me the handles, I realize her palms are covered in a mat of scars.

◈

I COULD TELL you now, of the moments that pass after that—day after day, week after week, grinding me away like an old tooth. The way the group slowly peels back its hard shell. The softening of Alena's glances, except for the night of the second hunt, when I came in without my sash, and she caned me so hard I couldn't sit for ten days. The next hunt, she fastened it to me with some kind of lock behind my back. Despite my best efforts, I couldn't tear the sash off.

I frantically learn vocabulary, adding each word to my repertoire like a weapon on a rack, as if sounds I can't produce can still somehow protect me. I want and fear understanding of their speech in equal measure.

I learn that the cycle of our lives will always have five days. The first day is marked by the man's short speech. The next days are all the same—work—until the fifth day, when we run for our lives.

I'm not caught by the creature, although there are many times it comes close. Times where I climb trees, or hide in bushes, or press myself to the earth in a shallow depression as its stench approaches. More than once, I am saved by a sneeze or the cracking of a branch—some other girl that has betrayed herself.

I should hate the creature, but I cannot. It is like the wolves that plagued our flock—an animal driven by natures it doesn't control and can't hope to change.

But the man I call *the fifth-day man* in my mind, even after I learn his name is Euolen? The more I know of their language, the more I hate him.

❖

I STUDY KALEN, the carding girl, who reclaimed her position once my hands healed. It happened quickly, Alena's ointment working some magic.

Kalen rarely looks at me. Ten hunts have passed since the morning she reached for the empty bed. I stay up at night, watching her elbows twitch, although I always fall asleep early the night before the hunt, some survival instinct dragging me to ground the way the creature did. On fourth-nights, I can barely keep my eyes open long enough to finish the meal.

Sometimes, the empty bed is in one of the other buildings. During our excursions to the kitchen, I've counted at least ten houses like ours, each probably full of girls.

The fifth-day man always comes to give his speech, but he only burns an object when the girl is from our house.

By now, I know enough words to occasionally guess the topic of conversation—the weather, the weaving, the cooking—but the girls still treat me like furniture. I rub my fingers against a candle-wick and write a single word, charged with longing—*hello*—but it's clear none understand. When Alena sees, she grabs it and berates me, a long combination of sounds that ends in *not do, not do, not do.*

After, that's what they all call me. *Not Do.* I'm driven mad a thousand times a day when those sounds prick at my ears, unsure if they're talking about me, or merely giving instructions.

When I was first captured, taken from my tribe and family—the loneliness ached, but fear kept my mind occupied. Now, during the four days I know we're safe, there's nothing to stop my heart from being ground like seeds under a pestle.

◈

I FEED MY loneliness by watching Kalen. I pretend she's my friend, that I know her thoughts. I invent stories of how she came here. She's a tribal princess, banished for being in the wrong inheriting clan. She's a criminal charged with assassinating a village elder. She's a sheep-spirit whose woolly pelt was stolen by these people, and she cannot leave until she reclaims it.

I learn that Kalen likes sweet foods. That she fidgets often with her sash, as if it refuses to sit right on her hips. That she avoids Wen. Wen always smiles, and her voice is always soft, but more than once, I see her light and cheery speech sends girls running away with tears in their eyes, which is how I know she's a snake.

If Kalen notices me watching, she doesn't confront me.

This kindles boldness in my chest, until one day, I resolve to communicate with her. I draw my eyebrows together and mime a series of actions—striking a match, setting fire to something from the bottom, my fingers wiggling like spiders as they crawl up. *Why*, I mouth, taking care not to show her my missing tongue.

I tilt my head, as if lying on my side. I close my eyes and reach forward, the way I saw her do. When I open them again, she looks stricken, as if I've just slapped her. She presses her hands to her face before running away, her braid swinging.

I'm devastated, but I deserved this. Kalen didn't consent to being my friend, to having me invent her entire history. I stand, steeping in my shame and the rapid knocking in my chest.

When I turn away, someone grabs my wrist from behind. My heart sings. I turn, sure that it's Kalen—but then my hope deflates like a bad bread. It's Wen.

I stiffen. I don't know if I should flee or fight, but I can feel that Wen is dangerous.

She shakes her head and speaks in small, broken phrases, as if addressing a child. *Not Do. You want knowing?*

My skin crawls to get away, but it's like a spell, hearing someone address me directly with anything other than *do* or *not do*. I feel like one of the wolves I used to hunt. I swallow and nod, and Wen lets me go.

Riotta. She bad.

I blink, and Wen repeats my gesture, spider-fingers climbing up a scarf. She points at the ceiling.

Always watching. Do bad, and creature happens.

She smiles, so sweetly I almost relax, but there is flint in her eyes, as sharp and bright as a new metal knife.

I nod. She goes back to her weaving, leaving me with the feeling that I have done Kalen some great, unknowable wrong.

4

PERHAPS I WAS wrong about lacking an interpreter. I step
through Wen's words and arrive at an understanding of
this place.

My parents' tribes both believe that those who make
mistakes should be given an opportunity to correct them.
Someone who cannot be redeemed reflects a failure of the
whole tribe. While we don't uphold these teachings perfectly,
this ideal endows us with responsibility and compassion
and dispels fear, because a wrong can both be created and
righted by our own hands. This is the way I was raised.

I study the girls as we cook, as we weave, as we flee from
the creature, as we disappear. I hold Wen's words up to my
eyes like a navigator's lenses, and I learn that these beliefs
aren't universal.

Samma drops a dish on the floor. She casts a fearful
glance, not at us or Alena, but at the door. Her eyes slide
skyward, as if she can see through the ceiling.

Menta and Deo converse in giggling whispers, until
Wen walks too close. From then on, they are silent,
although one glances furtively upward.

Kalen alone never looks up, and that makes me like her
more. I watch her elbows twitch in the night and burn to
know what she hides under the corner of her mattress—
but it feels wrong to pry. We have no privacy and own
nothing except the boxes, full of gray and white dresses
and whatever small trinkets we put together.

❖

HALF A YEAR passes, the warm weather sliding into cool.
By now, I've cobbled together an understanding of the
underpinnings of this world. The girls all believe—or
purport to believe—that the creature can smell sin. When
a girl is taken—and we've lost ten already from this house,

ten boxes opened and shown to us—the fifth-day man's speech gives us the reason, evidence of sin in retrospective.

I don't always understand the speech, but I don't need to. Common threads connect all these crimes. We aren't allowed to want or seek truth. We aren't allowed to be angry, only afraid.

Samma is taken for gossiping about the fertility ceremony, about what happens to the girls that line up before the hunts. Deo for harboring rage against Wen in her heart.

I come to believe that it doesn't matter what the fifth-day man finds in our boxes. There will always be some way for it to confess our sin.

❖

THE DAYS SHORTEN as we enter winter. It's colder than what I'm used to, and before long, I find an addition in my under-bed box—a thick wool cloak.

The snow is wondrous for the change it brings. I volunteer with a raised hand for each task that sends me outside, just to hear it crunch under my hobbled feet. By the end of the first day, my nose, hands, and feet are all burnt, and still, I revel in the way it renders the world still and peaceful.

That night, I hear Kalen's new neighbor whispering about how much harder the hunt will be with the snow. Then, I hate it the same as the other girls.

❖

TWO DAYS BEFORE the hunt, I'm stirring a massive pot of porridge. I've taken care since my disastrous encounter with Kalen to stay away, even though I cannot keep her out of my thoughts.

She's kneading some bread dough on the other side of the kitchen. She grabs the ball and turns—and trips on

Wen's outstretched ankle.

The dough sails through the air and lands on the floor. Wen says something I cannot hear, but Kalen stiffens. Tears glisten in her eyes as she sets the dough on the table, and then she turns and shuffles out the door, the hobble jingling furiously.

Wen's smile climbs her cheeks like vines.

I beg Alena for permission with my gaze. To my surprise, she nods. I exit and bow to the helmeted guard as I pass, before searching the clearing for Kalen.

A small gray triangle of cloth peeks from behind a tree-trunk, before bobbing up and down. How fitting that Kalen's elbow gives her away.

The snow crunches underfoot as I approach. I'm grateful that it's saved me from having to call out, from her hearing my voice of only vowels—but I wouldn't want to scare her.

I circle around the tree. She is bent double and silently sobbing into her hands, her body shaking. I wonder, not for the first time, if she was born into this life.

I lay a hand on her shoulder. After a moment, she straightens and brushes her eyes.

She turns, and something comes over her face—some boldness I cannot fathom. She leans forward and kisses me lightly on the mouth.

At first, there's a noisy rush of thoughts, but they're overwhelmed by the chalky scent of flour, the softness of her lips. I feel shot through with heat, like I can't draw breath. When she pulls away, air whispers from my mouth like the sighing of the girls in their sleep, and my whole body fills with longing.

She stomps away. I'm too stunned to follow.

When I look up, she's gone, and Wen is outside, talking to the guard. His helmet is off, and when I see his face my heart stops—*the fifth-day man*—but then I capture the differences. He's younger, his jaw sharper, his hair cropped shorter. He must be a close relative—a nephew, a son.

He catches my gaze, and it reminds me of the creature that first night, the whiskered nose snuffling at my waist.

◈

KALEN AVOIDS ME for the rest of the day, dancing away when I approach. I feel like I've fallen through a thick crust of lake ice, only to find hot water underneath. It cools every moment she ignores me.

◈

THAT NIGHT, I stare at her back and will her to turn over. For her elbows to start their dance. She's too still to be asleep.

Kalen. I mouth her name, the base of my lost tongue twitching. Something dark and made of longing thrums between us, something like the magic I once had. I almost cry with loneliness, for it and for her. *Kalen.*

She stiffens as if she can hear me, then shuffles around in the bed until she faces me. Despite the dark, her eyes are as round as the moon.

I reach for her. The gap between our beds is too large for my arm to bridge, but if she reached back, we could touch in the middle.

She doesn't. After a few moments, I let my arm fall and turn away. When sleep calls for me, I embrace it, if only to avoid my broken heart.

5

ON THE MORNING of the fifth day, the hunt hangs over us like an impending storm; tall, dense clouds of dread that threaten to drive us mad with the crush of their weight. Each week, I've felt it bearing down, but today, it's coupled with the rawness in my chest.

Worse, despite my fear, I'm drowsy, as if my longing has spent all night undoing the work of my sleep. I tell my heart that this silliness will get me killed, but it refuses to listen.

I spend the day in a fog. Perhaps the belief of these people in the punishing sentience of the world has some merit, because that night, Alena finds *Not Do* on the roster.

◆

YOU WANT THESE details. I know it—understand it, even. But I can't bear telling you what happened in the space from when I left to when I returned.

If it matters to you, I recognized the man waiting for me. His face was burned into my memory after Kalen's kiss—a face like the fifth-day man's.

◆

THE HUNT STARTS. My body doesn't run as fast as it can. It no longer fears the creature.

Within minutes, the girls are gone, and I'm alone with the trees and the snow.

At first, I'm aimless, but this changes. I've split my hunt-nights between hiding and investigating the wall that encircles the clearing. Tonight, I will throw myself at its poison, will clear it or die trying.

Before I'm halfway there, something grabs me around the waist and drags me to the ground. I have no time to scream before my face is driven into the muffling blanket of the snow.

"Be quiet, Not Do."

I still under Kalen's voice, so close to my ear. I would've guessed my heart couldn't beat any faster, but it does.

She helps me to my feet. "We have to hurry."

The weakest candle lights the dark; when Kalen takes me by the hand, my heart sings bright, despite the cold and the ever-louder baying of the creature.

She leads up a hill, down another, before pulling me behind a trunk. I blush as she lifts her skirt, but there is something thin and gray tied around her waist.

My mind fills, *crack-whoomph*, as I recognize it—a crocheted scarf, the fabric woven with a clever ripple. She removes it before holding me tight and wrapping it around our necks.

She murmurs warmly into my ear. "Be quiet, Not Do. It can't see us as long as we're wearing these, but it can hear us, and it will smell us if it comes close."

We stand, the contours of our bodies pressing together. I can't bring myself to breathe. There is much I want to tell her.

I kiss her lightly on the lips and turn away—but then her hands find my hair. She kisses me fiercely, and before I remember myself, my lips part.

Her tongue enters, soft with curiosity. I stiffen as she probes that empty space—but then she sighs, and I close my eyes and melt into her.

The horn sounds, startling me. She pulls away, and I realize the scarf is gone. I pat at my chest, my neck.

"A few minutes," she says. "Then gone. Have to always make more."

She walks away without looking back.

❖

KALEN AND I have conversations, time-delayed messages that are more like letters. When her eyes find me across the room, I mime my questions. Later, in the dead of night, she mumbles the answers, secrets only I hear.

We are only close during the hunts. There, her scarf around our necks, I have the chance to ask her anything I want—but in those moments, I can think of nothing but the feel of her hands and her soft tongue.

❖

THREE HUNTS PASS before I dare to ask about the girl she reached for after my first hunt.

That night, she lies facing the wall and ignores me. It feels like thorns are being pushed into my heart.

◈

THE NIGHT AFTER that, I'm the one that turns away.

◈

ON THE THIRD night, we lie facing each other. She holds up a hand before rolling over and pulling up the corner of her mattress.

The half-finished gray scarf hangs on the weaving hook like a flag of surrender. She rolls back over and puts it away, and my world is bright again.

6

The next hunt, I long to explore her with my hands, but she holds me too tightly, her head resting on my shoulder.

Her breath warms my ear. "I don't think the creature killed her."

I pull back enough to see her face. It's easier for me to understand their language when I can watch mouths move and see expressions.

Who killed? I mouth.

She presses her lips together. "I mean...I think they saw. They saw put on scarf. Scarf not allowed. So creature killed her."

I shake my head. I've already decided the deaths are random. If sinners were being struck down, we would've both died long ago.

Kalen pulls away. She cannot go far, not with the scarf around our necks, but the space between us feels unending.

I study her face. She looks sure—and she's been here much longer than I have, so who am I to doubt?

I write a story in my mind. Over and over, Kalen makes the missing girl a scarf. Kalen never knows if it's the scarf or luck that saves the girl from the creature. One day, the girl disappears. The next, the fifth-day man comes and burns the scarf.

If Kalen is right, they must mark us somehow. Mark us so the creature finds us.

My heart is so painful, I feel like its fibers are being pulled apart.

I'm dying, I think. *We're all dying.*

Forgive me, forgive me, forgive me.

I nod and reach for her. My hands travel her body, hungry to explore in ways I haven't dared before. I'm desperate to consume her.

We must be silent, and yet, she cannot, not always, not when she is shuddering against me.

When the horns call, I can't make my legs work, not until she kisses me on the forehead.

❖

THE NEXT FIFTH-DAY, Euolen looks at Kalen for a long moment before giving Alena the list. It's a hungry look. I know she'll be called.

We lock eyes as she leaves. I think again: *I'm dying, we're all dying, forgive me, forgive me, forgive me.*

I was so wrong, to ever call us girls.

❖

WHEN SHE RETURNS, her eyes find mine. There's something dead to them, something raw and hollow. I wonder if that's what the inside of my mouth looks like.

I shouldn't stare, but I can't look away. Not until I hear an odd sniff next to me.

I turn to Wen's stare, as hard and black as obsidian. She spins away as fear slides down my back, cold and sticky like spiderwebs.

◈

THAT NIGHT, AS the creature howls, I draw Kalen close. Our first kisses, Kalen explored my missing pieces delicately, with care. Now that she's the one with something cut out of her, I will do the same.

◈

SOMETHING HAS CHANGED. Alena and Wen watch us, so closely that I don't dare to glance in Kalen's direction. More than once, I look at Alena, only to see that Wen has already locked eyes with her, as if to say, *see?*

Days pass in which I cannot reach for Kalen, cannot sign to Kalen, cannot smile at Kalen. Days in which I hold my breath and wait for the hunt.

At night, Kalen faces the wall, strong and smart where I'm weak and desperate.

◈

TWO NIGHTS BEFORE the hunt, the dark pulls me down, my body pleading for rest, but I'm afraid that Kalen will acknowledge me, that I'll miss my only chance to see it. I reach for anything to keep me awake. I make fists and press my fingernails into my palms, small fires like sharp stones. I bite my lips. I mouth the silent spell that energizes an exhausted horse—and my mind clears, as if I've been blasted by cold wind.

Word-working spells only affect animals. They have turned me into an animal.

I mourn, bitter, but when I feel sleep coming, I mouth the spell, over and over.

The next day, I'm like a toddler sick with fever: running into walls, dropping things.

◆

THE NIGHT BEFORE the fifth-day, we have stew for dinner, but I can't eat. It feels like spiders crawl through my insides.

Alena presses me. When I shake my head, she grabs my jaw and forces spoonfuls down my throat.

It's not until I'm sitting on the bed, my head swimming, my body swaying, that I realize how suspicious this is. Alena circulates around the room, making sure we're all tucked in, and then she leaves.

I try to sit up, but my arms and legs refuse. My body feels impossibly heavy. I barely manage to mouth the spell before sleep rolls in—and then, I feel a slight reprieve. Over and over, I shape the words, slowly dragging myself aboard their raft.

When I'm sure I'll stay awake, I look for Kalen. Her side rises and falls in a rhythm impossible to fake—and this, more than anything, is evidence we've been drugged. Kalen never falls asleep before I do.

Something is going to happen. I'm sure of it. I mouth the words until my lips hurt, and my alertness solidifies like fat exposed to cold.

The door creaks open. I close my eyes. Fatigue swarms at me like a cloud of flies, making me almost sick with its force, but I keep my lips still.

Soft steps pad across the room, unfettered by a hobble—Alena. She approaches, and my pulse drums like hooves. *She knows, she knows, she knows.*

She passes me. I watch through my eyelashes as she opens the box under Kalen's bed—Kalen, who doesn't stir, not even when Alena drops the lid with a thump. Nobody does.

I risk a glance at Alena. In her hand is a white sash.

I wait until she leaves, and then I creep out of bed, mouthing the spell like a ward against evil. I open Kalen's box and pull out the sash. It looks the same, but when I bring it to my nose, there is something soft and bitter in its scent, and nothing of Kalen.

I quickly trade the sash with the one in Wen's box. I take care to leave it exactly as Wen's was, rolled into a neat bundle, nestled next to her weaving hook.

◆

DURING THE HUNT, cloaked by the magic of Kalen's scarf, I try to mime what happened. It's clear Kalen doesn't understand. I sneer and mouth the word *Wen*.

"Wen?"

I nod and wait for the whistle, the horn.

◆

THAT NIGHT, WHEN we return, Kalen's eyes find mine. They are round with fear, with suspicion. Although this hurts me, I'm glad. Glad it's Wen's bed that lies empty and not Kalen's.

7

AFTER THE FIFTH-DAY man pronounces Wen's sins—envy and vanity—he produces the proof: a small pot of dye for reddening the lips, one that wasn't in her box when I switched her scarf with Kalen's. The oils in the makeup easily catch flame.

Alena watches us even more closely. She must suspect I had something to do with Wen. I can't get close enough to Kalen to warn her. At night, Alena has taken to sleeping in our room.

Kalen avoids looking at me. I hope this is because of Alena. Other reasons reach up with bony fingers, as if from a dark pit. I occupy myself thinking of a way to save us, of some way over the wall.

The first and second days pass. It's not until the second night I formulate a plan, one so ridiculous it fills me with terror, but we're running out of time.

The next morning, I wait until Alena turns away. I go into Wen's box—still unoccupied, for she hasn't yet been replaced—and take the weaving hook I saw when I switched the scarves.

Later, I steal some yarn. That night, I keep my ears open for Alena's approach. I work as fast as I can without moving my arms, although I cannot stop my elbows from twitching.

◆

THE NIGHT BEFORE the hunt, I long to avoid the soup, but Alena watches me carefully. I don't want her to spoon it down my throat again. As soon as I eat, she looks away, long enough for me to palm the fork of the girl next to me.

The drug is already taking effect by the time our leisure hours start. Usually, I spend it playing with cards, or drawing on my mattress with my finger—but tonight, I sit back at my spinning wheel. Kalen gives me a sharp glance, which makes my heart flutter. She's been aware of me, even if I haven't seen her watching.

I look at Alena. Her eyebrows go up, as if she's waiting for an explanation.

I fidget and look at the door, which is a lie—although I'm nervous, this place has taught me nothing if not to be still. After having the weight of creatures upon me, it's impossible for me to be afraid of Alena the same way.

Her forehead wrinkles and her jaw twitches, as if she's biting down on something. She turns away. I'm glad for this.

I hope she feels guilty, because my list of monsters grows ever longer. A relief to imagine Alena's hand is forced.

I pump the treadle, weave thread, and wait. When I'm sure nobody is watching, I jam the fork into the machine, near the ends of the horseshoe-shaped flyer. The fork snaps.

Before Alena can come near, I pull the flyer and the bobbin off the maidens. She calls for me—*Not Do, Not Do*—but I pretend I don't hear. By the time she's at my side, I've taken half the machine apart.

I meet her gaze and shake my head quickly, mouthing, *sorry, sorry, sorry.*

Alena sighs and turns away. "Fix it tomorrow, Not Do. It's time for bed."

I take the flyer to bed with me, as if it's a stuffed animal, and wait for her to put out the candle.

◆

THE DOSE IS subtler, but sleep will claim me soon. I slip the wooden flyer under my pillow and mouth my spell.

An hour goes by. Alena enters. I lay still as she switches the sash in her hand with the one in Kalen's box, and then she takes a seat on the edge of my bed and waits.

I don't dare move my mouth. Before long, I lose the spell and fall asleep.

◆

THE NEXT MORNING, I awaken with a headache, although if that's from the drug or the sleep, I can't tell. I try to get Kalen's attention, but she refuses to meet my eyes.

Does she feel some guilt? Does she blame me?

Forgive me, forgive me, forgive me.

Alena stays close and orders me to help her with the cooking.

I chop. I peel. I wonder why she doesn't have us killed outright. In the end, I go back to my first explanation—that she, too, is a captive.

◈

WHEN THE HUNT starts, I run out the room first, tearing away so quickly I leave Kalen behind. I can't get stopped and questioned by Alena about why my dress doesn't sit right. I look back just long enough to see Kalen's stricken face—*forgive me, forgive me, forgive me*—and then the stampede of girls is behind me, so many bodies, there's no way Alena can follow.

I pull to one side and wait. Kalen emerges dead last. I sprint for her, grab her hand, and drag her toward the trees, despite the many eyes upon us.

She pulls back as if to fight me, but I'm strong, and terrified, and when she finally throws my hand down, it's only so she can match my pace.

We hide and don her scarf. My mind already ticks away the time. I rip her sash off and throw it on the ground. She responds eagerly, her fingers snaking into my hair, but I grab her hands and hold them flat to the sides of my head.

I try as hard as I can to tell her my thoughts. *Follow me, Kalen. We have to do this.*

She doesn't understand. She reaches for her sash, but when I grab her hand and pull, she follows, leaving it behind. We sprint together, a single body, the scarf stretching between us like a harness.

When we come to the wall, Kalen stops and turns toward me. Her expression is furious, and she points to her palms before backing up.

I fall to my knees and beg her, mouthing *please, please, please*, but she shakes her head.

I pull up my dress and show her the rope I've built at night. The horseshoe-shaped flyer is fastened to one end.

Perhaps not strong enough to hold our weight, and yet we'll try, *we have to try*, but still, she shakes her head.

"Please," I say. It comes out as mush.

She recoils, her lip curling in fear or disgust. It's the first time that she's ever heard my voice, and her reaction is a blow, but not enough to stop the clamoring of my heart. The sash's scent could still be on her. And if the creature doesn't kill her, Alena will.

I can't explain the feeling that comes over me. It can't be love: I don't know where she's from, and she doesn't know my name. We've never had time to do more than explore each other's bodies, no way to separate our passion from the boiling of our hurts.

But I think again—*I'm dying, we're all dying, forgive me, forgive me, forgive me*—and it's like I catch flame, *crack-whoomph!* If I'm going to die, I won't die scared. I'll die with a voice.

I open my mouth and breathe out the spell to calm a spooked animal. *"Aaaaa-maaa-baaa."*

It can't work. I know this now, know the spell keeping me awake at night was only my own fear, because we're not animals. I'm not an animal.

But something changes in her expression. She takes my hand.

I run for the wall. I hurl the rope and flyer with all my might. It sails over, and I pull hard, jamming the flyer against the wall. I yank to test the rope, and it holds fast.

I give it to her first. She shakes her head, but I kiss her, fiercely, as if I could pour my resolve into her—and when I pull away, there are tears in her eyes, and her brows have knitted together.

It's the most beautiful thing I've ever seen.

A bay echoes as she grabs the rope and starts to ascend. I don't care that it has tracked us, that it draws ever closer. I wait, my heart soaring, as she crests over the top.

She pauses, then, for she has not thought of this part, but I have. When she takes the rope and descends, it'll be on the wrong side, and I won't be able to climb up.

I hear another bay and look back. In the distance, I see the creature, a black form massive against the snow, weaving between the trees.

◆

IF THIS WAS a story, this is how it would end. I would sacrifice myself to the creature to buy Kalen time, and somehow, that would make everything worthwhile.

But this isn't a story. She throws the end of the rope at me, followed by a slim gray banner—the scarf. "Hurry!"

I look back. The creature has crossed half the distance between us.

I wrap the scarf around my neck and grab the rope.

As soon as the leather of my soles touches the wall, the poison starts to eat them away. I smell it first, a scent like mint and meat cooking, but I ascend, hand over hand.

Below me, the creature has slowed. My arms scream as I climb. Halfway up, I pass the end of the poison. A moment later, the scarf unravels into nothing, its magic spent. By then, I'm out of reach of the creature. It sees me and howls in rage.

As if in reply, a horn sounds. When the whistle comes, the fruits on the trees will all glow, and I'll be seen.

I crest the top, and the creature roars again. Kalen pushes me down and rips off my shoes. The poison has eaten through my left sole.

She drops the rope, and we climb down, together this time, because it doesn't matter if the flyer breaks, if we go hurtling toward the ground and shatter every bone in our bodies, as long as we are free.

As soon as we both reach the earth, light blooms on the other side of the wall, like a sudden sunrise.

Kalen gives the rope a strong pull, twisting her fingers as she does. Like the scarf, it unravels into nothing. We run, barefoot through the snow, away from the wall.

❖

We find a road, but we avoid it. We focus on finding water, on building a small lean-to. Kalen doesn't seem to understand surviving outside like this, but I have my training to guide me, and she learns quickly. I'm too afraid, still, to build a fire. At night, we curl into each other for warmth.

We travel four days, and on the fifth, we hear the faint call of a distant horn. I almost think I'm imagining it, except that I can tell from Kalen's face she hears it, too.

❖

That night, we finally have a fire. I dig a deep pit to shield the light and fan it constantly to disperse the smoke. We roast two fish Kalen caught in a freezing river with her bare hands. Even burnt, they're perfect.

When we're done, I put out the fire. We lie next to the warm stones. She touches her forehead to mine, and I stroke her hair.

I still haven't figured out how to tell her my name, to ask where she is from.

"I want to go back," she says.

I freeze like a statue, horror growing in my breast. I've heard of this, of captives being so broken they refuse to leave, even when the gate is open—but I would've never believed it true of Kalen.

She turns toward me, her gaze hard. "I think there are oils in the poison in the wall, like the makeup. I think if we tried, we could burn it down."

I imagine it catching fire like the scarf, *crack-whoomph*. My heart sings as I take her in my arms.

❖

It TAKES US four days to travel back. On the fifth, we wait for the horn, for the night the girls will be running without hobbles.

"Are you ready?" asks Kalen.

My heart beats, faster than a galloping horse. A dozen images flit in and out of my mind—Kalen's elbows, Alena's open mouth, the fifth-day man's sneer, the soft light of camp diffusing into the tent where I once slept, my mother telling a story to a group outside.

I nod and strike a spark. Fire roars up the wall like a braid.

Kalen and I don't stay to watch. We slip back into the night, two animals again made human.

Eulogy for a Brother, Resurrected

Carson Faust

Helek'shene tvhvsh' means, most literally, *breath of life*, which is what our brother lacks. The wife of one of Callum's many lovers drained it from his belly with her husband's bullet a few weeks back. Mid-September, Callum bled out real slow by Pump 3 at Carter's Fast Stop. Ambulances don't hurry out to places like Ridgeville, South Carolina. And why would they? We're just a bunch of mixed-up Indian cousin-fuckers, aren't we? Even if they tried to hurry, it probably would've taken them too long to get here anyhow. There was no saving him. Callum would've likely died in a hospital bed. Least this way, he didn't leave us with a bill. That said, it ended up costing us plenty to take care of Callum after Angela Ford gunned him down.

I can tell you the price of my brother's body.

Cummings Chapel charged us $885 to burn our brother down to nearly nothing. We paid $79.99 for the dark blue urn we poured him into once the chapel returned him to us in crinkled plastic that reminded me of a cereal bag.

Holding all that was left of him in my hands, Callum couldn't have weighed more than a few pounds. As we poured him into the urn, I tried not to spill a single wisp of him. Though he was so much less now, I wanted to make sure he was whole.

Before the fire whittled him down, the cops went through everything they found on his person at the time of his death. They were exact, so I will be too:

In his pocket, a dime bag of weed. In his right ear, a diamond stud—fake, but beautiful if the sun hit it right. A faux-leather jacket thrifted from some shop in Charleston. His keys, hung around his neck by a faded teal lanyard, and a keychain—a rabbit's foot, once white, now painted red. It made me wonder about all the blood he lost. How much of it left him before everything blurred and faded to black?

On the slab, Callum weighed one hundred and fifty-eight pounds. His skin, his jeans, his jacket, his shoes. Heart, lungs, brain, bowels, teeth—it all came to one hundred and fifty-eight pounds. All the blood left in him came to that. So how much would he have weighed if he hadn't lost any to the ground, to the cracks in the blacktop? Either way, most of all that rose up as smoke, and now we're left with the four pounds of him that remain.

In a place like Ridgeville, what happened to Callum isn't all that surprising. He insisted on loving men out loud, which is more than most folks like him could boast in this town. Any queer folks around here are quiet about it. Even more of them silent. Being the way he was had been dangerous enough in a town as small and Bible'd up as this one.

I always figured the earthly price for Callum's goings-on would be heftier than the unearthly one. I ended up being right, though I never wanted to be.

Helek'shene tvhvsh' can also mean *God*, which Callum also lacked. Church was a chore. To him, the man upstairs was just an imaginary friend certain folks never grew out of. The Bible was at least interesting. Snakes spoke.

Fire came down from the sky. Water turned to blood. Water turned into wine. Wine became blood. You drink.

In the Good Book, sons also came back from the dead. This makes me believe that not even death is permanent. But Callum believed in what he could hear, see, touch. He believed in only what his body would allow him.

When we were little, when he "he heard our parents scream at each other, he believed they might tear each other apart. A shove into the cabinet, a slap across the face, a fist wrapped around a neck. He believed they might tear us apart along with them. So we held each other together. If everything else was falling away, Callum made sure we had each other. So, if our parents were hollering, we tucked our small selves under my bed and counted paper flowers on the wall.

By the time he was ten and I was eight, we could count high enough to know that there were eighty-two daisies on the north- and south-facing walls and seventy-eight daisies on the east- and west-facing walls. We counted them each time. We kept counting until the day our father left. We kept counting when the house was finally silent. Eighty-two, seventy-eight. Eighty-two. Seventy-eight.

I have to assume that all those times we'd count the flowers on our wallpaper felt like prayer to Callum. Or, at least, the way I think of prayer. Even when you know the answer, even when you know what you need is right there, the praying helps. Though he knew those numbers wouldn't change, he repeated the counting each time. Just the same as me knowing that God is there, watching, listening. Though I know He's there, it helps to talk to Him. These rituals are just a way of reminding yourself where you are. Trouble is, now I don't know where Callum is. I know I should know. I know I should believe he's somewhere good. Somewhere better. But I don't.

All I know is: what's left of my brother weighs about four pounds.

Callum's body has been burned down to the dregs. This means, of course, that we need to build him a new body from scratch if we want to bring him back."

❖

Esv MEANS *HANDS* in the tongue that was first meant for us. In the language that our auntie Ina must feed me in pieces if we are to bring Callum back right. With ours, we pull muck from the Edisto River. Once the sun sets, my half brother, Kemly, and I go to the shallowest parts of the river and bring night-dark mud to the shore, collect it on an old blue tarp that we pulled off the top of Kemly's old trailers. *No shovels, no gloves, no nothing,* Auntie Ina told us. *Nothing but flesh can harvest the earth you plan to make the flesh out of.*

It is Auntie Ina who guides us. We borrow her knowledge. Her knowing is what makes the difference between Callum being alive or staying dead. So, handful by handful, we gather the earth that would become Callum's flesh.

❖

KEMLY AND I share a father—a man known to spread himself around. Spread himself thin. That may be why our father gave Callum his own name—he could see that this son would share both his wandering and his lust— though our father would probably turn over in his grave if he knew his son lusted for other folks' sons.

Callum and I share both mother and father, but it was Kemly who got the first call when Callum bled out—when his body went cold under the hot sun. Much as I don't want to admit, it hurt that Kemly knew first. Because I can't even be sure the knowledge hurt Kemly. I don't think it did. It was like he'd expected the call. Not in the same way I had. For me, *expect* wasn't the right word. For me, it was *dread*. For Kemly, to *expect* meant to *prepare*.

I was not prepared.

I fell apart. I lost my job. Clay Mound Elementary offers two personal days a year to all teachers. I burned through those, hardly noticing them pass. The administration figured it was easier to replace me. *You let us know if next year is more suitable. You just need to get better,* they said.

Nothing got better. Losing Callum gutted me. For weeks, I couldn't eat. All those dead-brother casseroles. All the dead-brother fresh-baked bread. Cobblers and pies and puddings. But in those weeks after, hunger never came. My body just kept eating itself, and I was glad to be disappearing.

I might have vanished altogether had Kemly not found me curled up on the kitchen floor of my apartment, passed out. He told me I'd fainted, and I wondered how long ago that had happened. After I refused food, he forced me to drink a red, sun-warm Gatorade from the back seat of his pickup. *You can't keep on like this, Della,* he said.

In that moment, I was amazed by how much clearer my head was. The hunger I couldn't feel and the faintness that protected me from all that grief had kept the world foggy. All that sugar rushing to my blood burned the fog away. And the grief, fresh as ever, replaced the haze. I knew the fog would swallow me up. But the grief would swallow me up, too.

He's not supposed to be dead, I said.

Kemly stayed quiet for a while, afraid his next words would break me open. He said them anyway: *There's nothing we can do.*

But I knew he was wrong. I feared I was wrong, too, but in a different way. Not that what I wanted to do was impossible, but that it might be unforgivable.

❖

KEMLY, CALLUM, AND I all have Auntie Ina in common—

our father's eldest sister. Earlier that week, after I begged him, Kemly agreed to drive me to her. *Only because you're in no shape to drive,* he said. *Can't let your next fainting spell be at the wheel.* What I think he meant was that he cared about me. He meant he hadn't prepared to lose me, and he was afraid that he might.

That's the only reason he'd agree to this. In our family, we're afraid of Auntie Ina. We'd always been told to be. Our mothers told us it was smart to fear her. And our father's avoidance of his own sister told us it was smart to listen to our mothers. *She's estranged because she's exactly that, Della—strange,* was all my mother would say.

Of all of us, Callum was closest to our auntie. You could even say that he was drawn to her. He used to go around our mother and invite Auntie Ina to family functions: our birthdays, high school graduations, even some of the Christmases when he was feeling brave. Not that she was partial to any of these gatherings. I always thought she came just to push buttons. Smoking Camel Reds on the porch as presents were being opened. Grinning smugly at our mother from across the room as folks filled their paper plates with beans, pulled pork, and potato salad.

The tension between our mother and Auntie Ina was no ordinary kind of familial disdain. It was a disdain that echoes through a lot of folks. All us Edistos here in Colleton County knew Ina was a conjure woman. A rootworker. Folks from other tribes might call a woman like her a medicine woman, but not here. Here, you either get God in your heart, or you don't. Those who sought her gifts might call her a fortune teller. Those who wished her dead called her a witch.

Auntie Ina lives about thirty minutes out from Ridgeville in a town called Cottageville. Took Kemly about forty minutes to get us there though, since he was driving all nervous. *You doing okay?* I asked. He usually drives like a madman. The fact that I feel safe as his passenger is strange. I asked, point blank, if he was afraid. *Nothing wrong with being wary 'round a woman who can pull your mind out through your nose.* Can't fault him on that logic. Based on what we were about to ask her to do, there was no reason she couldn't.

As we pulled up to Auntie Ina's house, I could see Kemly's hands trembling, despite his best efforts to hide it. We had never been here, though we've known Auntie Ina's address for the past twenty-some years of our lives. Callum found it in a pile of old envelopes when he was twelve or thirteen, and, like all forbidden knowledge does when you're small, the address stuck: 2833 Burr Hill Road.

We knocked, but Auntie Ina didn't come to the door. She beckoned us in with a holler, expecting us. We entered. And should I be ashamed to say I was surprised that the inside just looked like a home? No animal bones hanging from the ceiling. No feathers resting on the windowsills. No dolls dressed like us with needles poking out of the limbs. Just dark-paneled walls, a floral-print sofa, a coffee table covered by a white doily, and a small dining room table covered by a red cloth, surrounded by three empty chairs.

In the front room, there are bookshelves filled, not with books, but with pictures of family. Save for a few mirrors, the walls were full of family photos as well. There are several of Callum, Kemly, and me together, through various ages— toddlers, kids, teenage years. Even a couple of years' worth of my school pictures as Ms. Davis—my earlier years of teaching. Callum must've been sending Auntie Ina these pictures over the years. I'd never known. Kemly looked just as surprised as I was, even if his surprise was a bit more subdued.

We went through the front room, back toward her kitchen, which doubles as the little shop she runs. Canned peas and jams and beans—the berries and beans and roots all grown by her, prepared by her—filled entire walls' worth of shelves. At a small table by a window, crouched on a stool, Auntie Ina sat, painting her nails a bright cornflower blue.

Auntie Ina looked up from her nails, cocking her eyebrow. *Can't say I expected to have any visitors after Callum's passing,* she scoffed. *But it's good to finally see you kids.*

I'm sorry, I said. And I meant it. *That we never reached out after.*

Never reached out much, even before. You sorry for that, too? Auntie Ina asked.

We're not here to start shit, Ina, Kemly said, still on edge.

I know exactly why you're here, Auntie Ina said, focusing back on her nails. *Same reason you never came around before. And the reason you're scared shitless, Kemly. You can't start shit if you're shitless in the first place.*

Ma was right about you. Right to keep you at arm's length if this is how you act, Kemly growled through gritted teeth. I wanted to swat him upside the head. He'd ruin everything.

I speak my mind is all. Auntie Ina clicked her tongue. That's why some folks around here don't like me. She paused for a moment and added: *Sometimes I speak other people's minds, too. Yet another reason folks stay clear.*

Fuck this, Kemly said, beginning to turn back toward the front door. But I grabbed him by the shoulder. I felt him tense beneath my grip.

Fuck nothing, Kemly, I whispered, even though the whispering wouldn't mean that Auntie Ina couldn't hear every word, maybe even every thought. *This is all I have. The one shot I have to bring Callum back.* I felt Kemly relax a little, but I needed to make sure he stayed. I needed my next words to hurt. To nail his feet to the floor. *He could be alive if you picked up your damn phone.*

You and I both know he wouldn't've lived, Dell.

Then this is the only way we have, I said. *We owe him that. We both failed.*

We both knew that, as blood poured from our brother's belly, he called us.

Both of us.

Twice, he called me. Three times, he called Kemly.

The only two people Callum could think of calling as his insides poured out, making little rivers in the cracked blacktop.

I think it's still true that the ambulance would have been too slow. I think it's still true that Callum would have died, regardless. But I can't help but think that if Kemly tossed our dying brother in the back of his pickup, he could have gotten him to the nearest hospital fast enough that he might have lived. Even if he would have died anyway, he might not've had to die alone. If we had picked up, he would have known we cared. He would have known how much we wanted him to live. He died slow, and the whole time had no one.

Now there's only one way of letting him know how much we want him to live.

❖

It took weeks to convince Auntie Ina to bring Callum back. Kemly didn't stick to visiting her with me as we waited for her response. I came by her place every few days with flowers or family photos or anything I thought Callum might've brought her over the years. She seemed to chew on my request like a piece of cud, as if to make sure everything went down right. I knew it would take time and patience, but I also knew, deep down, that she wanted our brother back as much as we did. I knew that, like us, Auntie Ina felt Callum's absence deep in her chest. She told me as much, after October rolled around, when she finally agreed.

Callum was one of the few who came to me without needing anything. No curses, no cures. Just plain old company. She smiled, looking out toward her garden. *He'd tell me about you, mostly. Some of Kemly. He was proud of y'all. Sad often, too, for himself. But he was here. And, you're right, he still should be. But I need you to know that this ain't for you or Kemly, or even for me. It's bigger than that—than us,* Auntie Ina said, her smile fading.

And it ain't me this is going to take a piece of. That will be you.

Unable to help myself, I asked her why she was agreeing to this, and what it would take. Auntie Ina took Callum's ashes from me, and then she told me. This was what she was getting ready to tell me all this time. This was what she'd been chewing on. *Callum's the one who needs to carry the roots after I'm gone,* Auntie Ina said. *Was always supposed to be him.* But it seemed I would do in a pinch.

She took me to the kitchen, where she unlocked a cabinet in her shop I hadn't noticed before. This was where she kept the things she grew that weren't for eating. These plants were grown for spellwork.

Kemly will help us, too. He'll come back, I said, but Auntie Ina shrugged the words off, not all that concerned either way. She looked at me, content. As if, in me, she had everything she needs.

I can tell you the cost of my brother's body.

First, it takes time. Days to prepare. There is much I have to learn from Auntie Ina in order to be of any help. But I am a teacher, after all, which makes me a good student. Our language has never come easy to me, though. My folks never spoke it, could never give it to me, but there are pieces of it I must learn, and Auntie Ina knows it all well. *Because the roots work best when you talk to them right.* And so, while Kemly works at the truck yard in the days, I learn Auntie Ina's ways as best I can, as quickly as I can. When Kemly gets off, we all do a different kind of work together. It takes a lot of bodies to build up a new body.

After we collect the muck, the roots, and after we knead most of Callum's ashes in, we shape his body next to Auntie Ina's garden. With us, we have the ashes, a coffee mug, and bottles of water.

We begin, and October stretches.

As I follow Auntie Ina's instructions, it's easy to forget what's being built. That this mound of earth will become Callum's skull. This muck will be his chest, his belly.

The black water from the Edisto that's soaked into this muck will soon run through Callum like blood. It's so easy to forget. But that isn't the case for our brother. By week's end, Kemly is shaken. He does not look down and see what will soon be a body. He sees something completely inhuman. He sees something that will never be human.

We can't be doing this, Kemly says. But he's wrong.

We can. And nothing has ever felt more right. I am lighter than I've been in years. I think back to how my body fell away from me in those weeks after Callum first bled out. How hunger never came. How I began to disappear. My body feels far away now, but it is not despair that has pushed hunger away this time. It is not that I am losing myself. I am pouring myself into something better. It is not fog that blinds me. It is light.

I'll have no part in this, Kemly says, as if that changes anything. *This isn't holy.*

I say nothing as he leaves us. Let the crickets and the frogs sing him out. I have never felt holier.

But that is part of the cost—my brother's body has cost me a brother.

It doesn't matter for long, because I build a new one. Callum's new form is shaped. As Auntie Ina and I form the river muck, as we knead Callum's ashes into it, it firms up. It feels like clay, and becomes easy to shape, as if the earth knows how our hands want to guide it.

Vpel', his shoulders.

Vhvl', his arms.

Vpu'yv ekwel, skull.

Ehe'yv, mouth.

Kwvt, neck.

E'mv, body—the whole of it, complete.

Brother, kokenee'shv.

This body we build does not yet look like Callum, but at Auntie Ina's instruction, we sculpt the mouth wide open. Like a man dying of thirst, waiting for rain to fall from the sky.

But it is you who will drink, Auntie Ina says, because she can hear inside my head. As we build Callum up, as we get closer to completion, it seems easier and easier for her to step into my head. As the walls of Callum's self grow stronger, mine seem to weaken, but I don't care.

As we continue in Auntie Ina's garden, I watch as she sifts what's left of Callum's ashes into a coffee mug, pours water over them, and stirs it into a gray paste with her long pointer finger, her chipped, blue fingernail. She adds more water to thin it out and hands the mug to me. *Drink* is all she says, looking irritated that she had to repeat herself. I feel sick. Not sick to my stomach, exactly. More like a queasiness bubbling up in my throat. She probably doesn't need to step into my head to know what I'm thinking this time, so Auntie Ina just shakes the mug at me impatiently.

I drink it down.

It burns. As if the ashes are still scorching.

I heave, and hot blood rushes from my mouth. What else could it be but blood? What else could be so red? And it falls onto the clay chest. *Think back to the rain, girl,* I hear Auntie Ina say, and she grabs a fistful of my hair at the back of my head, steering me to the mouth of the clay head. Blood and ash drain from my mouth and into the sculpted face. I heave so completely that it feels like my ribs are shifting, breaking beneath my skin. I want to scream. Nothing comes but the taste of ash. The taste of copper. I hear a scream, but it isn't mine.

It's Callum's.

And as Callum screams, I think of the way babies scream when they're first pulled from their mamas. They scream because this is the first time they see light. They scream because it is the first time air touches them. They cry to rid their bodies of the world they left behind. I try to imagine that Callum's screams are shedding whatever came after he died. Imagine if all that came after was *nothing.* Just the same black that came before birth.

I don't have to imagine all that black falling away.

I am feeling it fall away. Hearing Callum's scream, I know the sound is not mine. But it is mine. Because I made it. I gave my own breath for it. I hear it as if it's coming from my lips. As if it came from my lips like all that ash. But that's not all that rushes in. In the screams, I hear the howl of the bullet that killed. Feel the blood rush from my belly, from my mouth. Feel my lungs lag and then stop. This is how it felt when the black crept in. Blur and then shadow and then cold from the inside out.

The screaming stops because I will it to. Everything will be fine now. Be silent. Be here.

I look down at a body that, moments ago, was not a body. And Callum looks just like himself. He stands. He looks just like me.

We share blood. We share breath.

We look at our auntie. We look so alike, she and we.

We are not a trinity. Nor are we holy, my brother and I. Though we are the father—for I am a creator, and this body that holds him was made by my hands. We are the son—for though I am a daughter, Callum and I are one now. We are Della, and a brother standing beside her, within her. The important thing is that we are not without. We are the blood in our veins and the ash in our mouths. We know what it is to be alive and dead—sometimes all at once. We know what it is to be apart and together, all at once.

Our auntie has given us a garden, which is more than we have been given before. Among her crinum lilies, the lantana, the marigolds and hollyhocks, we build what comes after both life and death. Our bodies are both earth and flesh. We are buried and we are alive. We nourish the roots that burrow into us. And when those we love fade away, fall to the earth, get swallowed up, we will take them in. We will soak up their skin, pull it up with the roots of the plants that wind through us, and they will be with us. We will not be trinity. We will be more.

Morning Star Blues

TESSA FISHER

N O MATTER HOW many times I looked out the viewport, I was always relieved to see the clouds of Venus swirling below me in the sunlight, elaborate shapes in the vapor giving rise to an other- worldly interplay of light and shadow. Before we had arrived, I had been worried that the skyscape below me would have appeared as it had from orbit—a bland, gray, uniform flatness stretching out to the horizon. I wasn't sure if I'd be able to to deal with that level of monotony, elite astronaut or not. Even Ashley's jokes could only keep me so entertained.

Admittedly, being sent to a boring planet wouldn't have surprised me; as the International Space Consortium began to ramp up its Mars settlement plans, it wasn't too difficult to imagine that post-gonadal women like Ashley and I were no longer as necessary as we had been a decade earlier, now that having kids on other planets was something desirable to the ISC.

Ashley's absent-minded humming drew me away from the skyscape. She was busy working away with a remotely-operated rover on the surface, trying to get as much geological data before the rover expired from the searing heat and pressure. I felt a little sheepish admitting it, but I liked her humming—she had a lovely voice, emotive and husky.

I shook my head, trying not follow that line of thought too far. I didn't want to think about her voice that way, lest I start imagining what she sounded like when she sighed with contentment, or screamed in ecstasy. The whole reason we were on Venus was because I wasn't prone to such potential mission-endangering urges, and neither was Ashley.

I turned back to my work console, looking at the readouts from the atmosphere probes that dangled below the *Lori Glaze*, our airship, strung upon kilometers of acid-resistant cable. My work was one of the biggest publicity boosters of the mission—Venus's upper atmosphere was actually fairly Earth-like in terms of temperature and pressure, if a little on the warm side (to say the least). There had been speculation for decades if there might be microbes living suspended in atmospheric droplets of dilute sulfuric acid. My job was to settle the debate, once and for all—or try to, at least. So far I'd gotten some interesting, but ambiguous, results suggesting the presence of complex organics, but no smoking gun as of yet. We had maybe a month left before the mission ended, and I was started to get more than a little frustrated with not having a definitive answer one way or the other. Too often now I was ending my work periods with muscles tightened and tense from aggravation.

I sighed.

"You feeling cold again?" Ashley asked. She was always teasing me about how I somehow managed to get chilled despite being in a balloon surrounded by a 60 degree Celsius atmosphere.

"No, just wishing I'd get something more substantial."
"Good, because despite what you might have heard—"

"If this is a joke about Venus in Furs, you're sleeping in the service airlock tonight."

Ashley blinked, slightly stunned, and perhaps a little deflated that I'd beat her to the punchline. "Dang, Kelsey, you know me too well."

"That tends to happen when you spend over a year in a metal tube with someone."

"Ah, the life of the astronaut, perhaps only surpassed in glamorousness by that of the first year college student."

I chuckled. "Hey, at least our food is better! Well. Marginally better."

"We had pretty good food when I was in college. There was even a sushi bar in the main dining hall—sushi! And omelet brunches every weekend. I was too much of a mess to appreciate it, really, but I remember it being quite palatable." I realized from the melancholy way she said "mess" and her downward gaze that she wasn't just talking about sleeping through the omelet brunch.

"Yeah, it was rough for me, too," I replied, gently probing the subject. It occurred to me I'd never really discussed this with her before. For having trained together so long, there was still a lot we didn't know about each other. When you're so focused on the mission, personal history is often left by the wayside—and, all too often, that history isn't something we necessarily want to revisit in the first place.

"Yup, I know what you mean—I had my share of difficulties, too. I mean, not academically—I was still a chronic overachiever. But psychologically, things were starting to get bad with the whole body dissonance issue. I never went suicidal or self-destruc- tive or anything— which is good, since I probably wouldn't have been picked for a mission if I had—but I was in a gloomy mood basically every waking moment."

"When did you reach your breaking point?"

"Not long after graduation. I just couldn't run from the truth anymore—especially since I was literally the only person holding myself back; everyone else in my life was totally supportive. And so I finally decided that maybe I deserved happiness, and started transitioning. And here I am now."

"Huh. Well, I'm glad you did." I smiled at Ashley, despite myself. "I can't think of a better woman to have as a crewmate."

"How about you?" Ashley inquired.

"Oh, well, it was unpleasant for me, too. I barely remember a lot of it—I was basically in a state of low-grade dissociation the entire time. It was like watching someone else go to class, get drunk on weekends, study for tests—but knowing that someone else was me. In my junior year I finally figured it out, and that helped tremendously—but then I had to deal with my parents, who were still pretty dubious about the prospect of me transitioning. I still went for it, though then, of course, they let me know how much harder my life was going to be because of it. As if I didn't already know." I swallowed hard, trying to keep the bitterness from spilling out too much, and reminded myself that at least they'd come to watch the launch. "Of course, I doubt they ever imagined I'd be flying around the clouds of a whole other planet. But then, I guess, most of us didn't."

Ashley nodded. "Yeah, I wanted to be an astronaut since I was a little kid—even got autographs from an ISS crew when I was in college—but being a trans astronaut never seemed possible. But then *Ares II* happened..." She shrugged. "Funny how things work out, I guess. I'm certainly not complaining."

I made an affirmative sound, and turned back to look at the newest batch of data from the atmospheric sondes. Ashley wasn't offended—after all, we had a tight schedule to keep to maximize the science return of the mission.

But really, I didn't want to think about *Ares II*. About how it was still the only case of a human killing another human beyond Earth in recorded history, even if that bastard would-be rapist had it coming. Because of that one incident, NASA and the ISC had developed such an aversion to sexual desires on long-duration flights that they went out of their way to find people who were willing tolerate chemical castration in order to fly—or, better yet, people who were literally castrated already. And I suspected a major reason—perhaps the *only* reason—I had been selected for this mission over thousands of other qualified applicants was because, over a decade earlier, I'd had my testicles removed as part of my sex reassignment surgery, and having not been interested in sex much previously, was happy to have my hormone levels tweaked by the flight surgeons back at Mission Control until I had just enough testosterone in my system to keep my bones from crumbling, but not enough to have that pesky libido.

That was the theory, anyway. But the longer I spent with Ashley, the more I looked at her, *really* looked at her, the more I doubted that I was the model eunuch astronaut they had hoped me to be.

I deliberately lost myself in my work, and spent the next few hours contentedly enough, humming along as I reviewed samples. Intriguingly, the mass spectrometer was picking up something that looked like complex macromolecules—I'd have to run some more analyses to get a better idea what they might be, and if they were biological in origin.

"I like the little singing you do to yourself," Ashley said nonchalantly, not even looking up from her console. "You have a really nice voice."

"Oh, thanks," I said quietly, "I put a lot of work into it." I wanted to say so much, about the challenges and frustration it had caused me, the intense dysphoria I felt about it from an early age, the agony and joy of learning to sing again—

but I knew if I opened up, it would only fan the fires of the feelings I had towards Ashley. For me, vulnerability was a dangerous substance, a doorway to desire. One of the nice things about being an astronaut had been that people tended to assume you didn't have any.

Before I could stop myself, I blurted out, "I like it when you hum, too."

Ashley blushed ever so slightly, before regaining her composure. "Well, that's good, I suppose. Otherwise we probably would've killed each other by now." I laughed, and tried to keep it from sounding hollow—*Ares II*, haunting us all again.

Thankfully, there wasn't much personal talk from there until the start of our sleep period, but even that small compliment she'd given me was enough to gnaw into my brain, with a warm rush descending towards my ever-so-slightly-faster-beating heart.

◈

"C'MON, BE SOMETHING other than pyroxene...aww, damn it." Ashley had a tendency to talk to herself when she was teleoperating one of the surface probes. It was hard not to find endearing. With an audible sigh, she glanced towards me.

"As exciting as the hunt for the answer to the Great Venusian Resurfacing Mystery is, I really would've appreciated some more variety. Everywhere you look, it's basalt, and not even particularly interesting basalt, at that."

"Didn't you do your PhD on basalts on Venusian worlds?" I asked.

"Well, yeah, but that doesn't mean I don't want to spice it up occasionally."

I chuckled. "Yeah, I bet." She already knew my opinion of rocks—namely, aside from the sparkly ones, they all basically looked the same to me.

"Hey, just because you can't appreciate the beauty of mineral thin-slices doesn't mean all of us are so unfortunate."

"Well, okay, I'll take your word for it. And I apologize for razzing you." First rule of a long-duration space mission: always apologize. A twenty-meter long cylinder surrounded by death is not a good place to nurse a grudge.

"You're forgiven. Lucky for you, I'm used to not being understood!" She paused and crinkled her brows. "Wow, that didn't come out right."

"Doesn't mean it's not true, though. Unfortunately."

She sighed. "Yeah. I mean, the world's better for us when we were kids—tons better. And hey, here we are, flying around on Venus!" She paused for just a second, inhaling with just a touch of exhaustion. "But, at the same time, I've had mixed feelings about the fact that we got to go because the astronaut selection office basically said 'We're sending you because you're not like all those other women.' Though I feel really selfish for saying that—since hey, we were picked, and a whole lot of other people weren't."

"Yeah, but it's like, it's exciting on one level, but very much Othering on another," I replied. "We're more than just freaks of nature to send on your dangerous missions without having to worry about another sexual assault." I paused, wondering how much farther I should push into proscribed territory. What the hell, you only live once. "It's weird to think that so much of this is just motivated by concerns about a single molecule or two."

"What, your part of the mission?" Ashley asked. She'd heard me go on about length about looking for nucleic acids and chlorophyll analogues, the best markers for non-terrestrial life that we knew of, sans radio broadcast and actual flying saucers.

"Oh, no, I meant hormones. We're here, in part, because they think they can fine-tune our emotional states for optimal mission performance by tweaking our endocrinology.

I mean, there are definitely advantages to that, not going to lie. But to get our fitness as astronauts reduced down to basic biochemistry..." I shrugged. "I don't know, it just seems a little dehumanizing. Plus, it's not like having zero testosterone means you're totally uninterested in sex, anyway."

"Right, exactly. I mean, you've never really been interested in sex, yeah? So it's not just your T levels."

"Well, yeah, mostly. I had a girlfriend or two pre-transition, and one afterwards, though nothing that really lasted. It just...didn't seem that important, I guess. What about you?"

"Mostly the same. For a little while I thought it might be that I was actually into men, so I tried that for a bit, but it didn't make a difference." She shrugged. "Honestly, for the last ten years or so, I've been so focused on making the cut at NASA that I just didn't think about it much."

Do you think about it now? a small part of me wanted to ask—but I quashed that impulse down. No, no good could come of pursuing that topic in conversation. Instead, I thought back to my own time as an astronaut candidate. The selection process had been intense—lots of interviews, physical tests (I had joined a swim club just so I could get the practice in for the water-landing survival exam), psychological evaluations. The whole being- trans thing didn't come up all that much, surprisingly—though I guess the administrators were trying their best to be respectful. On the other hand, maybe it was already a given—this wasn't too long after *Ares II*, and NASA, and the International Space Consortium in general, had become overconcerned about having testosterone in space.

"Yeah, I feel you on that," I said, thinking this was a safer topic. "Looking back at it, I certainly didn't have much brainpower left over for anything else at the end of the day. Did you ever start dreaming about the Venusian atmospheric entry protocols?"

Ashley laughed, a rich, melodic sound that I could listen to over and over again. "No, but I did have recurring dreams about probe deployment. Admittedly, I still do have them, but they were the most frequent during selection and training."

"While we're confessing our embarrassing training moments—you know something else? I'm still a little terrified to fly the T-38s during flight training. Not because it was an old design, but something about being a plane traveling faster than the speed of sound unnerved me. Like, you should never be that fast in an atmosphere, unless you're re-entering it from space."

"...I'll be honest, given you're the one flying this thing, I'm a little concerned. Or, I guess, I would be, if we ever went over 30 kilometers per hour. I guess it's a good thing they got you flying a balloon, then?" she said with a good-natured pat on my shoulder.

"Look, it's just at that speed, not only are your reaction times reduced, but what if you get a hole punched in your canopy?" I argued, pretending not to notice that her hand was still on my shoulder, hoping doing so would drown out the part of me that wanted so much to just lean forward and kiss her.

"You eject. Or, at least, I'd *hope* you eject. Though ejection isn't much of an option here. Talk about out of the frying pan, into the fire..." she trailed off, awkwardly removing her hand. She glanced downwards as if she could peer through the floor, and down to the hellscape surface.

I didn't want to think about that. I didn't want to think about what could happen if things went too far. I knew that I should just report this to Medical, and have them slash my testosterone levels further—osteoporosis be damned, I didn't want to risk the mission. But what happened if they lowered them to zero, and I still felt this way? Would the mission still be safe? And even if it was, would I ever fly again once we returned to Earth?

I think I already knew the answer to that last question, and it wasn't a good one.

◈

SWEAT CASCADED DOWN my neck and into my cleavage as I pedaled furiously on the exercise bike. Normally, I would have worried about stinking up the crew cabin, but Ashley and I had long since reached the point of no longer noticing each other's scent.

Well, at least not unless we made a conscious effort to—and that was something I found myself doing more often than I'd care to admit. The truth was, Ashley smelled good. I had noticed that when I first starting training with her, those few years ago, but I hadn't really thought about it much until now. Now, though, I was definitely thinking about it. I pedaled faster, and hoped that would provide a convenient explanation for why my heartbeat was accelerating in that moment. My exercise period was the only time I allowed myself to touch on these taboo feelings, however briefly.

While I pedaled away, she was sitting at the other end of the crew cabin, reading something on her tablet. Most likely a trashy romance novel, which somehow made it all the more endearing.

The timer on the bike chimed, and I began to slow my pedaling. Alright, mind back on the mission, Kelsey. Daydreams, lusty or otherwise, are for people who aren't flying above a hostile planet.

I grabbed a wash towel and ducked behind the marginal privacy curtain that divided the crew cabin, and did my best to clean myself up.

I knew that I should report this to Medical—but I didn't. I didn't want to. I hated to admit it to myself—fearless Commander Kelsey Hart, afflicted by a schoolgirl's crush—but I liked how I felt around Ashley. It was a feeling I hadn't really experienced before—

pre-transition I was too repressed to really feel much of anything at all, and my one relationship immediately post-transition had never had this intensity, this spark. I liked how excited she got about her work, how she never took herself too seriously, her oddball sense of humor, the way I felt like I could tell her anything at all and never worry she'd judge me for it. I liked the tawny brown color of her skin, her sparkling brown eyes, the way she gracefully flitted throughout the cabin, and flew in zero gee like she was born in it.

I felt the giddy rush in my chest, and quickly started focusing on my breathing, trying to return to my relaxed, just focused on the mission state. It was getting harder to keep these thoughts confined to my exercise periods. After all, we had well over a month left before we even departed Venus. I wasn't sure how long I could keep all of this under wraps. It wasn't that I was afraid of rejection—if anything, that would make life easier, if a little awkward, since I knew I'd be able to move on from it. It was the fact that the reason I'd been sent on this mission was to prevent this sort of thing from happening. I kept reminding myself that no matter what the mission PR folks said, I was selected above thousands of equally qualified applicants for one reason—and now I was failing at that reason.

◈

It was about a week later that everything changed. I had a sched- uled rest period and had been dozing on my fold-away bed when Ashley came galloping to the back half of the gondola cabin.

"KELSEY! KELSEY! Come see this!"

I bolted out of bed, and had to stop myself from following exhaustively-trained instincts and grabbing my pressure suit. I took a second to regain my composure, and followed Ashley to my console.

"What's the excitement about? Did you find something that wasn't basalt?"

"It's not what I found—it's what you found. The NMR analysis for your last batch of atmospheric samples just got finished. Check out the solutions."

I glanced at the screen, comprehension dawning. The most common molecule was a little different from the version I was used to, but the overall structure was startlingly familiar.

"Oh my God," I said. "Chlorophyll. It's chlorophyll—it doesn't have a metal ion, so I guess it's closer to bacteriochlorins, but still..."

There was only one thing known to make chlorophyll in the universe. Life.

The clouds of Venus were inhabited.

◆

I confirmed the NMR data, and started running isotopic analysis to make sure this wasn't just some freak non-biological process that was producing the chlorophyll. My mind was utterly focused on the revelation—me, Kelsey Hart, discoverer of aliens. Admittedly, there'd already been some microbes found in the deep Mars subsurface, but that didn't lower my excitement. The solar system now had three life-bearing worlds, and I'd found one of them.

With a cocky grin, Ashley shoved a small bottle into my hands. I was in such a daze of wonder that it took me a few seconds to focus and read the label: "Champagne."

"...I didn't think we were supposed to have alcohol on board," I said as I poured us each a glass.

"We aren't. Didn't stop *Ares IV* when they found the Martian deep ecosystems. I smuggled these on board for the same reason."

"You were that confident we'd find life?"

"Kels, I've known you for over five years now. You've never not accomplished something you've set your mind on." She paused, gazing into my eyes for what felt like minutes. "Honestly, it's something I really admire about you."

"Thanks, Ashley. That means a lot to me," I said, holding her gaze. And suddenly I couldn't look anywhere else. I was drowning in her eyes—they were pulling on me like gravity.

The next thing I know, her lips are on mine, my arms around her waist, her hands cradling my face, my heart is racing and I'm in love and my mission, my purpose, my identity is spinning, spinning into pieces.

❖

I woke up the during the next wake cycle, feeling a contented buzz, and the delightful warm softness of naked skin pressed against mine. I could get used to this, I thought.

That thought was quickly dashed as I opened my eyes and took in my surroundings, the cabin lights of the *Lori Glaze* shining above me. I was naked. So was my crewmate. My gorgeous, bril- liant crewmate, who gave me a rush of emotion even as she just lay there, peacefully sleeping.

Oh no. Oh no oh no oh no.

I started focusing on my breathing, trying to keep the growing mixture of panic and guilt at bay. It had happened during a rest period—where normally Mission Control tries to give us a bit more privacy—but I had no idea if they'd have picked up on it or not.

How had I let this happen? I should've been stronger, should've just told her to wait until we got back to Earth, should've told Medical to dial down my testosterone when I had the chance. Missions had rules for damned good reasons, and I'd just broken one of the biggest.

Ashley made a soft, contented noise as she stretched out, and sleepily opened her eyes.

"Good morning, Kelsey," she said with a grin.

"Ashley," I said, as evenly as I could, adrenaline making my heart hammer in my ears. "Look, about last night. I'm sorry, I shouldn't have allowed that to happen. I'll take full responsibility, and I can even sleep in the airlock if that would make you feel more comfortable—"

"No," she said, gently but firmly, her brown eyes glittering gold.

"What?"

"No. You aren't going to be sleeping in the airlock. I mean, I suppose if you really want to, I can't stop you, but you don't need to. As far as I'm concerned, you haven't done anything wrong. I know Mission Control might see it differently, but I don't."

"You don't? But, we were sent on this mission precisely to avoid situations like this—" I fell silent as Ashley put her hand up. "No, Kelsey, we were sent here to avoid situations like *Ares II*. Which was non-consensual, whereas last night, I gave you my full consent. Rather enthusiastically, and multiple times, if memory serves." Despite the gravity of the situation, I felt my lips turning up into a smile at the memory. "So, no, this isn't what Mission Control has nightmares over. This is two people sharing how much they feel for each other in an entirely regular way."

"We say that now, but what happens if things go south? There's a reason they don't usually let couples fly on the same mission." Ashley smiled at me. "Then we sit down and we talk it through like reasonable adults—like we're doing right now. Don't forget, I've spent a lot of time with you, Kelsey. Last night wouldn't have happened if I thought there was a chance of it ending badly. Yes, it's a risk, but so is flying to Venus." She gently reached for my hand and squeezed. "It'll be okay, I promise."

"How can you be so nonchalant about this?" I replied, surprised by the rising frustration my own voice. "We willfully violated one of the most basic protocols of our mission—even if it's one that you don't think is necessary. We can't just ignore rules we don't happen to like out here, it'll get us killed!"

Again, Ashley showed remarkable calm. "Kelsey, I know you're upset, and I understand why. I get it. Women like you and me, we're used to being under the microscope, whether it's because we're trans, we're women scientists, or because we're astronauts. I know how much the wrong decision can cost me, professionally and personally. But I'm not saying we should ignore the rules that keep us alive—I'm certainly not going to start climbing around the airship exterior without a safety line. But," she said, leaning closer to look me straight in the eyes, "there are some things in life that are worth breaking a rule. As far as I'm concerned, you're one of them."

"You're willing to risk your career as an astronaut, your professional standing, all that—for me?" I asked, a little bewildered.

"Yes," Ashley answered, without any hesitation. "Like I said, this was a decision I spent a lot of time thinking about—I didn't come to it lightly. To me, being with you is worth any amount of risk." She suddenly went quiet, and her face began to wrinkle with concern. "I mean, you do feel the same way, right? If you don't, I'll understand, but I need to know, especially after last night. You can walk away from all this, protect your standing in the corps. But do you want to?"

I lay there, thinking. Picturing returning to Earth, us going our separate ways, never speaking of what happened between us again. Staying in NASA's good graces. Continuing my stellar—but undeniably lonely—career.

"No," I said finally, my voice thick with emotion. "No, I don't want to walk away from this. God help me, I'd give up ever flying again if it meant having another night with you."

I took a second to compose myself—astronauts aren't supposed to tear up on duty, after all. With a sigh, I continued.

"We still have to tell Mission Control. They'll figure it out eventually, and the longer we keep it from them, the more it'll blow up in our faces."

Ashley looked at me sagely. "We'll face that reckoning when we come to it." Her voice was full of a confidence I wished I had.

◈

BEFORE WE CONFESSED anything, however, mission priorities came first. I'd just detected life on another planet, after all, and disseminating that bit of information seemed far more important than our personal foibles.

I'd gotten more samples, and even begun extracting DNA for analysis. It looked as if some previous suspicions had been confirmed—the microbes were suspended in microscopic droplets of dilute sulfuric acid, suspended in the upper atmosphere. My best guess was that they used some form of anoxygenic photosyn- thesis, probably taking in hydrogen sulfide or some other reduced sulfur compound, and putting out sulfate as a waste product. They were also only present in extremely scarce quantities. This wasn't surprising, given how water and nutrient-poor their environment was; it also explained why they hadn't been detected previously. Their DNA appeared to use the same bases ours did, but the primers for the normal sequencing amplifiers didn't work, so I had to switch to nanopore sequencing instead. The ship's computers were still analyzing the genome, but so far it seemed very different from most terrestrial life—which suggested that if Venus had been seeded by meteorites carrying bacteria from Earth, it had happened a long, long time ago, or that these cloud microbes were the descendants of indigenous life that arose on Venus completely independent from terrestrial life.

Both were tremendously exciting possibilities, and for a time, I managed to avoid thinking about the judgment Ashley and I would inevitably face. That isn't to say we stopped having sex or sharing affection—we certainly didn't—but whatever was going on between us seemed utterly trivial in comparison. For example, at the moment I was trying to prepare for my first media interview on the Venusian cloud life.

"You'll be fine. Just relax and let your natural passion shine through. They'll love you, I know it!" Ashley said to me cheerfully.

"I hope you're right." I thought that stigma can take a long time to die. "Alright, first question is coming in now."

"Hello, this is Chantal Owens, reporting. Speaking with us is Third Venus Expedition pilot and scientist Dr. Kelsey Hart, who discovered life high in the clouds of Venus' atmosphere. Dr. Hart, what can you tell us about these Venusian microbes?"

Good, I thought, nice easy open-ended question. I cleared my throat and spoke. "Well, the upper atmosphere of Venus is surprisingly similar to Earth's, at least in terms of temperature and pressure, so the idea of there possibly being life there isn't new. And sure enough, that's where we found them—living in tiny droplets of dilute sulfuric acid floating up in the clouds. They're not too different from algae on Earth, except instead of taking in CO_2 and putting out oxygen, they take in hydrogen sulfide—the stuff that smells like rotten eggs—and put out sulfate." I hit the send button, beginning the lightspeed-lagged delay until the next question appeared. I wasn't sure if I felt confident in my delivery—my voice tends to drop a bit when I'm talking about my passions—but Ashley gave me a reassuring smile.

"Was that okay?" I asked. "Did my voice sound okay?" Even though it's been years since I went through voice therapy to learn how to feminize my voice, it was still a nagging insecurity.

"You were fine, absolutely fine."

"You sure?"

"Yes, I'm sure," she said warmly. There was an awkward pause—as it turns out, it's hard to maintain a conversation when you know you'll be interrupted less than two minutes later. Soon, however, Ashley began to hum a song—one that I'd taught to her, "River of Birds." It was a favorite of mine from when I sang in a chorus in grad school. Without a second of hesitation, I joined in, singing the lower soprano line in harmony. Singing with her, hearing our voices intertwine as they reverberated through the cramped airship cabin, helped put my mind at ease.

Just as we finished through the last section of the song, the next question had arrived. The rest of the interview went smoothly, and I was smiling to myself by the time it wrapped up.

It was only later that we found out our impromptu duet had been beamed to Earth along the rest of my Q and A.

❖

BETWEEN THE ANALYSIS, taking new samples, documenting everything about my findings, additional media interviews, and the occasional duet, I kept busy—so much so that I was almost shocked one morning to discover that more than a month had passed, and we had reached our day of departure.

Ashley and I piled into the tiny, cramped departure vehicle, sitting in front of the Venusian escape rocket that easily made up half the *Lori Glaze*. I knocked softly on the *Glaze*'s outer door as I climbed in.

"Going to miss her, huh?" teased Ashley.

I shrugged. "She's been a good ship." The fate of the *Glaze* was still being decided—there'd been some murmurs that the ISC would remotely gather up the Venusian airships us explorers left behind and use them as the foundation for an eventual base for longer-duration missions. While nothing was set in stone, I found myself hoping that'd be the case—that some other brave souls would sit in her pilot's seat, tinker in her lab, harmonize with their crewmate in her crew quarters.

Finally, after running through all the departure checklists and putting the *Lori Glaze* into hibernation, there came the stomach-lurching moment when the escape rocket dropped away from the airship, and the millisecond of fear that inevitably occurred before the rocket engines ignited. We plowed upward into the darkening sky, where our relatively more spacious transfer ship, the *Cybele*, waited, ready to take us home.

As the planet's swirling clouds receded below me, I felt a small pang of sentimentality—it seemed all too fitting that I had had to come all the way to the Goddess of Love to finally fall for someone.

We docked with the transfer ship, took it out of hibernation, ran through a multitude of checklists, and, a few hours later, lit the engine for Earth.

All we really had to do at that point was just wait and let gravity bring us home, and with nothing else pressing to worry about, I became aware of the knot in my stomach that I knew had nothing to do with reacclimating to zero-gee.

"We should tell them," Ashley said, just matter-of-factly.

"I know," I sighed. With no small amount of reluctance, I readied a transmission for Mission Control. "Alright, we might as well get this over with. Recording will be on in three...two...one."

I took a deep breath. "CapCom, this is Pilot Kelsey Hart. Just a personal update, the Commander and I thought it would be prudent to inform you that, ah..." I struggled to find the right words.

"The Pilot and I have initiated an intimate relationship," Ashley jumped in, going straight to the point.

"Yes, what Commander Gutiérrez said. We acknowledge that this is a breach of normal mission protocol, and are willing to face the consequences of our actions." There was an awkward pause as I tried to think if there was anything else I could say, anything that could somehow make this better. After a few seconds, I gave up, and simply ended the transmission. Between the two and a half minute trip time it took for radio waves to reach Earth from Venus, processing the signal, and allotting time for Mission Control to decide on a response, I figured we had about eight minutes or so before we heard back from them. I waited restlessly, fidgeting as I floated in zero gravity.

Ashley reassuringly stroked my arm. "Hey. It's okay. We'll be okay."

"I hope you're right. I'm sorry for putting us in this position."

Her hand gripped my arm. "Don't. Don't be sorry. You've got nothing to be sorry for."

"Ashley, we could be ejected from the program." "So?"

"So, this is the thing we've spent years training for. You can't tell me that you wouldn't regret giving that all up just for me."

Ashley smirked at me. "Try me."

"I'm serious, Ashley."

"I am, too. Now, tell me, if we get kicked out, would you regret it?"

I started to speak, then reconsidered. I thought, remembering the moments we'd shared. Ashley and I had been through so much—rigorous training, dealing with a press that was not always forgiving of who we are, the months-long voyage to Venus, and the cruise over the planet's cloud-cloaked surface itself. The feeling of safety, of comfort, that I felt with her arms around me. The world-shaking pleasure she'd given me. The fact she challenged me, because she knew I was capable of becoming more than what I was, rather than just letting me rest on my laurels.

"No," I said. "No, I wouldn't. You're the most exciting thing I've discovered on this mission."

"Flatterer." She stuck out her tongue at me, and I couldn't help but smile despite my nerves.

"I'm being completely honest, though."

"I know you are," she said, gently. "And that's why you shouldn't worry—like I said, we'll be okay. Besides, you're Dr. Kelsey Hart. You discovered life on Venus. I doubt they'd just throw you away, y'know?"

A ping from the communications system cut off further conversation.

"*Cybele*, this is CapCom. We received your, ah, personal news." You could almost hear the blush in the CapCom's voice—while I couldn't see Chang, I was sure his face was scarlet. "Mission Control hasn't fully decided on a response yet. Obviously, while we can't stop you from doing anything out there, we do urge restraint and good judgment. Your continued flight status with the Consortium will be determined upon your return after your full debriefing."

Makes sense, I thought. Don't want to demoralize your astronauts before they get home. "Acknowledged, CapCom," I replied quietly.

"Well, if we're going to get grounded for inappropriate relations, we might as well make the most of it, you know," said Ashley deviously, as she leaned in to me and started gently nibbling on my earlobe. "Besides, after that, I'm pretty sure we could both use something to lower the tension."

A few minutes later, there was a cloud of discarded clothing slowly diffusing through the crew compartment. Ashley never did fight fair.

❖

WE MADE IT back to Earth safely, and without killing each other— if anything, despite being locked in a tin can for four months, we were closer than ever. Immediately after we were cleared by Medical at the Human Spaceflight Center, we were separated and debriefed by the standard assortment of interchangeable ISC and NASA staff in suits.

I did my best to explain everything that had happened, the good and the bad. I made no excuses for our actions. I shifted as much of the blame to myself as possible.

Towards the end of the debriefing, one of the Consortium higher-ups who had been circulating in and out of the room chuckled at my latest attempt to fall on my sword.

"You know, it's funny," he said. "In the other room, Gutiérrez is saying the exact same thing." Despite knowing our attempts to cover for each other were likely ultimately futile, I couldn't help but feel my heart sing at that bit of information.

Hours later, they finally let me go, and I returned to the barely-furnished on-site apartment where I was staying until I got my next directive from the ISC. A few of my colleagues stopped by to welcome me back to the homeworld, but most of them seemed to ever-so-slightly keep their distance—what had happened between Ashley and I wasn't entirely public knowledge, although I'm sure there were suspicions. Regardless, everyone involved with the astronaut corps knew we were the subject of a significant inquiry.

Ashley and I were both reacclimating to Earth-normal gravity, and so I mostly stuck close to the apartment. The first few days, I was too exhausted, and too anxious, to even really think of seeing anyone else. My major forays were either to eat (I had missed fresh-cooked food more than I realized), or for physical therapy to help speed along my recovery.

After the first day we'd been released, I heard a knock at the door, and discovered that Ashley had wobbled her way over. We spent the evening just curled up on the couch, eating pizza and streaming cheesy movies.

We didn't talk about Venus, and we didn't talk about how the higher-ups might be deciding our case. She spent the night—and the next few nights. Early on, I thought I'd try to conceal our relationship, but soon realized, hey, what did I have left to lose?

A week went by. I was getting stronger, and figured I'd probably be through the brunt of my physical reacclimation within another week or two. There'd been still no word from the ISC. I should've been nervous, but honestly, I was enjoying my time with Ashley too much to care— and too tired. I found myself a mess of emotions: The mixture of novel euphoria from this still-intense relationship. The fear that our relationship would suffer that we were no longer forced to share the same space-craft, and the relief that this was proving not to be the case. The exhaustion from the emotional rollercoaster that I'd been on for the last six months.

Eventually, I found myself, surprisingly relaxed all things considered, standing next to Ashley in HSC's weight room. Getting up from the machine —I'd been spotting her while she did her leg presses—she slipped and almost fell. Thankfully, I was able to catch her before she hit the equipment—and there we stood, my arms wrapped around her, until the sound of a throat clearing grabbed both of our attention. Before us stood one of the smartly dressed ISC rep that I remembered from the debriefing. Dana Sánchez, I think her name was.

I remained remarkably calm, waiting for the inevitable bad news. Ashley's face, however, was anything but calm; I grabbed her sweat-drenched hand and gave it a soft squeeze in reassurance. At this, Dana's face seemed to soften just a bit before returning to her normal Important Official expression.

"Dr. Hart, Dr. Gutiérrez, I'm here to inform you of the preliminary findings of the ISC inquiry on the Third Venus expedition."

We both looked at her, not sure what to say. After a few awkward seconds, she went on. "Based on your actions, in direct violation of ISC protocol for long-duration spaceflight, we've removed both of you from the roster of any future Venus missions."

Instantly, my heart plummeted into my stomach. Rationally, on some level I'd known that this was probably coming, despite Ashley's attempts to reassure me that my status as discoverer of the Venusian atmospheric ecosystem would provide me some cover. Ashley herself looked like she was on the verge of tears.

"It's alright," I said to her, quietly, not caring if the ISC rep heard. "We'll still be together, and that's the important thing." Part of me had worried what would happen to our relationship if Ashley had been grounded and I hadn't; I now had the bittersweet comfort that I wouldn't have to worry myself about that.

Dana cleared her throat again to get our attention—she had more to say, and seemed oddly pleased about it.

"*However*, I am authorized to offer both of you positions at Robinson base."

"What?" Kelsey said, staring at the ISC official like she'd grown a second head. I was equally perplexed— Robinson was a planned Mars colony, the first long-term, permanently crewed settlement beyond the Moon.

"You're joking, right? Why would you want us for that? We broke the rules!" I almost threw my hands up in exasperation. What kind of cruel trick was this?

"It's no joke, ma'am. The official reason is because of the success of your mission with the *Lori Glaze*—we want people of your calibre involved." The official paused, ever-so-subtly glanced around, and then continued in a quieter tone. "Off the record, the general consensus of the inquiry board that after *Ares II*, the ISC was in a near-state of panic, and didn't make what were necessarily the best decisions. We've realized that there's no way we're going to have people spend years, decades—maybe even the rest of theirs lives—on Mars and not have them couple up. With that perspective, it became obvious that you two are exactly what we want—stable partners who have already shown that their relationship can withstand the close confines and stress of being off-Earth. As an added bonus, we won't have to worry about any unexpected pregnancies, either."

"That's a bonus?" I asked, still a little confused. "Don't colonies usually require, you know, reproduction, at least in the long term?"

"In the long term, sure—but in the first few years, it's imperative that we make sure the infrastructure isn't strained by a sudden increase in the population. Once the ISC feels comfortable that Robinson is sufficiently close to self-sustaining, we'll probably ease that policy." I stared at Kelsey, her at me, both of us trying to process such an unexpected opportunity.

With a slight trace of awkwardness, Dana continued. "Might even be able to get one or both of you ladies a uterus transplant if you'd like, provided the medical facilities there can handle it."

I was a little stunned by all of this—it seemed almost too much to take in, and oddly, I react quickly to worsening situations, but good ones tend to take me off-guard. Ashley, thankfully, kept her head, and within a few seconds, I found myself in her tight embrace. "Kelsey! We're going to Mars! Us!"

Dana smiled. "I'm glad you agreed to remain with us, both of you, if for PR reasons if nothing else. I don't know if you've realized, but that clip of you two singing went viral. There are a lot of people out there who are looking forward to seeing you two on Mars."

The ISC rep left at some point after that, I think—I honestly don't know. I was too busy holding the woman who I knew, without question, that I'd be spending the rest of my life with——and there was not a planet in the Solar System that could contain us. And someday soon, I knew the red cliffs of Mars would echo with our duet.

Parásito

Ana Hurtado

They crawl on trees, antennae twirling. Bodies form a crooked path of shimmering brown up the bark of a tree so old the students can hear it exhaling, a long sigh lingering in humid air. Spider monkeys hoot nearby; toucans croak. Under a canopy of greens and browns, Professor Torres' river biology class watches their teacher capture one of the ants with the tip of his grimy fingers and shove it into his mouth, his lips closing in on his nails. He drops his mandíbula and allows his pupils to observe the tiny creature wander around his molars. It is uprooted and displaced, curious about its new wet home: the breath of this house envelops its entire exoskeleton, and so la hormiga runs in circles, searching for answers. Its movements tingle Professor Torres' tongue and he closes his jaw, crunching. The ant lets out a little scream. Professor Torres swallows his snack and smiles.

So tart and sweet, he announces to the class, pointing at the line of lime ants on the ancient tree, and invites his students to join in: grab a living being off a tree, watch it squirm trapped within your grasp, and bite.

Emi stands near the professor, waiting for her turn to feed. These ants remind her of the lime she likes to squeeze into ceviche. She picks out a juicy one and doesn't hesitate. It plays around in her mouth, sliding under her tongue, but she manages to catch it between her teeth and eats. Un mordizco de limón.

How are you not freaking out right now? Irene asks Emi, pointing at her throat. She, too, has selected her little ant and cannot bring herself to eat it.

What do you mean? Emi asks back.

It feels so evil, she replies, observing the little hormiga de limón she picked off the tree explore her wrist. It gets lost between the cracks of her skin and her tiny arm hairs. Emi watches Irene eye her ant and sweat. Today, she wears her hair in a giant braid; it sits on her shoulder mimicking the anaconda—one recently fed, podgy and rotund—they spotted outside their cabin last night.

I feel bad eating something that's alive, Irene says.

Well, you calling the hormiga some*thing* should help with that, Emi responds, grinning. Just do it. It tastes so weird.

Irene shakes her head and decides to return the ant to its family. She wipes the trunk gunk on her pants and proceeds to photograph the ceiling above them—a braid of branches, twigs, sharp and soft verdant blades—and walks off, her head raised to the sky.

It won't feel a thing, te prometo! Emi says to her best friend who doesn't listen.

Emi then picks up another victim and places it delicately on her tongue; she wonders if any of them will bite her before she bites them. When she pierces the ant with her molars, Emi feels something cold slither out of the creature. It leaps down her throat, and she swallows instinctively. Her eyes widen, and she begins to choke. She coughs so loud, some monkeys nearby howl in response. One of her classmates approaches her with a mouthful of lime juice and asks her if she's okay. She walks it off, her sweaty palm grasping at her throat, and finds relief next to a colossal tree root. Emi leans on the radicle, some of the tree's fungus rubbing against her butt. She manages to breathe again.

As Emi recovers, she spots her best friend Irene talking to Professor Torres in a place beyond the hormigas de limón tree. Irene's palm exposed a little brown thing moving in circles tracing the lines of her hand, and Professor Torres leaning his torso on her shoulders, close in on her snake. The hand that he used to pick his prey off trees now rests in the small of her back, and Emi feels like she's choking again.

◈

THE UNIVERSITY CAMPUS in Quito drowns with rain. It overflows gutters and storm drains, something to be expected around noon in the capital; it's a rite of passage to be drenched by rainwater, to succumb to the cries of an Andean sky. Water falls on all of Quito, on every invasive eucalyptus tree that occupies its parques, on cars stuck in locked intersections, and now rainfall inundates Humboldt Hall.

Doric columns line the entry path towards the Biology Department housed within the great hall named after the white explorer. Scotch-taped posters on new species findings and brown bag seminars flood these shafts, their bases muddied by footprints of students who lean on the pillars while smoking. Cigarette butts mix in with the rainwater, and a stream carries ash and burnt stubs down a drain that vomits its insides into one of the city's most polluted rivers a couple of blocks away.

Emi rushes past the Greek columns in her Ecuadorian university campus, sometimes slipping but not falling on the terracotta tiles; her brown hands tanned by last week's fieldtrip sun hold her woven backpack tight over her head. Inside the classroom, a couple of students, hairs drenched, hoodies sodden, sit and wait for their professor to arrive.

On the whiteboard, thunderbolts illuminate an anatomical drawing of a prokaryotic cell: a long flagellum looping around, the one that students like to nickname its tail, and tiny hairs that stick out of the body labeled *fimbriae* with cursive handwriting.

Emi arrives before her instructor and spots Irene sitting in the back row, her wooden chair creaking as she wobbles. In her notebook, Irene sketches tiny flowers. She then plops down on the neighboring seat and takes out her smartphone: she stares at herself via the front-facing camera and clears her throat every now and then. Something feels stuck.

Emi notes how the rain dragged her black eyeliner down to her cheeks; she's a racoon. She pulls at her skin with her fingers, trying to remove her makeup.

Oigan, does someone know when the midterm is? Ignacio asks his peers as he scrolls on his phone. His short-sleeved shirt reveals arm hairs combed over by rain.

I think the syllabus date hasn't changed, Emi replies, hiding her face in her hands.

Ugh, Ignacio utters. We *just* got back from la amazonía and now we have a test next week?

Is it going to be on the Napo river only or—another male student asks, someone Emi doesn't know quite well. She thinks his name is Felipe. Or Fabricio. Something with *F*.

Is it me or are the tests like stupid hard in this class? Ignacio asks the *F* boy.

Emi lowers her hands and smirks. The first test was easy. I don't think the midterm will be hard at all, she says.

The male students laugh and exchange glances. Ignacio chortles, too.

What's so funny? Irene asks, looking up from her notebook. It *was* easy.

Ignacio and *F* boy turn their heads to face the young women.

I mean it was easy for y'all; Professor Torres takes it easy with girls, Ignacio says.

That's sexist, Irene responds.

Yeah, shouldn't you be, like, man enough to accept that we're smarter than you? Emi laughs.

No, that's not what we mean, *F* boy replies. A silver crucifix dangles at the bottom of his throat, picking up the classroom's fluorescent lighting. His lips are chapped, and his eyebrows meet in the middle.

Then what do y'all mean, Fede? Irene follows up. *Federico.* Emi was never going to guess that.

Let's face it, Professor Torres has a reputation of going easy on girls so he can, you know, Ignacio says with a smile that soon disappears into a frown.

No, I don't know, Emi says.

Yeah, what is it? Irene asks.

So you'll say yes when he wants to sleep with you later, Federico says, grinning. The male students chuckle and shake their heads as Irene and Emi look at each other. Professor Torres walks in. Irene gulps.

He steadies his sharp umbrella next to the instructor's desk. While removing his coat, Professor Torres shakes the excess water from his salt and pepper hair and beard. From the class's back row, the young women witness how a cloudy sky highlights the deepest shades of blue in his eyes.

Let's begin, chicos, he announces.

From their classroom in Humboldt Hall, Emi observes the university's biggest pond. Tiny fish create bubbles in its murky green surface. Her mouth dry and craving. In the window's reflection, she studies a curious Irene staring at the whiteboard, at Professor Torres' hand and how he outlines the Napo riverbank they visited last week. Emi then spots Federico the *F* boy raise his hand; Emi rolls her eyes at him. And in her own reflection, she looks at her face: the skin underneath her eyes still so dark from her eyeliner remnants. It looks as if she's been crying. Her nostrils expand as she sighs, and her right one quivers with her breath. Emi feels a sneeze coming on but instead of feeling any relief from sneezing, all she finds is an ache that lingers in her face. The window shows her how she frowns from pain, how her brows scowl and mouth pouts. She then detects a dark and slimy little thing wiggle in and out of her nariz, almost waving.

◆

She stands in the bathroom stall and listens. Doors smash and creak open around her, high heel taps echo alongside muddy boot stomps. Taps run hot water and paper towels are pulled and ripped from the wall. Lips are pursed in front of a foggy mirror, shades of lipstick smeared across skin. It's the ten-minute break between classes, and the first-floor bathroom of the Guayasamín Arts Department is the most popular at this hour. Emi stares at the water bowl below her and feels sick. It's not the stillness of the water that sometimes bubbles when neighboring toilets flush that revolts her; it's the fact that she wants to dive her head in there and drown.

Emi waits patiently for a knock she knows so well. After last night's text, she tries putting the puzzle pieces together: a huge hand lingers on Irene's backside out in the rainforest, Irene smiles when Professor Torres calls on her in class, and el mensajito de anoche: *I need your help*, received around two in the morning.

She spots Irene's maroon military boots hovering beneath the stall door. And then the knock, the passcode. Emi unlocks the latch and pulls her best friend into the stall. Other students outside protest, *Ey, ey, ey! I was first!* And *Go make out elsewhere, I gotta pee!*

Irene and Emi stand facing each other, their bodies touching. She looks down at her Irene who always was a couple of inches shorter than her and asks, Qué paso, Ire?

Irene finds a way to not look at Emi while they're stuck in the tiny stall, their faces inches away. I don't know where to start, she replies. Her breath smells like mint.

What is it? Did something happen last night? Emi asks.

I think you know about my crush, Irene confesses, her stare now set on Emi's eyes. Emi nods in response. So, Irene continues, I thought this was what I wanted. To be flirted with and kissed, but *this* isn't what I want at all, she says. Toilets flush and punctuate the end of her sentence.

What happened with Professor Torres? Emi asks.

Ssshh, please, don't say his name here.

Okay, what happened with Professor Idiot? Emi insists.

After yesterday's class, he asked me out.

And this was what you wanted, right? To go on a date with him?

Yes, but then he asked if I could meet him at his place down in the valley of Puembo.

Oh, Emi says, catching on.

Yeah, Irene responds. This is when I said something like I'd rather meet in Juan Valdez. Like, have some coffee and talk. We're both adults. We don't have to hide or anything, right? Her tone looks for assurance from her bestie, and Emi stays quiet for a while before responding.

Right, she whispers, nodding. Nothing wrong. Emi rolls her eyes. You'd just rather have shitty coffee than go to his house, totally understandable, Emi says. That sounds so fast, though.

Irene bites her bottom lip and then mutters, He got mad. Said I should stop playing games with him and then told me his address. Urbanización Jardínes.

Emi is glad to know where this man lives. What did you say back? she asks.

No, gracias.

Oh? Emi smiles.

And then he said, I don't appreciate being teased. My body ran cold. I told him I don't tease. He asked me if I was calling him a liar. She stops to inhale and exhale.

Someone taps on the bathroom stall. They both yell, *Ocupado!*

What else did Profe Imbécil say? Emi asks.

Irene sighs. Something about my last exam; my performance didn't showcase my best efforts and that I should stop by his house to make sure I do well next time.

What? Didn't you get an A last time? And how will going to his house guarantee an A? What is he talking about?

Irene hesitates. Because if I don't go, I'll fail. At least that's what I think he insinuated, she says.

Umm, yeah, that's quite an insinuation. Sounds like coercion to me.

What's that? Irene asks, pointing at Emi's face.

What? Coercion? It's—

No, estúpida. Something's dripping from your nose, Irene insists.

Emi places her ring finger on her warm nostril and feels something smooth slide back inside her.

It's nothing, she responds. Escúchame, Ire, she says. We need to tell someone.

Irene leans her head on Emi's chest and tears stream from her cheeks onto Emi's breasts. They hold each other and listen to the bathroom and hallways quiet down as classes begin.

❖

THE SIMÓN BOLIVAR library houses the biggest collection of books in Ecuador. Sheathed by a grand section on larvae, Emi sits, taking notes. She's surprised none of Professor Torres' students are here, cramming before their test. She knows Irene's stuck in Ceramics class, presenting her midterm project and will join her soon, but, right now, Emi feels alone and unsettled. A worry that grows from her stomach up to her throat and extends into her arms.

She holds her pencil, leaning hard as she retraces the *R* in *Río Napo* over and over again. She remembers the cold river water, their speedboat roaming the brown canal, headed deep into the amazonía. She remembers some droplets landing on her lip and when she licked it off, the notable salt in its grit. She's suddenly so parched. Then the memory of a bite of limón sourness gurgles up some saliva in her cheeks. Emi can hear the crunch of the ants she bit in this silent library. As other students bury their heads in books, she keeps smirching her biology notes with the smudgy graphite pencil, looping the o's aimlessly.

It first feels like pressure. Her index finger reddens, her nail and pencil tip drenched by a layer of thin blood. A tailed and slimy creature is birthed from underneath her fingernail. Emi drops her pencil. The thing pushes through her carne and stretches out, reaching, wobbling about. Emi resists an urge to scream and holds her hand close to her chest, the little animal unfolding its greasy self on Emi's other fingers, tangling itself on her fingers.

She stands up, her chair falling sideways. And before she decides to run to the student health center, the creature who smells like ceviche slithers back in, her finger swollen and gushing. Emi passes out and topples over, her body almost taking down the library's oil painting of Simón Bolivar straddling his white horse, preparing for battle.

❖

THE SIGN ABOVE Emi's head reads #BájaleAlAcoso. A hashtag tacked across every corkboard in the university's health center and taped all over the female bathrooms. The sign represents the university's anti-femicide campaign, and its rhetoric aims to give victims of harassment and assault a voice. There's a blurry number underlined beneath the hashtag. Emi stares at it, her hand pulsing, and wonders if Irene has thought about calling.

A nurse stands bedside and takes Emi's blood pressure. Her touch is cold.

Emi stares at her inflamed hand and her heart beats fast. She then hears footsteps headed towards her and braces herself for an angry Irene. Her bestie pulls open the curtain to Emi's bed and then barely closes it behind her. Irene wears rainboots and a short skirt; her knees a little grey.

Is she okay? she asks the nurse and then rushes to cradle Emi's head. Qué te paso, idiota?

She fainted, the nurse answers on Emi's behalf. And looks like she cut herself with something sharp. The nurse's eyes jump from Emi's bleeding finger to Irene's legs.

What happened? Irene insists. Emi looks up at an Irene who hasn't slept: the skin beneath her eyes a little green, her eyes red with a flood of tiny pink veins.

How was your Ceramics show and tell? she asks, smiling.

The midterm? Fine, whatever, Irene replies. She looks at her watch and then back at Emi. We're so not gonna make it to the river bio midterm, she says.

That's seriously the least of my problems. Emi exhales. The nurse finishes up her notes and fixes the clipboard next to Emi's bed.

The doctor will be in a few minutes, she says.

Gracias, Emi responds.

And, chicas, please beware we've been getting reports of harassment out by the university entrance; so, I wouldn't wear *that* to campus. Irene and Emi look down at Ire's skirt. The nurse walks away before they can say anything back.

That's, that's so great. Emi sighs, placing the palm of her hands in her eye sockets. I hate everything, she says.

I told them, Irene announces. And didn't go to Ceramics workshop.

Told whom? I'm confused.

I told the office of Equal Opportunity. I had to skip Cerámica to do it.

Oh, you mean you went to the Do Nothings, Emi replies. She laughs and then becomes silent. I'm sorry, she offers.

Está bien, whatever, Ire replies. I don't know what I was expecting, she says.

Okay, but what did they say?

They didn't believe me.

Oh.

They didn't believe me that it's coercion. They said I should feel flattered Professor Torres has taken an interest in me.

Wow, Emi says, her hand pulsing

There's nothing we can do, Irene says. Just stay away from him. But—

But what?

But what about our grades? Ire says. A tiny tear exits her eye and lands near her nose. Emi uses her bloodied hand to pick it up like she did with that hormiga.

So, we'll fail, it's fine. We can take it next semester with someone who is *not* a creep.

Oh, but then we wouldn't feel complimented that he has taken an interest in us! Irene laughs. Emi joins in, too. But, are you sure? Irene asks. Cold rainy air rushes in through the building's open windows and the tiny hairs on Ire's legs stick up.

Sure about failing? Wouldn't be my first time. Actually, it would be, but it's fine, Emi reassures her.

No, no. Sure about failing with me? For me?

Now *that* I'm cien porciento sure.

❖

THE SEATBELT STRAP strangles Emi's body. Her insides shift and fight for space as she tries to focus on the conversation. Irene sits in the passenger seat, playing with the radio knobs. They're parked in the entrance of Río San Pedro's beach for its monthly clean-up, an extra-credit option written in Professor Torres' syllabus. The young women theorize their grades will tank with a missed midterm exam, and maybe volunteering today can help them pass the class with a C.

My GPA is going in the toilet, Irene murmurs. She raises and lowers the volume of the radio.

We shouldn't worry about that now, honestly, Emi says. Her last word gets snarled by her mouth, and she feels like vomiting.

Irene looks up at her. Emi smiles, lips closed.

Vamos, Irene says.

They exit the car and carefully walk down to the river beach where other students gather. They form a chain, like las hormigas de la amazonía. Some students crouch down on the sand and stretch their arms towards a smelly river: they pick up parts of car tires, political flyers from past elections, deflated soccer balls, and other trash. The students fill up their burlap sacks and aim to save a river that will never be fully cleaned. But the extra credit will suffice.

As they carry on, a blue Volkswagen pulls over, windows tinted black. Professor Torres emerges and waves. Emi wants to talk to Irene, wants to ask her if she's okay, if they should leave, but she can't move her tongue: it is petrified inside her mouth, caught in a lattice of slippery black wires. She can only nod in response when Irene tells her, Estoy bien, I'm okay. Emi smiles, mouth closed, and extends her gloved hand towards Irene's. She taps it back.

Other students eye Professor Torres as he heads towards them. He skips down the quebrada, as if he's done this a million times, the bottom half of his blue jeans browned by dust. Emi hears a couple of female students she hasn't met exchange words; through the babbling of the river stream, she hears them say, *I thought he wouldn't be here. Why is he here? Should we go?* It's a common conversation in every friend group, a list of shared terrors.

Irene stoops next to the riverbank, her knees soiled in gunk. With a cupped hand, she collects bits of plastics that float on the water that would have later ended up in the Pacific. Today, she wears her hair as two snakes that rest down her back. Emi observes Professor Torres make his way over to her best friend, and, when he's close, she becomes unleashed, surrendering to the call of the water: with a single leap, Emi tackles Professor Torres, and they both fall into Río San Pedro, more trash added to its once pristine waters.

In the depths of the river birthed by volcanic glaciers, now clogged by city trash, Emi is freed. Her eyeballs are pushed to the side by a wormed black beast flailing hundreds of boneless limbs as it exits her body, leaving behind a shell of Emi to sink with the weight of her carcass. El parásito then swims, a tangling web whirling and dodging waves. It heads towards a thrashing Professor Torres. It catches him with its shifting netting and penetrates the professor's mouth. It dives into him, and Professor Torres becomes paralyzed from the outside in, the black mass conquering his being. El gusano exits through his pores, exploding the professor's flesh. Black and white peppered hair reaches the surface of a brown river now veiled in maroon. The parasite floats away, hunting for a mate.

Mandy and Lulu Welcome Walter

S. M. HALLOW

JUST FOR THE record, I was *very* clear. I was literally like, Lulu, I will become your vampire bride on one condition, and she got down on her knees—you know how she is—and she was like, Name the price I must pay for your love. It was super cute, actually—she was so eager for me to finally say yes that she would have agreed to *anything*, and looking back I totally could have milked that. Like, I could have told her I would only move into her Edgar Allan Poe murder mansion if we could start our own multi-level marketing scented soap scheme, and she would have been totally on board even though she doesn't know what any of those words mean. *Anyway*, my one condition was simple. I was like, Lulu, I will become your vampire bride as long as you promise me we *never* get a cat, and she started laughing, and she was like, That is all? You make marriage easy.

And so like, I thought the matter was totally settled. That's what you would think too, right?

So you can imagine my surprise when one day I came home with a local virgin farm boy—her favorite!—and there was Lucrezia. On the couch. With a cat. In. Her. Lap. I was like, Are you serious right now? And she was like, Darling, you brought me virgin farm boy! And the virgin farm boy was like, Cool T.V. He was totally oblivious, as far as victims go, which is probably for the best, but I immediately lost my appetite. I was like, He's all yours, and I stormed out of the room.

Protip: if you want to successfully storm out of a room, live somewhere small enough that your every step makes an impact. By the time I got to the staircase Lulu couldn't even hear me storming off, and what's the point of storming off if not to make sure everyone knows you're not happy?

Anyway, about thirty-three minutes later—because *yes*, I *was* keeping track of how long it would take—Lulu showed up in our bedroom. Holding this little brown tabby cat. In her arms. Like a baby. And she was like, Mandy, what is wrong? You did not even touch the farm boy.

And I was like, Lulu, do you remember what I asked you before we got married? And she was like, You did not want cat.

And I was like, What are you holding?

And she looked at the cat, then looked at me, and she was like, Walter is not cat. Walter is Walter.

And I was like, Walter? The Walter who saved your life? The Walter who helped you pull off the Great Diamond Heist of 1899? The Walter you camped out with at Woodstock? *That* Walter?

And she was like, You remember!

And I was like, He's a fucking *cat*?

And Walter meowed like, Pardon me, good madam, but Lucrezia the Defiler, scourge of Transylvania, vampire of yore, just told you I'm no mere cat: I'm Walter.

❖

So you know how cats have nine lives?

Yeah. About that.

Apparently Walter and Lulu have known each other since she was a Little Match Girl street urchin. That was Walter's first life. Every time he dies, he searches for Lulu in his *next life.* Yeah, okay, it's very noble, and I *get* that they're attached to each other, but *come on.* Every single story I have ever heard about Walter makes him sound like a *human boy.* For the entire time we have known each other, Lulu has *conveniently* forgotten to mention that Walter is a *cat.* And you *know* how I feel about cats. I grew up with golden retrievers! There's just no comparing which animal makes the better pet.

I tried pointing this out, and Lulu was like, Walter is not *pet.* Walter is only family I have, and you *hate* him? And then—and this was horrible—Lulu started *crying.* She never cries. Her cheeks were all blotchy, her blood-tears were everywhere, and she was like, This is Walter's ninth life. Soon he will *die* die. You expect me to forsake him? Because you prefer *stupid golden dog?*

And I was like, Great. Just great. I wasn't going to keep my wife and her magically reincarnating cat away from each other. I'm not that much of an asshole. So I wiped Lulu's tears, and I was like, Obviously Walter can stay.

And she was like, But you do not like him. How will he feel at home if you are menacing him with your bad vibes?

And I was like, I will control my vibes. I will learn to like Walter.

◈

Within three days Walter was using the leg of my velvet couch as a scratching post. Lulu was like, He is doing very good job with his scratchies! And then she saw my face, and she was like, I buy scratching post for him. He will like that better.

Well, he *didn't* like the scratching post better. And every dawn, as Lulu and I climbed into our coffin, he *insisted* on joining us. The first time it happened, I closed the lid and let him meow, but Lulu was like, Mandy, darling, he needs somewhere to sleep, and I was like, Uh, like the cat bed I just bought? And Lulu was like, Does the cat bed offer undying love?

And who do you think Walter woke up in the middle of the day when he wanted out of the coffin? Who do you think helped him into the sink when he refused to drink from his water bowl? Who do you think put on sunglasses and kept him company while he stretched out in a sunbeam?

Not Lulu, with her undying love. *Me.* Just like it was me who took a moment to read the label and discovered what was actually *in* Walter's cat food. Corn gluten meal? Wheat gluten? Chicken *flavor*? Um, *as if.* My wife's cat was *not* going to eat like a pauper. He'd had enough of that in his first life. If this was his last one, I was going to make him feel like a king.

Cat tree? Check. Water fountain? Check. Catnip toys, cardboard tubes, battery operated mice to chase? Check, check, and check. Lulu was *so* happy. She was like, Look, Walter, Mandy does love you!

And, like, I thought *love* was a little strong, but I wasn't going to correct her. And then one night, as I was putting together cardboard boxes for a DIY cat condo, Walter rubbed his head against my arm. And pushed his way into my lap. And I was like, Um, excuse me sir, but I'm kind of making you a castle right now, do you mind? And he just like, curled into a little ball on my lap. And started purring.

And I was like, Oh, shit, I think I *do* love him.

❖

WHICH MADE THE whole ninth life thing depressing.

I mean, Lulu got all of Walter's nine lives, and there I was, skating in at the end, only getting one. And Lulu wasn't handling his last life well either. She was like, I have never lived without Walter for more than a few years. What do I do when he is *gone* gone? And like, I've lost pets before, but none of them had been century-long companions. I think if Daisy or Butterscotch had seen me through the advent of electricity and two world wars, I would have simply laid down and never recovered when they passed.

Which is when I was like, Um, Lulu, we're *vampires*. Why don't we just make Walter a vampire?

❖

WE THOUGHT ABOUT it for a long time. Obviously Walter was very well taken care of, and the vet called him a model cat, so it's not like we had to *rush*. But Lulu couldn't decide what she thought of the idea. Sometimes I would find her crying, and she would be like, I cannot deprive him of sunbeam. Other times, she would dance around the living room with Walter in her arms, singing about being family forever. So it was, like, a pretty confusing time for us both.

And then one morning, as the three of us got comfortable in our coffin, Lulu started counting. She got to eight, and then stopped. And then she was like, Mandy, I have made grave error.

And I was like, Is this about the taxes?

And she was like, I think this is Walter's *eighth* life.

And I was like, Oh my *God* Lulu, you *better* be sure.

And she started listing off lives. And by the time she finished, she only got to eight. We went through it three more times, and still: eight. That night, Lulu pulled out a century's worth of diaries. We spent the next weeks poring over every single detailed page in every single musty, water-stained journal, just to make sure there was no chance we'd be losing Walter for good. And Lulu was right.

This *was* only his eighth life.

So I was like, What does this mean? What do we do?

And Lulu was like, We let him have all nine lives. We let him have sunbeams. So he still had the rest of this life, and one more to go. Which was, first of all, a huge relief. Now we could press pause on constantly worrying about the ethics of turning an animal into a vampire. (I tried reading *Bunnicula*, hoping for some guidance, because I thought it was about a family that owned a vampire bunny? Let me just say it did *not* help.) But it was also, like, a huge joy, because we still had *so* much time ahead with him. I was so overwhelmed by how ridiculously happy I was that I started crying—I mean full out *sobbing*—and I picked Walter up and held him against my shoulder like a little baby. Walter closed his eyes in a slow, scrunchy blink, and tucked his head against my neck, purring, and Lulu was like, Look at you. He is king and you are serf.

And I was like, You know what babe? You're right. I have embraced feudalism for this cat.

Which is, like, the way I think it's supposed to be.

Three Nights in Orissa

Sean Robinson

STARED AT THE map and it didn't change. The sunset light through the arrow slits was red like poppy juice and a shaft of light struck the table, struck the map, struck the city of Orissa. It painted my city in bloody contrast.

"My lord?" Medeav stood in the doorway. "She's here."

My heart sank, and as it did fear moved up from my stomach to fill the space.

I was not ready. We were not ready.

I wanted my mother, my father, my brother.

But there was only me. I nodded to the city commander and rose. The armor I wore was heavy, but not any heavier than the crown on my head. I made my face the cold mask of a king, and forced the fear from my chest.

Or at least I tried.

When I stepped out onto the barbican, the sun was setting into the sea, bathing the Orissa plain in light. The Orissa plain and the army that had marched down the road. Marched down all the roads, and left emptiness behind it.

It filled the valley, up into the hills. Men and women, horses and caravans, rough-built siege towers and fine-wrought catapults. An army that had broken city after city, leaving only the dead behind it. It had come for my home. It had come for Orissa.

"What news of my brother?"

"No word, my lord," Medeav said.

He had donned a helmet of beaten bronze and would command the defenses, as he had for my mother. The old man would lead our warriors, and show the invaders that ours was not a soft city. Good men and women stood ready to defend Orissa with their lives. We were ready to die for the people who could not fight, those that hid behind our walls, in the towers and manor houses, in the slums and along the canals of Orissa.

They were mine, and I would be damned if I let the city fall.

Beneath my feet, I felt them all.

I felt them when I rested a hand against the rough stone of the wall. I felt Orissa, as alive as any warrior, prepared to wage war to protect its people. Its song was a carol, a war song, a chant. It whispered in the language of cities to our warriors. It whispered out down the road to the enemy. I was its King, and it whispered to me.

Orissa was the Heart of the World, and the Heart of the World would not fall to the woman who had brought her army to us.

I expected the enemy lines to part, but when they did, it was like a river parting around a stone. Her soldiers bowed as she came forward. I watched them clutch their hearts and dip their heads to their queen, hands across the crimson badge they each wore.

Althair the Red came to Orissa.

Her red hair free in the wind, her gown wrapped around her like an ocher breeze, I could say that she was beautiful. Perhaps the most beautiful woman I had ever seen.

She had snuffed the lights of other cities, had left aching wounds on the face of the world where good places had been.

As her army parted around her like a great ocean wave, she burned.

I did not know her, but I hated her.

"Hail to the people of Orissa!" she called.

Her voice was strong, the lilt of her words gentle, toying. But the City shuddered beneath my feet and I tasted the power of Althair the Red. It was bitter juice, tanged with blood. I let it roll on my tongue as if it were wine and when I drank it down, Orissa rumbled and the power inside me roared.

"Hail to the Red Queen," I said, and every rock and cobble and stone spoke with me.

My hands shook with power.

I was my mother's son, and would not bend to an invader. I would not bow to a queen who had not birthed me, nursed me, bled me. Althair was not Queen Vast, and though she was a terrible beauty, I was not cowed.

"Open your gates, my lord," she said. "Open your gates and let us be friends."

I laughed. It was not a kind sound.

"You are no friend of Orissa. No friend brings death as her drumsman. No friend brings blood as her herald. Only Althair. Only the Red Queen. No, we will not open our gates for you."

She laughed in return, and the bloody sunset clung to her until her hair sparkled, as though it had been woven with bright rubies and dark garnets, as though she dripped in burning, crimson light. She stood like a bonfire. It hurt my eyes, but I did not shut them. I stared into the woman who had come to take my city and forced myself to see nothing more than a woman, nothing more than an army.

"I have come to the city, my lord," she called. "I may come in peace, or I may come in war. Throw open your gates and welcome me. I am your Queen!"

There was more of her bloody magic on the wind. The soldiers on the wall felt it. Old Medeav felt it beside me. But when her magic tried to swallow me, there was Orissa beneath my feet, against my hands where it held the stonework.

I struck the stonework of the wall with the flats of my hands. When my heart beat a second time, I struck again. On the third heartbeat, Medeav joined me. Again, and it grew. The men and women in their armor struck the rock that defended them. The ranks at the gate stomped, or clashed their swords against their chests. It grew until Orissa thundered to my heartbeat.

I did not look away from Althair's great magic.

"I am Orrin, son of Vast," I said, and let the magic flow to the beat of the gathered arms, down into the bedrock, in the dark places of Orissa that I didn't dare go, not even as king. I drew it back as the beat grew louder, until Orissa was a bell and defiance was our peal. "I am King in Orissa."

"King no longer," Althair said. "The Red Queen comes!"

The magic of our refusal was almost too much.

Sweat dripped down my face and my heart thundered with it, pulling it tighter and tighter. Orissa was the Heart of the World, the hub around which all cities turned.

It was mine, paid for with sweat and blood. It was mine, in oath and deed. It was mine, honor and responsibility. The air tightened into one last agonizing moment.

I nodded and Medeav roared.

The archers on the walls loosed their bolts. My magic followed in a torrent, soaked into every arrow head and fletched-feather.

Her magic rose, but not enough. All along the invaders' line, the arrows found their marks, and as the enemy fell, my magic gripped the wood. And as Althair's army died in ones and twos, the arrows sunk roots into the ground and I forced them up.

The soldiers had just enough time to scream before they died.

The thorns grew higher, their dagger-studded vines climbing toward the sky from trellises of flesh and blood and bone.

But they did not touch Althair.

The thorns grew around her, but she did not look away from my eyes. The rear line of the army did not move. They held as their fellows died.

I pushed again with my magic and the battlements answered.

Every stone, every joint burst into light, as blue as the queen was red. The air chilled as the front lines broke, throwing themselves into the light, I heard more screaming. The soldiers' flesh gave way to hoarfrost and ice.

I did not look away from the queen in red until she turned and strode back up the lines.

There was a call from the rear of the lines, and a second figure moved forward. It was taller—he was tall— and armored. His helmet was a jagged obsidian piecework. He raised an arm and the army at the feet of my city tensed, as though they were an arrow and he the archer.

The Butcher. Althair's Beast. Her General.

I gathered the last of the magic, enough for a third push.

The thorns still grew, but slowly. The soldiers were slow to throw themselves against the ice-rimed wall. There were enough in the valley for Althair to build a siege wall with the bodies of the fallen to break Orissa upon her knee.

The Butcher threw his sword forward and the army charged.

I flung my power into the ground.

The road moved beneath them so their feet brought them no closer. It flowed backward as my magic made land between us, as it forced the army back. It grew grassy hillocks and fields between us. The magic was a wave and it drove them back. Adding distance, farther and farther.

Not far enough, but it would buy us time.

A little time.

My knees buckled, but I clung to the stone.

"It won't be enough," Medeav said.

Beneath us the army cheered.

"Have the walls reinforced," I said. My voice was thin. It was hard to breathe. "See if we can't get a breast wall in between. Make sure the scouts are careful. There was maybe ten leagues in that spell. It won't take long for them to march back. Mother could have done better."

"My King," Medeav said. "It still won't be enough."

I smiled at him and placed a hand on his shoulder.

He had been a father to me when I was a child and heir to the throne. I looked into his eyes and let myself feel what I was forbidden. I wanted Mother, my terrible, awful, powerful mother. I wanted magic enough to keep my city safe.

I wanted to not be King.

"Have hope," I said, instead.

Medeav nodded and turned.

"Medeav?" I said. "Get a messenger out before she closes the road."

"It will be done, my King."

I shut my eyes. Althair stood there in my mind all in bloody light and magic.

"Tell my brother that he will be king after all."

Most of all I wished that I was not alone.

◈

I walked the streets as night fell. People watched me pass. Some called out my name, some begged for aid. But most locked their doors, barred their windows, and prayed. I could feel those prayers, like tiny licks of fire inside my chest.

They prayed to the city, to the unicorn, and to the phoenix.

But there was only the City left. The City and me. Orissa had no phoenix, no unicorn. We were not enough. Not when the unicorn and phoenix had fled Vast and her cruelty. Not with an army like a red-metaled ocean at the feet of the battlements.

I walked the streets, though my mother would not have done it. It was as important as battle planning that every person knew—every person in Orissa—that they were not alone. I would not abandon them to the witch at the gates.

"Bless you, my lord," a young woman said as I passed her. She carried a small child on her hip.

"Bad night to be out," I replied. "Best get home."

She nodded and moved faster. There were a handful of people farther down. A few shopkeepers trying to sell their goods. A few alehouses and wine shops in the Old Quarter doing good business.

We were facing death, who could blame them?

I stepped inside the Cobalt Weaver, its blue spider dangling from the sign, legs against the handle of a beaker.

"If I die tomorrow, I might as well say that I've drunk my fill," I said to myself. I'd been young the first time I'd passed into the tavern's cramped interior. It had been Medeav who'd found me, sweet-to-bursting with honey mead, and Medeav who had been unsympathetic when the mead-sickness started.

Life comes full-circle.

A half-dozen men sat at the table near the hearth. The ceiling was low, and one of the men slammed a tankard onto the scarred wood, and stood.

"Old Vast, she'd've 'et that red-haired creature. Would've gulped her down and picked her teeth with the bones. Not like that stripling. A king? He ain't no king. I heard it from my cousin who was on the wall. He only pushed them back. Waved his hands and made a right fool of himself."

I shook my head.

The night I decided to get drunk at the Cobalt Weaver, Vast had threatened to get me herself. People liked to forget that. They liked to forget that Vast was her name, and vast was her hunger. Vast was her cruelty.

She might have 'et Althair the Red, but she'd have eaten Orissa to do it.

The tavern had one other person at it, shoulders hunched forward, front pressed against the bar. I couldn't see his face, but as I sat and the barkeep pushed a full tankard in front of me, he leaned back. He smiled, nodded, took a sip of his own drink and promptly ignored me.

We were quiet for a while as the table by the hearth grew louder and louder. They cursed the city as their voices slurred. They cursed my mother. They cursed the phoenix for her desertion, the unicorn for his absence.

I sighed into my cup.

The man beside me turned on his chair.

"So loud, a man can't even hear himself think," he said. His voice was soft, like snowfall. His face was wide, with a strong jaw. I noticed his hair, dark, falling across his face.

A fist struck me hard. Followed by a second, forcing me off the stool and onto the floor. The boot that followed wasn't fast enough and as I twisted, the loudest of the table drinkers fell cursing.

But he had friends and they were on me fast. Each one drunk and cursing.

"Phoenix burn you," one hissed. I did not let him hit me. I did not let the others hit me. My cheek was cut and my nose was bleeding. "Don't need your kind in here."

No, they didn't need my kind in here.

I couldn't draw my sword. Drink tainted the air, and I could see how scared they were. Scared like a child without a mother, and twice as angry.

I couldn't let them beat me, or the barkeep, or the other man, either. But as I pulled for the flicker of power deep in my chest, the man at the bar stood. He was taller than I was, and broad.

"Tonight's not the night for fighting," he said in his snowfall voice. He touched the shoulder of the man coming up behind me. "Not when there are enemies at the gate."

He touched my shoulder too, and I felt myself relax. He helped one of the fallen men—the one who said my mother would have 'et the witch'—from the ground and set them on their way.

They left without a protest, not even looking back. The man returned to his seat, hunched over his ale.

"Thank you," I said as I took my own seat back.

"Guess you shouldn't complain about them complaining," he said, smiling.

"I think that was you. I was just minding my own business," I smiled back at him.

"Is that how you Orissa folk treat people just looking for a drink at the end of a long night?" he asked.

"Not usually," I said. "What brought you to the city?"

He took a sip from the ale. "I had been traveling. The army was marching, and I needed somewhere to go. Orissa seemed as good a place as any."

"Aside from the locals," I said, looking back to where the small group had huddled over their cups by the hearth. Now the cups were scattered and there was mead on the floor.

"Can't blame them though," he said. "No one expects an army at their gates."

"No. But it doesn't change that there is one."

"Not quite the gates, I hear."

"By the morning." The ale burned as I drank it. It wasn't enough to stop the slow burn of fear. Dawn wasn't far off.

"You're one of the defenders?"

I caught myself looking at the curve of his chin and the shape of his eyes. Then I was looking for the color of his eyes. They were pale, but deep.

He smiled when I nodded.

"They say the army has never been stopped."

I sipped the ale again, embarrassed. "We'll stop them."

"How?"

I didn't know. And when I shut my eyes, I saw the army like a blood-specked wave and Orissa a seashore about to be overrun. I jumped when I felt him touch my shoulder.

"Lost you there for a moment."

"I'm sorry," I said, shaking. "It's been a long day."

His eyes were pale circles of silver, dappled, like pitted metal.

"Tomorrow will be worse, if I've ever seen a siege. And I've been through my share."

"Tell me your name," I asked. Because he was beautiful. Because I liked how he smiled, because there was no reason not to. And when I looked at him, I had forgotten—for a breath—what waited with the dawn.

He smiled. "Ask me tomorrow."

"I might not be here tomorrow."

"Survive and ask me again."

He set the mug down on the counter, as though it were the most precious thing in the world, and then left the quiet tavern, the cold of new snow behind him. Like first winter. I didn't even mind when the barkeep asked me to pay for his drink.

◈

I WAS THINKING of him as dawn came too soon, and I was atop the battlements again.

The spells on the stones had held through the night, but no longer. The brambles fell in the first hours of sunlight, and the cold lasted a bit longer.

Althair's force-marched army drove ladders into the corpses of its fallen, and tried to scale the walls with ropes. We did not let them. Althair's soldiers were brave, but we were braver. As the red-badged soldiers made the wall, they were cut down. Their ladders broken, and their lines shattered.

I thrust the point of my sword into the chests of the men and women who would hurt my people. Who would raze my towers. I did not stop until they had all retreated, or were dead. The world collapsed down into blood and battle and desperation.

A cry rose up around me as I cut down another red-badged soldier and looked for the next.

We had held.

Medeav was quick to find me as he directed the disposition of the fallen. Our soldiers were brought off the wall, wrapped in samite and laid in state. We ripped the badges from Altair's forces and threw the corpses over the battlements to join their siblings below.

And feed the crows.

Unicorn remember, I hurt. From a sword thrust I'd barely parried, from cuts and scrapes and the weight of armor, and of so manydeaths. The sun was setting and there were friends of mine among the fallen.

"Where was your head?" Medeav said in a hiss too quiet for anyone else to hear. "You let them take the wall!"

I swallowed hard. The old man was angry, and there was a cut bleeding down from his eyebrow.

"Let's get you looked at——" I started.

"It's a war, boy! A war! And where were you last night?"

He was getting louder. Loud enough for the healers and the soldiers to start looking at us.

"King of the city and no one can find him. You should have been planning with the generals. You should have been helping keep watch. Yet you wander in at dawn! How foolish are you?"

"I was walking the city," I said. "Seeing people."

"You were in a tavern. You were in a brawl. If your mother were still alive——"

Something brittle snapped inside me.

"If my mother were still alive, I would answer to her. I do not answer to you," I said.

My words were cold.

I was tired, so tired.

Things were not what I'd imagined them to be when I was still my mother's heir. Kingship was heavy.

"If my mother were still alive she would still be eating sapphires like blueberries and powdering phoenix feathers onto her morning chocolate. You will excuse me, Lord Medeav. We both have business to attend to."

I left the man who was almost my father stuttering and angry and bleeding. I left the battlements and the aftermath of a hollow victory. Althair's force had been outriders, whoever had been fastest. The rest were coming.

Still coming.

My footsteps were light and quick as I made my way to Old Town.

◈

The stars were out by the time I made it back to the Cobalt Weaver. The inside was quiet. Only the barkeep, running a rag up and down the counter, kept watch.

He looked up when I walked in. As I sat he put a thin cup of beaten bronze in front of me. Inside were three fingers of dark drink.

I smelled it.

Blackberry.

The barkeep poured another three fingers into his own cup.

"Ale's run out. So's the mead. Only thing left is the kind of drink no man looking Sabbaeus in the eye would want. But I've been saving it for a special occasion. Seems like a special enough time, don't you think, your highness?"

I shook my head. "Just Orrin."

He drank his blackberry wine in a single long draw.

I sipped mine more slowly and it unfurled on my tongue. It tasted of autumn and the promise of bronze leaves and the air coming crisp after a warm summer. If I were chasing death's city, I wouldn't be sipping it either.

"I don't suppose you've seen the man from last night?" I asked, pointing toward the seat he'd taken the night before with my chin.

There were footsteps behind me, and when the barkeep looked back, I turned. My stranger was heavier on his feet than he had been the night before. He still wore dark clothing, and a vest of tooled leather. He smiled at me, and I felt myself smile back.

"Looks like you made it," he said.

"It's good to see you again."

Oddly enough, I meant it.

He sat beside me, and he still felt like snowfall. The barkeep poured him a copper cup as well, but the man didn't take it. Instead he turned his pale eyes on me.

"I'm Jerrod," he said and smiled, the bow of his lips curling at the edges. "How bad was it?"

"Bad enough," I said. I tried to forget the ache in my arms, in my legs. I was tired. So terribly tired and I didn't want to think about what dawn would bring.

"You could join her, you know," Jerrod said.

"What?"

"Just slip out. People have done it. There were some in the tavern before you came in. They say all you have to do is walk out and they'll take you to her. You promise to fight for her and her cause, and she'll tear a piece of her own gown for you to keep as a token. Until the war is over, or you die, or forever after."

"Did they say just where you might join up?" I asked.

He laughed and shook his head. "I think they would notice the King of Orissa coming, wouldn't you?"

"I'm sorry," I said. My cheeks burned, but Jerrod kept smiling. "If you'll excuse me."

I stood and turned. Embarrassment curled in my stomach, followed by shame. How had I been so stupid? Death was camped at the gates of my city and I was in a tavern. What was I doing?

My mother would have been appalled.

Before I was two steps away, he grabbed my hand.

"You came back," he said. His smile had almost disappeared, except for the corners of his mouth, which curled.

His hand was warm in mine.

"It only seemed polite," I said, not pulling away.

He laughed. It was the sound of ringing bells.

The world was falling apart around me. We would die when Althair's army came again. We couldn't last. But Jerrod's hand didn't leave mine.

"Have you seen much of the city?" I asked.

He shook his head. "Can't say I have had much time for sight-seeing."

"Would you like to?" I offered. "You don't have to feel obligated. You don't have to if you don't want to."

"I'm not someone who does anything I don't want to," Jerrod said simply. "Not for kings, or queens, or baronets who think they're beautiful."

He stepped close to me. I could feel his warmth. His hand moved, and as it did, he wove his fingers between mine. I had never felt anything like it before. Vast had never let me, and there had not been enough time for joy as a King.

"Then perhaps I might show you some of the sights?" I asked.

"A private tour by the King? I am both honored and delighted."

Not as delighted as I was. Not as happy as I was as we left the Cobalt Weaver and passed into the star-stitched darkness, into the quiet Orissa streets.

◈

NO ONE WANDERED the cobblestone thoroughfares but tightly formed squads of soldiers, fast marching their patrols. No one trusted Althair and her army. I did not think that they would be able to penetrate the wall, not yet. The magic of the ramparts still hummed in my bones.

"Where are you from? I asked.

"A little village that was nothing more than a handful of houses beside a riverbed and a road," he said. "Nothing so grand as this."

I laughed.

There had been days, growing up, and since becoming king, that I had wished for a hovel and some chickens. I wished that my greatest concern was whether the birds would lay enough eggs to feed me.

"Do you miss it?"

"Never," he said, "and if I did, there is nothing there to go back to. It didn't even have a name, and in the years since I left, it's withered and died. Anyone left is there because they are too scared of what the road or the world might have beyond their mud walls."

"I've never been too far from Orissa," I said. "My brother—he's the adventurer. We get letters from him, sometimes. He's in Aspice or Ellyson. He's on the road from some place you only hear about in stories, doing things that become stories."

I smiled, thinking of Scander. I missed him. I did not know if he would like Jerrod. He would have challenged Althair in single combat. Odd thoughts for so dark a night.

"I've heard of the Scander Prince," Jerrod said. "More than a few minstrels and bards seem to favor his adventures."

I laughed.

"I hope they get the good parts right when they write songs about us. I'm sorry you weren't able to see the city at its best."

"Who says I've not seen the best Orissa has to offer?"

The lilt of his voice made my heart beat faster and my head grow light. What was I thinking? There was an army at the gates and my people fought and died. Dawn was coming.

Another troop marched in front of us.

Their boots rang off the cobbles.

"They didn't even look at us," Jerrod said.

"The patrols are perfunctory. Nothing's getting over the walls."

"You seem pretty sure of that," he said. He grabbed my hand again, but I pulled away.

"The city will hold," I said, and then softer, to myself, "It has to."

He nodded, the smile gone from his face. "I'm sorry. This is your city. Your home."

I sighed.

"If they break the wall, my people will die. There aren't enough soldiers on our side. We'll be overrun. Althair the Red will take Orissa. I can't give my people over to her."

Jerrod said nothing. He was still, like a pond, like the first snowfall of winter, when the world is quiet, sleeping.

"They're just people," he said. "They love and bleed and die and dream. But they're just people. They're not any more special than anyone else. There were people in Valdez and Foy and Rasia, too. The Queen came, people fought, died, and the city fell. The Queen remained."

"She cannot have Orissa," I hissed. "I don't expect you to understand."

I had wanted him to understand, though. But I couldn't explain why.

"The shopkeepers? The children? They can't fight. Not the way I can. Not the way my brother can. Or my mother. They don't deserve to be hurt because one woman thinks she can rule the world."

We walked more, in silence, not touching. We walked along the canal, beneath the Old Town towers, and threaded our way to the docks, which were as quiet as the rest of the city. There were no ships along the quay. The counting houses were shuttered. If a ship could be bought, traded, or pirated, we had packed who we could aboard, and let them sail out into the Ossean Sea. There had not been enough.

He stood beside me. Close enough that I could feel him. His eyes were pale in the moonlight.

"My mother used to bring me here," I said. "We would watch the ships and she would tell me that our salt came from quarries up the coast and that our sugar came from Cadien on the ships. I always liked to watch the sailors. I thought that they had the most amazing job in the world. They touched the things that other people wanted, and helped them get what they needed."

Jerrod was quiet, but I felt him in the dark, almost against my skin. Standing, but not quite touching me.

"They wouldn't let my mother work. My grandfather was a vinter. He made blackberry wine. But he couldn't help us after I was born. So she did what she could to keep us fed. When I was old enough, I went hunting. And when I was old enough, I left."

I leaned into him, just a touch of shoulder and elbow and wrist. Barely anything, but something in the dark, with only the stars to see us.

"My mother—" I started, but I couldn't finish. I couldn't get the words past my mouth. I loved her and hated her and feared her all in equal measure.

Instead of pushing, I felt Jerrod move and suddenly he was behind me, a warm weight, his chin resting on my shoulder, his arm wrapped around my waist, pulling me tight to him. He was warm, so terribly warm.

I leaned back into that weight and let him hold me. Because we stood at the shipless dock. Because Vast and Althair and the Butcher were far enough away as to be a memory. I let out a hiss of air and leaned back into the strength of him.

We stood there, wrapped in one another, for a time.
I didn't know or care how long. I did not think about
the dawn or the blood. I only thought of the firmness of
him, and the ache inside my chest that,for a few stolen
moments, had eased. I was not alone.

Jerrod kissed me.

I leaned back to meet his lips. They were thin and cold,
but warm too. I kissed him in the darkness where we could
be just the men we were, where there was no reason at all
not to, and a great army of reasons to take what little joy
we could have.

He pulled away. My heart sank for a breath as Jerrod's
head turned from the sea and toward the shuttered
counting houses, the dark-windowed warehouses.

Jerrod's eyes reflected silver in the moonlight.

His nostrils flared, the way a horse's will sometimes.

"I smell fire."

"Fire?" I asked, pulling away and turning too. "I don't
smell anything."

He was scanning the buildings with his eyes, his head
turned until I could only make out the profile of his face in
the darkness.

"Footsteps," he said, and he pulled away from me.
"Oil."

"I don't—"

Then I saw it. A flicker of red. A moment passed and
the flicker grew, along the roof edge of a warehouse.

I ran toward the burning buildings.

Jerrod was a step behind.

"They're grain houses," I said. They were holding bags of
grain, piled almost to the ceiling inside each building. They
were siege rations, in case Althair tried to starve us out.

If the grain caught, it would explode.

I reached for the place inside me where man and city
blurred. Where I was Orissa and Orissa was me. Before Vast,
there would have been a Phoenix and a Unicorn as well.

Each of us bound in service to the city, but no longer. I was alone, except for Jerrod, who stood beside me like a pool of silence.

Orissa's cobblestones were my skin. Its ramparts were my bones. I could feel the fire and I reached out to it with magic, cold and still. I reached for it as a city, I reached out for it as a king, but nothing happened.

The fire was spreading, licking along the timbers of the storehouses.

But there were footsteps. A dozen of them.

I lost hold of the city.

"Watch out," I said to Jerrod. "They're coming in fast."

They came out of the darkness like wolves. Their feet were quiet on the stones, but their swords were sharp. I had enough time to pull my sword loose from its scabbard before they were on us.

I blocked the first blade, and turned into the second. The third I ran through, tangling the attack up as I moved. As the warehouse fire grew, I could make out the attackers better. They wore the motley armor of Althair's troops.

My blade struck fast. I opened one of them across the stomach and blocked a mace with my forearm. It hurt. Hurt enough for me to miss the downswing of a knife. I saw its edge reflect in the firelight and took a breath, knowing that I couldn't stop it.

Jerrod charged them.

He was faster than anything I had ever seen, and he was bare-handed.

I watched, dumbfounded, as he struck the blade out of the attacker's hand. He grabbed the arm that had held the knife and twisted it. There was the unmistakable snap of bone, and Jerrod threw them away.

I pulled my sword back up, bracing against the pain that radiated down my forearm.

We were surrounded and the warehouse was burning. It lit up the cobbles and chased away the smell of the sea.

"You cannot have this city," I snarled. They wore mismatched armor, but a red patch of fabric was stitched over the heart of every one of them.

Jerrod had his back to me.

"I'm sorry," he said.

I leaned into him, so that I could feel the weight of him against me.

"Don't give up yet."

There were too many. Even though cries were rising as the fire spread, it wouldn't be enough. It would take too long for the wall guards to make it so deep into the city.

The world slowed as the soldiers rushed us.

I stepped into the nearest attacker, bringing my sword under his guard. It cost me momentum, but I brought the man down.

Behind me, there was a sound I had never heard before. I turned, then stopped dead.

It was black.

A great mane of silver ran down its neck like moonlight. Its tail was just as silver. Four legs ended in hooves like dinner plates. From the center of its head, a single horn rose like a spike. The unicorn was as tall in the shoulder as I was.

And where it danced, death followed.

I couldn't speak, even as the attackers rushed it.

They fell to the unicorn's hooves, its teeth. The swords struck against the horn. But it was not enough. I could feel its magic, pulsing out as its feet struck the cobbles.

I watched as it slit a throat with the tip of its horn. As it trampled another man's body. As it brought its great forelegs up and dropped its weight on a fallen attacker.

When they were dead, it turned to look at me with eyes ringed with molten silver. There was blood on the unicorn's muzzle. Darker things coated its horn.

It stepped forward, a hoof crunching bone.

I stepped back, unthinking, then realized. But it was too late.

The fire in the warehouses had razed the roofs.

I turned my back on the unicorn and reached for the flames again with my magic. But even as I did, I could feel the heat. There was too much of it, and it resisted. I struggled, trying to snuff the fire, drive it away, anything. But it was not enough.

The unicorn stepped past me.

I watched as it tossed its head back. Watched as it pawed the ground. Watched as it danced, black-pelted but etched with firelight. And with it came magic again, but stronger. So strong it drove out the scent of burning wood and grain the way the fire had drowned out the sea.

It smelled of the first snowfall of winter, when the ground hadn't quite frozen.

"Jerrod," I said.

But the unicorn didn't stop. His power rose as his hooves rocked off the stones. As he lifted and jumped, the power built and built. And finally, he hurled himself up. When he landed, the magic broke.

The flames went out. Snuffed as if they had never been.

And where there had been a unicorn, there was a man. A man I had kissed in the starlight. A man I had held, and let hold me.

I crossed the space between us in the time it took Jerrod to get to his feet.

"Are you hurt?" I asked. But when I tried to take hold of him, to draw him close, he held me back.

"I'm sorry," he said. "This was unbidden. It was forbidden. How dare they?"

"Jerrod—"

He didn't look at my face. Instead, he looked back at the carnage. A dozen bodies bleeding in the dark. There was noise, too. More footfalls. The Orissa soldiers were coming.

"It wasn't supposed to be like this," he said.

I could not name the look in his eyes when he finally gazed at me. Gone was the smile on the edges of his lips.

Gone was the self-assured languorous humor.

"It's all right," I said.

Jerrod laughed, but it was hollow and strange. He shook his head. "No. No sweet king, it is not all right."

He pulled away from me.

"I need to go," he said.

"Please," I called after him. That time it was me who pulled his hand, drew him back to me. "Stay."

He shook his head.

"Then meet me tomorrow," I said.

"It will be magic tomorrow," he said.

"What?"

Jerrod brought my hand up to his mouth. He laid a kiss on the back of it, not caring that it was dirty with dust and blood and grime.

"She will attack with magic," he said. "Be safe, Orrin. Please be safe."

He pulled away and left.

I tried to follow him, but couldn't. He moved too fast and between one breath and the next he was gone. Leaving me with the dead and the burnt and more questions than answers.

And an ache inside me that I could only name to myself.

❖

Dawn found me bleary-eyed. I felt like a too-taut bit of string. As though I was one bard-strum away from breaking. But I had planned with my generals. I had eaten, I had slept. I had thought and thought. I had dreamed.

I greeted dawn on the battlements.

Althair's army had lain camp. They had felled whatever was left of the brambles and they stood like a silent, unmoving sea. Shifting as heartbeats passed, but waiting.

Medeav was beside me.

He looked as grizzled as I felt. He had not slept. Instead he had spent the night scouting the city. Cajoling. Demanding. Conscripting.

"One of our scouts made it through the lines," he said. His shoulder was close to mine. I did not look at him. Instead I was looking across the field, trying to make out faces. Searching.

"And?" I asked.

"Prince Scander is on his way," he said. "Two days out, riding as hard as his mount will take him."

My mouth was dry. My skin was cold despite the heat of the morning sun and the weight of the armor around my shoulders. It felt like a lifetime since I had walked without hauberk or pauldrons or vambraces.

I nodded, but whatever words I might have spoken died.

Up the hill, Althair's army parted.

"Here it comes," I said.

They made a clearing, wide enough for anyone on the Orissa wall to see. It was empty, except for a handful of figures. They were bound and wore the colors of Medeav's missing scouts.

Our scouts struggled, but she came.

She came like a bloody heart all in red, in a dress that clung to her like a second skin. I could see it all. She strode barefoot across the hard-packed dirt and I knew as she did it, there was a smile on her lips.

There was murmuring behind me. Medeav's conscripts shifted on their feet, out of sight from the wall. I would have shifted too, but I watched and waited.

I did not have to wait long.

"Two days have passed, King of Orissa," she called. Her voice was magic, hot and spiced like perfume. It carried across the field as though we stood barely apart. "Do you not open your gates to me? Give yourself to me and I will leave the city untouched."

As she had left Valdez untouched, or Orissa.

Untouched perhaps, but dead. Dead and emptied, scraped clean of life and love and magic like a pomegranate was scraped of its arils.

I did not speak.

"No?"

Her thin-arched brow rose and the smile faded from her lips.

"And you?" she asked the kneeling soldiers.

Medeav tensed beside me, ready to command our warriors to battle. But it wasn't the time yet. As much as I wanted it to be, as much as I wanted to cross to Althair the Red, it was not the time. We were not ready.

"Will you swear to me?" she purred. "Will you cast your foolish king aside and take your place next to me?"

The first spat at her. I could not see his face, but pride spiked through me. And rage.

She struck my scout down. And the second. And the third. Seven of them. She struck them down with her own hands. She reached to them and rent their flesh with her fingers until her bare arms were covered in blood.

I felt her magic on the wind, growing with each death.

Medeav ground his fingers into the stonework, still and frozen. We would have our revenge. The lives we lost would not be for nothing. We would survive and the seven fallen scouts would be remembered.

I swore it to myself, to the city. To the people.

Althair's army cheered. They roared as our captured people fell and died within sight of our city—their city— and there was nothing we could do for it.

"Now," I said.

Behind us were the people we had found as the nighttime fled. A girl still in braids, a man hunched forward, clinging to a staff for balance. A mother who had walked from her house because her city had asked her to. Because if she did not come to the wall, her babies would die like our scouts.

There were not enough. Not nearly enough. But magic had been coming thinner and they were all we had. The strongest magic workers in Orissa.

The little girl's name was Roura, and at Medeav's command the magic that flowed off her was the cold of a mountain stream in high summer. It was bracing, and she gave it up without hesitation.

Badric—the old man—followed. He planted his staff and joined his power to the little girl's. His was different. It was the sharp, mirror-perfect crack of ice-covered snow. It was jagged edges and hidden deeps.

But it was the mother—Zallannah—who forced her power into the sky. She was a glacier, a bottomless crevasse, where the screams of the fallen echoed into the depths.

Their power flowed over the battlements.

I watched as Althair's magic rose on the backs of our dead.

"She's using death to power it," I said.

Medeav nodded.

It was hot magic. The kind of heat that brings disease, the kind that brings delirium and death. It was bloody copper and she smiled as she cast her magic toward the city.

Althair's spell met the cold of Zallannah, Badric, and Roura. At first, I thought it wouldn't be enough. How could three stand against the queen?

I ached to put my magic into it, too. But there was not enough left in me. Not if the gambit failed.

The air was heavy as the two powers met.

Between one breath and the next, clouds charged in as the magics roiled in the air above Althair's army. They were a sickly green, and there was wind. It tore through the attacker's line. And lightning followed. Except it struck the battlements, and it struck the attackers, and it struck the gates.

Both sides broke as the hail fell. As we were battered by wind and rain. I clutched at the rockwork, but it was not enough.

A blast of wind knocked an archer from their post along the wall. Lightning danced across the ranks of Althair's soldiers.

"Enough," I called down.

Roura was on her knees, Badric beside her. Both bled from their noses, their eyes. Both gasped for air that struggled to come.

"Medics!"

The storm grew and grew.

Those at the foot of the wall scattered.

I watched as Althair hissed toward us, but no other motion followed. She turned as well, flanked by her guards, and moved away from the battlefield. Back to wherever she was bivouacked, anywhere but on my doorstep.

"Where is her Butcher?" I asked. But the wind tore the question from my mouth before any answer would come. "Where is her general?"

The medics were carrying away the little girl and the old man. I knelt beside Zallannah, whose magic had been stronger than the rest. Whose children I swore would know of their mother's bravery. She stared into nothingness. She did not breathe. I remembered her face from the first night. She had wished me well as I walked.

I did not cry. Orissa could not afford a king with tears in his eyes. But I remembered her. I would not forget.

◈

MEDEAV DID NOT lecture me as I walked into the night. He said nothing and there was nothing left to say. Not when we had seen the army. Not when we knew that our third day was over. Not with Althair coming.

"Let them do what needs doing," he told me. "Let them make peace with it."

But I could not make peace with it. I stalked the parks as the sun set. They were quiet. Whoever might have wandered the tree-lined paths was absent. And that was good.

My heart was heavy.

It was hours that I walked.

He sat beside the canal. Dark except for where the moonlight traced the bridge of his nose, and the edges of his clothing.

"No Cobalt Weaver?" I asked.

I sat beside him, curling my arms around my knees.

"You survived," he said.

"Others didn't," I said. "A woman whose children will only know her from memory. There is a little girl who may never walk again because she gave too much magic. Seven scouts who only wanted to keep their city safe. She tried to use their deaths to fuel a spell to kill the people they loved."

Jerrod said nothing.

I breathed. Deep breaths that tasted of Jerrod's snowfall and the brighter smell of herbs along the canal, of trees that hadn't yet given up their blossoms to the changing of the season.

"You're a unicorn," I said.

Jerrod said nothing.

"They say that one of the Herd has joined her," I said.

Jerrod said nothing.

"Not someone. You." He was too tall, too slender, too much. No full-blooded unicorn had coiled muscles like Jerrod had. None of them stalked a street like a beast. "You're hers."

"I've been hers for a long time."

"You don't have to be," I said. "You can choose something different. Here and now, you can choose to be something bright and beautiful."

"This was not what I planned," he said. "I didn't expect to meet you. I didn't expect to feel—"

I reached toward him.

"I am not a child who needs saving, Orrin," the unicorn said, pulling away. "I am the darkness against the moon. I am the night your children are told to fear. I walked into the bloody rain with my eyes open. I am a monster."

"Then I love a monster," I said. Because there were no other words today, and I felt the sun rising through the trees. Orissa caroled and the light was bright and warm. It painted Jerrod's face, and even the black of his hauberk turned gold.

"I am not safe to love," he said, and stood.

I took his hand. "We are neither safe to love. But if not here? If not now? When? She comes with the sunset."

"We come with the sunset, my king," he said. He said it gently, but he pulled away from me.

"Then love me," I said. "Love me, my unicorn. Love me for today, because we are not promised tonight."

"You don't know what you're asking," he said.

"I'm asking that we be happy," I stood beside him on the bank of the canal. The water trickled behind us and the grass was gold and green in the light. "I am asking that when sunset comes, we can say that we took the time we were given, because we aren't promised more."

His hair was gold in the dawn. It reflected off the panes of his cheeks and even the bottomless pits of his eyes were tinged with gold. His fingers were clenched into fists, but I reached out my hand to him. Because he was as lost as I was and it didn't matter what the sunset would bring. It didn't matter to me.

"I've waited all my life," I said, hand out. "I didn't know what I was waiting for until now."

"She'll kill you," he said. "She will kill you and she will make me watch if we do this."

"I'll see you again," I said. "If not here, if not Orissa then somewhere else. Somewhere that even the Red Queen cannot go."

He shook his head. "There is no such place."

"Love me," I said.

Jerrod had no reason to. What were we? A handful of nights, a few stolen kisses. But, oh, I ached for him. I ached for his arms around me and to be strong for him.

"You will die."

"Then I will storm the City of the Dead, Jerrod. I will remake the world if I must."

He kissed me, all lips and tongue and strong hands against me.

"I will not stay," he said.

I pulled the vest from him, and the shirt beneath it. I ran my hands down the pale skin of him. And I kissed him.

"I did not ask you to," I said. "I only asked that you love me."

And he did. We did. In a forgotten corner of Orissa, where my mother and Althair were far away. Where the war had not touched, where there was only Jerrod and I and the morning light and the tiny, fragile, thing that had grown up between us.

It was enough. It was all that there was and all there would ever be. But it was joy. At least there was joy. And we were not alone.

◈

THE MORNING FADED to afternoon and we lay on the grass. I ran my fingers through Jerrod's hair, but he was looking away, out toward the wall and the army and what waited.

"How do I stop her?"

"You can't," he said, but he grew still. "Nothing can stop her."

"She will kill us all," I said.

He turned to me. Still beautiful. Still broken. I could see it now, in the daylight. I could see the hollow need in his eyes, the desperation. I had felt it in him and he had shown it to me.

"You're asking me to betray my Queen."

"I'm asking you to help save lives."

He shut his eyes. "Lives are replaceable."

"Not yours," I said. I traced down the edge of his cheek with my finger. He was warm, so terribly warm.

"She will drink you down," the unicorn said. "She will drink your life down and it will fuel her magic. If she can drink it down, pull blood and death down inside her, it will fuel her. It has always been her gift."

"I love you," I said.

We kissed again. Made love again. And as the sun westerned, we dressed in our armor and were what we had always been.

I watched him walk away, our eyes not leaving each other's until the distance between us stretched and broke. And then I was alone again.

We were both alone again.

◈

THE GATE WAS breaking. Each crash against it was the sound of thunder, a wall of percussion. I felt it in my magic, felt it with my senses.

"Hold," I said. The soldiers around me clutched their weapons. Some prayed, but most watched. The great timbers shuddered and the silence was broken by the sound of splitting wood.

"Steady!" I called again.

She was there, on the other side. She was the hot wind that melted frost. She was false-summer in the endless winter. She was coming.

And somewhere, out beyond the gate, was a man with pale hair, who was gentle snow. Who loved me.

The gate broke, the timbers flew and she came.

Her warriors flanked her. They wore mismatched, pieced together armor. Their swords had been honed down to a thin edge.

And beside her, a step behind, was a man taller than the rest, his armor black ink in the light.

"Take it," she said, and the rest swarmed around her, like ants, like a red-badged tide.

The men and women around me roared.

"For Orissa!" I heard, and it was Medeav, who had been the nearest in my life to a father. They charged. I watched as the gold of his armor disappeared in the throng. I lost sight of Jerrod as I followed my people, and then there was nothing but blood. I didn't see faces. I didn't hear voices. I gave myself to the sword and the battle.

If it wore a badge of crimson, or carnelian, or poppy, or rose, I slew it. I slew it until my sword was wet with blood and my side ached where I had been cut, and my chest ached with every breath I took.

I watched Medeav break through the faltering line. We were losing, there were too many to hold. Althair stood like a rock as her attackers continued to pile through the broken gates. Medeav charged her, like a star of gold.

But Jerrod was there before he could strike the Red Queen. He moved like water, his axe an extension of his hands. Medeav was not as fast.

On the downswing, as my old mentor watched the falling arc, the unicorn's war axe met my blade. "They are not just game pieces, Jerrod." I said.

I let myself be cold. I let myself be ice and winter and I let the way he looked into my eyes and the memories of him above me, beautiful in the moonlight, freeze in my heart. I would keep them safe forever, but we were not Orrin and Jerrod anymore.

I pushed him back as Medeav rose, and he went.

The tide had slowed, but the Orissa line had broken. We were overrun, but for where we stood, Jerrod, Medeav, and I. And Althair who walked on bare feet, whose eyes didn't look at the slaughter. Who smiled.

"Do you yield?" she asked. "Yield and I will spare the rest. Yield and learn to love me, Orrin."

Medeav threw himself forward before her magic wrapped tighter around us. Jerrod followed, and Althair and I, until we fought. Althair ripped the sword from Medeav's hands, its edge not cutting her skin. Jerrod's axe was too fast, and it struck the old man down.

"Bring me his head, my Butcher," she said.

Medeav fell to the ground and the unicorn advanced on me. I watched the light fade from my mentor's eyes. He watched me until the light was gone, and there was only a man I had held hands with in the moonlight, and the queen who had broken the world.

I did not want to fight him. I wanted to hold him. I wanted to wake up and have the fear in the pit of my stomach be a dream and the dead around us be anything but my people and his.

"And you thought he loved you," she said. "He has always been mine."

Jerrod made a feint, a half-swing with his axe, and then caught the edge of my blade with the haft of his arm, locking us in close. His face was a mask, but his eyes, his eyes held tears. I pressed my face forward, until my forehead touched the place where a horn would have grown, if life had been different.

I released my sword, dropped my hands away from his axe, and pivoted.

And as I did, I called the cold. I called it up from the flagstones, and the skin of the dead, I called it in my heart and in the heart of my city. I called the magic and it answered.

It answered, and I made myself a spear of magic, one that Althair could not melt, one that would not break or falter.

I could not look at Jerrod, but I met the bloody magic of his queen.

Her smile failed when I closed the distance between us.

"Jerrod!" she screamed, but there was no answer as I grabbed her by the neck. Her power burned my skin and where my fingers met her flesh it leeched the cold from me.

"I will drink you down." And she tried.

Desperate, I forced the power into her. I gave her the feeling of the ramparts beneath my fingers, the taste of ale on my lips as Jerrod kissed me. I gave her Orissa with its gentle parks and my mother looking down on the docks. And I gave her the cold, and it was too much.

She screamed, and I still forced the power into her, until there was blood in her eyes and in my mouth and I did not know where I began and she ended.

Althair tried once more to rip herself free as the ice and fire gave way to darkness, and even then, I gave her the power that made my legs stand, my heart beat. I gave it all to her. Because there was no other way but to burn her out.

I fell and there was quiet. I saw her, bloody eyes staring into space.

"He is mine."

And I gave her the last of it. Jerrod and I walking along the quay, his arm across my shoulder, pulling me close. The touch of his lips against my cheek, the warm weight of him behind me, as we looked out to the sea. As the moon turned the wave-caps silver.

"Mine," I said.

I faded into the dark, the sound of the first snow fall of winter following behind me.

Please Mind the Poltergeist

TEHNUKA

THE FIRST SIGN of haunting was the door relocking itself.

"Is it broken?" asked Appa on attempt six. "Should you call Miriam?"

Such an ordinary door for a haunted house—peeling green paint, taped-over bell button.

"She's on her flight. I've got it." Vani wedged a foot between door and frame and squinted along the corridor. A decorative vase lay on its side beneath an empty picture-hook.

"I'll unpack, you rest."

"No, Appa. I'll do it." Convincing her parents she'd manage alone was hard enough without mentioning the ghost. No reason to tell them on moving day.

He returned to the car for the cooler. She leaned against the door, uncertain she had the strength to hold it open.

Appa hated night-driving. When she switched on the porch light, he lost enthusiasm for unpacking. She promised to invite her parents over once she was settled, waved goodbye, and sat on the cooler. A clanging arose from the kitchen.

Her first night alone in a year—except she wasn't alone. She shouldn't have agreed.

But after so long in her parents' spare bedroom, free accommodation elsewhere was a miracle, even when Miriam explained it was more ghost-sitting than house-sitting.

The metallic noises stopped. A gust rattled the doors.

Miriam knew she'd hated moving back to her parents'. Miriam was also about start the fieldwork that had been allotted to Vani, roaming the mountains, sleeping in a tent...Her gratitude conflicted with envy.

"You'd just be monitoring breakages," Miriam had said on the phone. It was the first they'd spoken since Vani's farewell party, a year earlier. "Sort any urgent repairs, so it's livable when I return."

"Does it break much?"

"The mischief mostly happens when I'm out. I don't think it needs me, specifically. It's probably frustrated, being tied to the house. Having someone who's home more might help."

The hallway light flickered out.

"Oh, come on!"

She needed to eat, unpack her pyjamas, and find her room. She couldn't exhaust herself—crying could wait until she was in bed.

She pushed the cooler towards the sound of water. The kitchen glowed yellow in lights she hadn't turned on. She found dinner in a lunchbox in the cooler, along with vegetables for a week. Appa had included a napkin-wrapped fork.

When she opened the lunchbox, the lid whipped out of her hand and splashed into the rapidly-filling sink.

"Please don't." She gripped the box, eyes filling. Her fingers ached. "Throw Miriam's stuff. She said you would. I'm too tired for this."

The lid returned, spinning like a frisbee, and landed beside her elbow.

❖

Next morning, she re-fastened the bathroom window she hadn't opened, gathered plate-fragments around the house, then had a nice, hot shower to ease her muscles.

She should have known better. There wasn't even time to rinse out Miriam's shampoo before, vision fading, she crawled onto the floor and flopped on her back. The floral stink in her hair made her nose itch.

So much steam. Shouldn't have closed that window.

A clatter.

She pushed herself up to see spaces in the condensation on the mirror.

They read: *RU OK*

"Uh…yeah. Low blood pressure."

Her toothbrush floated up, scraping against the mirror.

"You really don't have to use my toothbrush."

111?

Her trousers—her phone in the pocket—flopped onto her lap.

"No, no ambulance. I'm lightheaded. I'm not dying or—sorry. Dying might be fine for, some—I'm fine. Thanks. It's kind of you."

The toothbrush dropped into the sink. She pulled a towel over herself.

"Also, do you mind not coming in when I'm showering, please? I know being incorporeal, you mightn't have… vision, but I'd rather be dressed around company."

❖

After that the poltergeist stuck to breakages, clogging the sinks with a grey-green slime Vani hoped was just ectoplasm, and moving furniture. She sat on the floor if the sofa was upside-down, scooped ectoplasm into a bucket to feed the compost when she could—letting dishes pile up when she couldn't—and wrote down what was broken.

❖

For solitude, Vani sat on the garden bench, thinking this also gave the poltergeist solitude to express its feelings.

The first time, she got locked out. After that, she always went inside once the doorbell shrilled.

❖

When her parents rang, Vani took her phone outside. "You can visit soon," she said. "I want to cook something nice, but I'm having a flare-up. No, don't bring food. Being independent, remember?"

The summer weather was glorious—could she just host them outside?

❖

Vani found the missing corridor picture face-down under her bed while hunting a sock: a glacial valley, sharp-peaked, green-forested, scree-sloped; braided river winding through, crossed by a swing-bridge.

Her chest ached.

"I climbed mountains," she told the poltergeist. "Hard seeing something you'll never get back."

She slid it back under the bed.

❖

The ghost broke every plate and dented every piece of cutlery, except Vani's. She ate from her lunchbox with her hands, or the fork Appa packed.

❖

When she wasn't up by noon, a mug of water appeared

at her bedside. Hadn't the ghost broken all the cups? She didn't ask.

◈

THE GHOST RAN out of things it wanted to break.

Vani woke to hot cocoa in the last remaining mug.

"Thanks," she said. The lights blinked.

"You're a lovely housemate," she said, and felt the slightest tickle on her palm. "I hope you'll write to me again."

◈

THE GHOST DID write to her again.

◈

WHEN SHE COULD think, she read aloud, or they played Scrabble. When she was too tired, the ghost brought meals in bed, packed in her lunchbox, a gust of wind sliding it onto her duvet.

◈

THEY CHOSE NEW crockery together online.

◈

"I DON'T MIND if you want to hang out in the bathroom. You could write on the shower wall."

◈

WHEN SHE LAY on the bench in stale summer heat, a breeze blew out the open door, cooling her skin. Nothing else moved.

"WANT TO MEET my parents?" she asked.
The ghost squeezed her hand.

A Record of
Lost Time

Regina Kanyu Wang

TRANSLATED BY REBECCA F. KUANG

HOW DID WE end up here?

The humans before me had the same physiological traits as I did, yet still we had no means of communicating with one another.

I couldn't understand what they were saying. Words and phrases spilled from their mouths, a torrent of sounds bleeding into one another, syllables pouring out in a drum roll, unending and uninterrupted. To their ears, my speech was perhaps like an endless song; syllables dragging at an agonizingly slow pace over a never-finished sentence.

I couldn't see their faces clearly, either. The high-frequency movements of their facial muscles blurred their features, and their waving hands left behind after-images like the fluttering of insect wings. To their eyes, perhaps my own movements were like those of an action figure with a dying battery; propped up on its last bit of energy, but never able to reach the position it desired.

I knew that if I waited, then their black hair would rapidly turn white, that wrinkles would grow on their faces, that their teeth would fall out, that their inner organs would sicken and cease to function. They would be like the plants that surrounded them—rapidly growing and rapidly deteriorating; rotting in the mud, then replaced by the next generation. And that next generation's speed would be even greater. Their lifespans would be even shorter. Yet still they would not sense that anything was out of the ordinary.

When all was said and done, entropy would reach its maximum level and heat energy cease to circulate. There would be no distinction between past, present, and future. The heat death of the universe, the collapse of time—all would grind to a complete stop.

There was nothing we could do to stop it anymore. This process couldn't be reversed. We once had an opportunity, but no one had really tried. We saw it all happen with our eyes wide open—some actively, some passively, all racing to the end of the story.

I don't know what to do, except to record a few people and their words. They're like me: the slow and lonely ones among the masses, the ones who chose not to speed up of their own accord. They'd all glimpsed a hint of what was coming from the start, and they'd tried to escape their fate by refusing to accelerate. But they hadn't expected the whole world to be swept up in this madness.

We were strangers who had come together by chance in the slowest dimension. We met, we spoke, and then we parted ways. I don't know where the others are today; or which speed dimension they're living in. The specific year, month, or day holds no meaning; our old conventions of marking dates and times don't work anymore. But I'll do my best to record how they appeared when I first met them, and to record everything they told me. I'll try to leave some archival material for future generations.

That is—if there are any future generations.

MO XIN, ABOUT TWENTY-SEVEN YEARS OLD, METAMEDIA STREAMER

PEOPLE IN MY line of work were FastForward's first users.

Back then the FastForward had just been approved to go on the market, so the company was reaching out to lots of streamers to push their product. They launched a marketing campaign on every social media platform, targeting every audience group. I got the sense that they simply hadn't thought through how best to position their product, so they'd opted for the simplest strategy: pouring buckets of money into advertising.

I was ranked in the top twenty on BiJie.com in terms of site traffic, and my follower loyalty and conversion rates were pretty good, so my fees and stipulations were pretty demanding for potential brand partnerships. At first, I was a bit hesitant when their marketing rep reached out to me. I'd mainly done promotions in fashion and cosmetics, and those had little to do with the FastForward. But they told me that the FastForward would be the start of a new era, that it would set off a time revolution, that everyone everywhere would want to speed up. They were, therefore, hoping to leverage my influencer reach and elite status to kick off this revolution. I was quite flattered by this. Around that time I was also trying to expand and transform into a lifestyle brand—and the compensation they were offering was quite generous besides. So I said yes to a brand partnership.

Before their first time on the FastForward, every new user had to go to a FastForward Acceleration Center for a complimentary physical and equipment installation. The physical was very simple—they just measured your heart rate and blood pressure, and if they didn't flag any problems, then a store assistant would fit you with a headset.

The FastFoward involved the newest generation of semi-invasive brain-computer interface technology, known to be the safest possible prototype on the market. It was even safe for use by children and the elderly. The device looked like a small, delicate shell—you could customize its shape and color. It was installed behind the ear, corresponding to the location of your cerebellum. Stored within the shell was a small amount of T-42, a natural element extracted from rare meteorites. It was completely harmless to the human body, but it could, by speeding up neuron activity, increase a person's thinking and reaction speed within a unit of time, thereby increasing their efficiency.

All this I could rattle off with ease. I was a beauty streamer; I typically had to memorize even more details about the ingredients of cosmetic products I was promoting. I also knew that these ingredients and their supposed effects were just marketing phrases, something to boost the product's premium. In this regard, I thought the FastForward was pretty clever. They weren't just selling equipment, they were selling the necessary components and services. Think about it—this little toy was just like a skincare product. It could be used up, and therefore would need to be replenished. It wasn't like clothing or handbags. If a customer bought one, they weren't very likely to buy another, identical product. You had to keep designing newer versions. Everyone in this industry knew that to the average consumer, mid-to-high end skincare products had a lower entry threshold than clothing did, with strong customer loyalty and a high repurchase rate of the same product.

FastForward claimed that it could provide only a small amount of T-42 to each user every month. It was stored in the shell, and every time we needed to use the device, we would simply press down. The dose would be injected into our brains and start taking effect. It would only work for a set period of time; but when the period expired we could press it again immediately. However, when the T-42 ration was used up, we'd have to wait until the next month for a refill. Their reasoning made sense: they wanted to prevent customers from becoming addicted and misusing the product. The ingredients were so rare they were difficult to acquire, and the timely rationing would ensure the best experience ... Of course, I knew that all this was just to manufacture scarcity to justify higher prices.

I streamed my first visit to the clinic and my installation process on my Bijie.com channel. The total number of viewers reached fifty million. When my device was installed and I tried it out for the first time, the number of simultaneous online viewers exceeded thirty million.

I still remember the feeling of that first time. When I pressed the button on the shell, the live broadcast feedback I saw to my left suddenly slowed down. The netizens who'd been vigorously flooding my screen fell silent all at once, and it seemed to take forever for their comments to start reappearing one by one.

How does it feel? Has time sped up for you?

Xinxin's too cool, even high-tech products like these want to partner with her. Truly my idol!

The previous comment was wrong—from Xinxin's point of view, time should feel like it's slowed down.

God, finally caught up! I'm here to witness Xinxin making history!

A fan has sent a gift heart.

...

To the right of my display, I could see the viewer count steadily ticking up. A smile twitched across my mouth. I faced the holographic camera suspended in the air before me. "Thanks, everyone! I feel pretty good. Time indeed has slowed down. It's like I'm watching a movie in slow motion. Here's the store assistant helping me today. He's lifting his left hand very slowly right now, which is funny."

More sporadic comments popped up again in the left of my display.

Xinxin's talking so fast! Cuuuute

Cut the bullshit and give it to us straight—does that thing work?

Watch your language. Don't come into our Xin's channel if you're going to be rude.

The store assistant's hand had finally reached his head. He touched the shell behind his ear. Accordingly, his movements sped up to normal from my perspective.

"Miss Mo, may I ask if you're feeling all right?" he asked.

I nodded. "I'm fine. It just seemed like the world had suddenly slowed down."

"That's normal—it means that the product is working. Our experiments show that the FastForward can triple a user's perception of a unit of time. During this period of time, your efficiency also triples. Currently, one dose of T-42 works for an average of thirty minutes. When that runs out, your perception of time returns to normal."

I noticed that the broadcast duration counter to my right display was also ticking up three times slower than usual.

"This feels *amazing*. I recommend everyone try out the FastForward if you're eligible. I can already think of so many ways to use this. It's not just good for everyday work or study—you can also use it when you're playing video games and shooting monsters, or when you're running late getting ready, or if you ever get into an accident, or if you're in danger. If you use it at the right moment, this might even change your future. I have a discount code today, which I'll share with everyone..."

After that livestream, FastForward made over $100 million in sales.

And then? And then I myself became a loyal FastForward user. Who doesn't want to be more productive? By investing just a few thousand RMBs a month, I could get more work done in a single unit of time. I could create more content, draw in more fans, and earn more money. I got my value back for my investment.

At that time, my Bijie.com ranking rose by five spots—a whole five spots in half a year! I wouldn't have even dared to imagine that before. I immediately renewed my FastForward subscription for three years.

If Mandy hadn't noticed the wrinkles around my eyes, I probably would have kept using the FastForward forever.

That night, we were snuggled up on the couch watching a movie. By then I hadn't watched a movie on normal speed for a long time, and I thought the pacing was too slow. But Mandy liked it—she said that old movies deserved to be watched slowly. I forget what that movie was called; I remember only that it had to do with being in love and growing old.

As we watched, I fell asleep on Mandy's shoulder. I didn't wake up until the closing credits. I lifted my head and saw that her face was covered in tear tracks, with more tears spilling out the sides of her eyes. I reached out and wiped her face, and she turned towards me. The fluorescent lights from the TV screen reflected in her glistening tears, rendering her both pitiful and adorable. I wanted to kiss her.

She gazed back into my eyes. Suddenly, her expression changed. She turned on the light, wiped at her cheeks with the back of her hand, and grasped my chin to take a closer look at my face.

A few seconds later, she declared, "You've grown wrinkles!"

Mandy dragged me to a beauty salon for a skin test. The results indicated my skin indeed appeared two to three years older than it should have given my age. I'd prematurely developed wrinkles. Usually I pay a lot of attention to my skincare routine. I've never stayed up late, I only use the highest quality beauty products, and I never pull at my skin; I always rub it as gently as I can.

When she saw me and Mandy heatedly debating what had caused my wrinkles, the beauty technician asked, "Do you use the FastForward?"

I nodded.

"That's it, then." The technician had a knowing look on her face. "We've seen a lot of clients like you recently—their skin prematurely ages after they use the FastForward. They've sped up time, after all. Keep an eye on it, try to reduce how often you use it, and take extra care with your skin. We've recently developed a new protective cream for FastForward use—it can help slow the skin aging process. I can give you a sample today ..."

I bought the cream, but I stopped using the FastForward. At first, withdrawal was terribly painful. I felt sluggish at everything I did, and I was always fighting the impulse to press the empty space behind my ear. But Mandy was always by my side. Our relationship grew stronger and stronger. I also pivoted successfully to a career as a lifestyle influencer, which meant I didn't need to spend so much time every day selecting products to promote. The pace of my work slowed down, which meant of course my income also got smaller.

But I'd thought it through. At the end of the day, speeding up time meant also speeding up aging and death. Would you think that was worth it?

YAN DONGDONG, PERCUSSION INSTRUCTOR

It was during a rehearsal that I first noticed something wasn't right. That rehearsal left a very deep impression on me, because I rarely have such embarrassing moments.

I'd graduated from a conservatory with a concentration in percussion, and my grades were middling to low. After graduation, I became a teacher, and spent several years teaching percussion to children—mostly those who needed to pass their extracurricular music exams. After a while, I got increasingly bored with it, and I began missing performing on a stage. With a resume like mine, I couldn't imagine joining a premier orchestra—they only accepted top graduates. But after looking around for a while, I finally joined an amateur orchestra. There were about fifty musicians—it counted as a fairly small symphony orchestra—and I also quite liked their repertoire.

That day, I sat as usual at the back of the rehearsal hall, looking over the dark backs of everyone else's heads, closely following the conductor standing at the front. He wore a rather ill-fitting black suit that frayed at the elbows. His shirt ran up whenever he raised his hands, revealing his potbelly. It probably hadn't been tailored for this performance. Probably it was a suit left over from a wedding or something—a suit he'd been pulling out of the closet for years. It seemed serious and perfunctory both at once, just like everything else in this orchestra.

"One more time! With me—five, six, seven, eight!"

The conductor's hand moved, and the violin and viola began playing from the sixth measure where we'd left off. I counted the beats silently in my mind—*one, two, three, four; two, two, three, four.* They got faster, then faster. The clarinet joined in, matching their rushing rhythm, but the conductor seemed not to react at all. Anxious, I furrowed my brows. What was going on? The pacing had gotten out of control—why wasn't anyone yelling stop? *Seven, two, three, four, eight, two, three, four* ... my entrance was approaching. I lifted my mallets, counting down the bars to my approach. *Dong, dong dong, dong, dong. Dong, dong, pause, dong.*

"Stop, stop, stop!" The conductor made an impatient fist. "Bass drum, what's wrong with you? Why is your beat dragging? You're supposed to guide the rhythm of the entire piece—how is anyone supposed to play if you're going so slow?"

Everyone turned around to stare at me. My cheeks burned; I heard a sudden buzzing in my ears. I was the slow one? How could that be? I'd obviously come in at the speed on the score. I pulled up my score again, flipped to the beginning, and confirmed—*allegro moderato*, a moderately quick tempo, with a BPM of about 120. There was no mistake—120 quarter notes per minute. It was the other instruments that had gone too fast—their BPMs had increased to at least 180. They were playing at *presto*, really ...but how could this piece be played at *presto*?

"All right—we'll stop here for today, and get back to it when the bass drum has figured out what rhythm is. Remember—you're delaying everyone's progress, not just your own. Keep that in mind when you go home. I don't care if you studied at a conservatory or not—in my orchestra, all that matters is how well you can actually play. Dismissed!"

The conductor turned and left the rehearsal hall. Some players' holograms disappeared—they'd been attending rehearsal remotely. One by one, the others leaned over and began packing up their instruments. The strings went back into their cases; the brasses were cleaned of spit, and the woodwinds were broken down. I sat staring blankly ahead, trying to calm down.

I knew the conductor had a problem with me. He knew about my background, and when I'd first joined the group, he'd asked me out privately several times, insinuating that he could promote me directly to first chair. I'd declined. Later, he'd sent me several nonsensical drunk texts. I'd blocked him right away. Now I only ever saw his group notifications to the entire orchestra.

My friend Dong Xuan leaned over and whispered, "What's going on, Dongdong? Why do you keep messing up?"

She was first chair in the percussion section, and she was in charge of the snare drum for this piece. She was the only person in the orchestra I was close with. I had refused the conductor in the first place because I didn't want to steal her position—and it goes without saying that I had no interest whatsoever in the conductor himself.

I hesitated a moment, and then asked, "You think I'm

the one who messed up? You don't think they were going too fast?"

Dong Xuan's eyes widened. She reached out and felt my forehead. Her hand was cool to the touch. "Do you think you might be sick? Everyone else's rhythm was fine, it's just yours that was slow. Dongdong, is it because you're under a lot of pressure right now? Do you not have enough time to practice?"

"I—I suppose I'm a little busy." It was summer term just then, and I did indeed have a full schedule of classes to teach. I had no spare time to myself; it was hard enough to carve out time to show up to rehearsal.

"Have you ever thought about trying the FastForward? Lots of people are using it nowadays. Catching up on a report by the end of the month, packing for a business trip, finishing the boss's errands—people use it for all sorts of things. Me, I have time to exercise now—I'm really close to my weight loss goal! Why don't you give it a try? It's really popular right now, and it feels really cool to be one step ahead of time."

I shook my head. I knew about the FastForward. Some of my students' parents used it, but it was banned at school, so none of my students had it installed. In my profession, there's no point in speeding up time. Besides, it was too easy to destroy one's sense of rhythm, so I was never interested in trying it out. "No, it's okay. Relax, I'm fine. I've been beating these drums day in and day out. Maybe I'm having an off day. I'll go back and make some adjustments. I'm sure it'll be better next week."

"All right—we'll talk again after you've given it a try. I'll send you my referral link—you'll get a discount that way. Goodness, look at the time—I've got to run to my spin class. See you next Saturday!" Dong Xuan stuffed her mallets into a bag emblazoned with a gym logo and hurried out the door.

I blinked at the empty concert hall as, slowly, I packed

my things. My mind wandered to the past. At school, I'd been like this too. The percussionist was always the first to come in and the last to leave. We were situated at the far back of the orchestra. Most of the time we just waited. To the rest of the orchestra, it was like we didn't exist. But I liked it. I enjoyed surveying everything from the back of the stage, leading the rhythm. Some said that the percussion part was like a second conductor on stage; that everyone in the orchestra depended on the drums for the rhythm. When I'd first started studying the drums, I was also criticized by my teachers for dragging behind the beat, for my hands moving with uneven force, for my uneven triplets. Day after day, I slowly corrected these problems in practice, until I could play everything with assurance. I'm not sure I believed the conductor when he said I was slow, but I also didn't understand why even Dong Xuan thought everyone else was on beat.

When I got home that day, I turned on my metronome and set the BPM to 120. *Da, da, da, da.* The metronome sounded out a clear, even rhythm. *Da, da, da, da.* But the rhythm wasn't quite right—this beat was obviously too fast, approaching 180 more than 120. I examined the settings for a moment, but the needle was indeed pointing to 120. Was my metronome broken?

I turned on my holographic field, pulled up an online metronome, and set it to BPM 120. *Da, da, da, da.* I turned on my analog metronome. *Da, da, da, da.* The two rhythms matched up perfectly. The problem wasn't with my metronome—but that meant the problem could only be with me. I was greatly dismayed. I'd practiced for so many years—how could my sense of rhythm have degraded like this?

I had no choice but to practice some basic skills with the metronome. Right, left, right, left; left, right, left, right; right, right, left, left; left, left, right, right. A single beat, followed by a double beat. Right, left, right, right; left, right, left, left; left, right, right, left; right, left, left, right.

I practiced all sorts of combinations of compound beats. Then came the triple notes, the drum rolls, the crescendos, the diminuendos. I stopped for a break only after I'd stabilized my sense of rhythm. I'd broken out in a small sweat, and I was getting hungry.

Most of the time I cook for myself at home. Because I'm a percussionist, I can estimate time with great precision. If the recipe says I ought to stew something for three minutes, or stir-fry something for ten seconds, I can do it without a timer, and I'll never take something off the heat more than an eighth note late or early. All that to say, I'm a pretty good cook.

That night, and every night that following week, I burned the dishes again and again. Back then, I thought it was simply because I was distracted.

The next week, I went back to rehearse with the orchestra, played at the speed of that week's rehearsal, and once again was told I was too slow. But I knew very clearly—it couldn't be that I was too slow. During that week, I'd gotten up early every day and practiced for at least an hour—my speed was most certainly correct. But why would the conductor and other players all think I was too slow? Was it that I was indeed slow, or were they too fast?

Suddenly, a thought flashed through my mind like lightning. Everyone in the orchestra was playing too fast. My metronome was too fast. My food was getting burnt. Could it be that the world itself was speeding up? I shuddered at the thought, and the conductor's criticism seemed to fade into the distance.

The world had gotten faster, and was getting faster and faster all the time.

What happened afterwards proved me right.

WEI WEI, ABOUT FORTY-ONE YEARS OLD, CORPORATE SOCIAL RESPONSIBILITY CONSULTANT

FastForward contacted me after that incident.

Who wouldn't know about that incident? At that time, all of the major media and social media networks were abuzz about it, how a so-called completely harmless natural substance had a radioactive period, which affected not only the users' minds and bodies but also impacted their surroundings.

The mother was just an ordinary FastForward user. While she was trying to get pregnant, she hadn't stopped using the FastForward—if anything, she used it beyond the typical time restrictions. At her company, using the FastForward was an unspoken rule. After she became pregnant, though she herself stopped using the FastForward, she still went into work and was therefore exposed to the environmental radiation caused by her coworkers' use. She gave birth at just twenty-three weeks after a difficult labor. But the child didn't exhibit any of the health problems typical of premature babies; in fact it was as healthy as a fully mature infant. Its height and weight were about the same as a baby born at forty-three weeks. But the mother suffered a torn uterus during labor, resulting in heavy post-partum bleeding. Though the doctors did their best, ultimately they couldn't save her life.

The situation raised multiple angles of suspicion—the workplace conditions of pregnant women, employee exploitation, the doctors' failure to perform a C-section in time, etc. But most of the blame fell on the FastForward. There were three questions at play: first, how could that company have obtained excess FastForward rations for its employees? Second, how did the FastForward impact pregnant women and their babies? Third, how could the FastForward be radioactive?

Clearly, FastForward knew this was going to be a problem. They immediately put a press release expressing their deepest sympathies over the woman's death. They would donate a sum of money towards the newborn's care, and cooperate with internal and external bodies to conduct a thorough investigation as soon as possible.

Their crisis PR team did pretty well. They must have met overnight, discussed countermeasures, put together a list of names, contacted people, and formed their incident response team. They phoned me at four in the morning.

I had fifteen years of experience in CSR and ESG—that is Corporate Social Responsibility and Environmental, Social, and Corporate governance. At the start of my career, I'd worked in the procurement department of a factory, focusing on social responsibility in the construction and auditing of the supply chain. Later, I moved over to the sustainable development department of a foreign company, focusing on the impact of corporate production on vulnerable groups such as women and children, as well as the environment. Now, I worked as a CSR consultant. I helped companies build environmental, social, and corporate governance-related systems, issue CSR reports, and give the relevant training to their employees. There was no shortage of Fortune 500 companies and publicly listed companies on my client list, and I had the right CV besides, so it was no surprise that FastForward's people found me.

There were six people on the crisis management team. Aside from me, there was the Sustainability Department Manager, the Chief R&D Engineer, the PR Manager, the Sales Manager, and the Product Vice President of the entire company. Everyone was very professional, and our meetings proceeded smoothly. On the first day, we drew up a response plan, listed our various priorities and deadlines, and drew up a list of experts external to the company.

That evening, FastForward issued a second statement explaining that the company in question had been using a commercial version of the FastForward that was still in trial phase, designed to help employees increase their efficiency. Even if its usage exceeds the monthly designated rations, it should have still been harmless to users. In light of this incident, FastForward would temporarily suspend all trials of the commercial version, recall any commercial products on the market, and strongly recommend that companies avoid pressuring employees to use any version of FastForward while at work. Moreover, FastForward would set up a nonprofit foundation for public welfare and invite labor law experts to act as consultants to help defend the rights of employees who had suffered unfair treatment at work.

Obviously, this statement had been workshopped to death. What on earth was a commercial version of FastForward? And of course excessive use of the FastForward would have side effects. What's more, FastForward would never actually recall its product. FastForward and the dead woman's employer had made sure their stories matched—this was the least damaging rhetoric for both parties. As long as none of their employees spoke out, they wouldn't risk exposure. Of course, everyone was asked to sign non-disclosure agreements.

A few days later, FastForward put out a third statement. Due to current limitations in sample size and available data, and the lack of clinical trials, it was still impossible to confirm whether the use of the FastForward while the user was attempting to get pregnant would impact the health of the baby or the mother. The instructions "PROHIBITED DURING PREGNANCY AND BREASTFEEDING" would be prominently displayed on the FastForward's packaging, as well as the instruction booklet. Users were supposed to read carefully and use the FastForward as appropriate for their respective physical conditions. During follow-up physicals at FastForward clinics, a sales specialist would emphasize the risks of FastForward use during pregnancy. Moreover, FastForward would collaborate with several obstetrics and gynecology experts to establish a working group to care for the premature baby. They would closely monitor their physical condition, and care for them until they'd matured.

Announcing the FastForward's radioactive effect on time was a more difficult matter.

To begin with, this concept was still very new. T-42 was currently the only material in the world with "time radioactivity." Even scientists weren't quite in agreement about what this phrase entailed. But to the general public, it was broadly understood that "time radioactivity" meant that the substance didn't just affect the way the user-perceived time, but also the time perception of people and objects in the user's surrounding environment. The impact was not immediate, but rather lingered in human bodies and the environment over an extended period. What's more, the effect could accumulate. Time radioactivity did not only affect one's subjective or mental experience, but also had material effects—it would indeed actually speed up people's metabolic and aging processes.

One could almost say that the material T-42 had been invented by the scientists at FastForward. The meteorites from which it came had been on Earth for several years now. They'd fallen from some comet pulled onto Earth's surface as it passed by. During its descent, atmospheric friction transformed it into a rain of meteorites. Quite a lot of these meteorites made their way to Earth, and at first they hadn't aroused any special interest. But a member of the meteorite research team accidentally discovered that the meteorite could alter a person's perception of time, and thus resigned from his research institution to found the parent company of FastForward. He obtained all similar meteorites that were on the market, extracted the crucial substance T-42, and put it to commercial use. FastForward was only launched several years ago—the scientific community hadn't done nearly enough research on T-42.

Moreover, it was hard to even quantify time radiation. FastForward could precisely determine the user's perception of time acceleration while they were using the product, but they had no way of measuring the effect of time radiation. What was its range? What about the length and intensity of the exposure? All this data could only be obtained from observations on past users. After all, FastForward couldn't do human trials, and humans were the only species that could clearly perceive time.

In the end, FastForward had long known about the time radiation effects of T-42, but had deliberately concealed it from the public. There was no way we could spin this. One might say that what they were doing now was the human trial: a large-scale, unscreened, uncontrolled, human trial on a global scale.

This was where I started butting heads with the rest of the incident handling team.

They were all FastForward executives, so I could understand that all they wanted was to protect the company's long-term profits. But as a CSR consultant, my obligation was to guide companies towards sustainable development and actively take matters of social responsibility into consideration. Here, FastForward's position was quite firm: do not admit fault, do not apologize, and treat everything as rumors and conspiracies.

This was unacceptable to me.

I was most struck by the words of the chief R&D engineer: "T-42 fell to Earth in meteorites long ago, which means the effects of this so-called 'time radiation' also began long ago. We're only using it to benefit mankind in a fair and reasonable way. We've increased individual productivity rates and simultaneously sped up society's development as a whole. We've already successfully extracted even higher-grade T-42. In the future, we'll be able to put out new products that can speed up the user's time perception even more, letting them create more value in a shorter period of time. The whole world will enter a new era of time differentiation. If the masses panic at this critical juncture, the price will be unbearably high for all of human civilization."

All of human civilization? Were they joking? In the end, I resigned from the incident handling committee and invited them to hire someone more qualified. My NDA? Fuck that. The world was ending; what did I care?

Everyone inside FastForward had known for a long time that time radiation was real. Every time T-42 interacted with the environment, it emitted chrono-particles—essentially, a type of energy that increased the entropy in its environment, which thus created the acceleration effect. It was not the kind of thing that would dissolve naturally into the environment.

FastForward products had been on the market for eight years, with a total user base of six hundred million people, and a total sales volume of twenty-four billion monthly rations. How many chrono-particles had they released into the environment now? No one could say.

The impact of time radiation went far past anything I'd initially expected.

People have long begun to wonder: is time speeding up? Winter has gone, spring has come, and time keeps slipping suddenly away. You blink, and another year has passed.

It's real. It's happening.

Are other people speaking more quickly? Are you finding more gray hairs than before? Are your pets living a shorter lifespan than you expected? Do your cyber prosthetics need more frequent maintenance?

It's all real. It's all happening.

Time rushes past, sweeping everyone along like a great flood. If you can't keep up, you can only fall behind.

And that flood's destination?

Doomsday.

CEN XIAO, ABOUT THIRTY-FIVE YEARS OLD, ECOTOURISM GUIDE

The impact of time radiation wasn't only limited to humans.

I work in eco-tourism. All year round, we take groups into the wild and teach them about nature. These past few years, the changes to the environment have been quite noticeable. Plants are blooming earlier than they should be; insects are laying eggs earlier than they normally do, and the migratory patterns of birds and fish are all out of sync. Even the four seasons themselves have gotten shorter.

This has had a big impact on our work. We can no longer count on our years of experience—rather, finding a particular species in nature has become a game of chance. Even if we find something during an exploratory survey, there's no guarantee it will still be there the next time we bring in a group.

Some of my colleagues are partially to blame. In order to track, observe, and photograph wild animals, they sometimes used the FastForward. And the FastForward was so easy to use! All you had to do was press a button, and your movements and reflexes would become so much faster, which made tracking animals so much easier. New tour guides didn't have to go through painstaking training in basic observational skills or accumulate practical experience over time. All they needed was a quick crash course, and they could start leading tour groups right away. They could even catch frogs, butterflies, praying mantises, and the like with their bare hands, which delighted small children to no end (though this wasn't very good for teaching them about ecology.)

Our biggest problem was poachers. Using the FastForward, they doubled their efforts to hunt protected species, escaping after their exploits without a trace. I'd heard that in a wild bird sanctuary in a neighboring city, patrollers had found four different waves of poaching gangs in one day. They didn't interfere at all with one another. It was as if they'd made an agreement—they went wild poaching in their own designated territories, sweeping through like lightning. The wardens still didn't know how many birds were killed that day.

In order to deal with the poachers, patrollers and the

volunteers they'd recruited also had no choice but to use the FastForward to keep pace and rescue the animals before they were killed.

That meant a lot of humans had moved through those habitats by now, and the animals had long been exposed to time radiation. Gradually, their actions became faster and faster, which made them better at escaping from hunters. A new balance was found between humans and animals. Nature was like this—as long as it had time, it could always find a new equilibrium.

On the other hand, this only made our work harder. How were we supposed to track down animals affected by the FastForward without using the FastForward ourselves? Just thinking about it made my head hurt.

We get a lot of families on our eco-tourism outings, which means we meet a lot of little kids. They chirp and burble as we lead them about, like a flock of happy little birds. Their reflexes are generally faster than those of us tour guides, and they can never keep calm—it's hard to get them to quiet down and listen to our explanations. They're easily distracted by anything that flies by, runs by, hops by, digs by, or swims by. Sometimes they just get up and start chasing things, or plunge headfirst into the water without thinking. It's as if they're testing our ability to respond.

I always thought that kids nowadays were just like this. Times were different. And the kids were younger than us; more agile and faster to respond than we were. I thought this up until one encounter, when I met a very particular child.

That day I was leading an elementary school class on their spring outing. A little girl stood at the end of the line, and she walked more slowly than her classmates. Gradually, she lagged further and further behind the other kids. She didn't speak to them, and they ignored her. My partner was leading the team at the front, and I was overseeing the rear. The gap in the line was getting a bit unwieldy, so I tried having a chat with her.

I spotted some wiregrass at the side of the road and pointed it out. "Look—over there! Its leaves are long and thin, with a fringe branching out at the top. Do you know what that is?"

She wasn't shy at all. She stretched out her neck, stared for a moment, and declared, "It's goosegrass, isn't it? Haven't you seen goosegrass before?"

I was a bit startled. There were few children these days who could identify wild grasses. "Of course I've seen it. But I've never seen it here before. Are you familiar with this grass?"

"I'm from the village," she responded easily. "There's lots of them in the orchards."

"You're from the village? Me too. When I was a kid, I was always helping my family harvest rye. If I didn't harvest enough then my parents would scold me. And I was never allowed to play when I got out of school." While we spoke, I began walking a little faster, hoping that she would follow along.

Sure enough, she kept pace. "But that's normal, isn't it? I also have to help my brothers wash their clothes. Boy's clothes get so dirty, they're really hard to wash. And I have to make dinner, do the dishes, and boil water for washing our feet. Then after I'm done with all the housework I have to do homework. But I've always been the first in the class, and Teacher likes me the best." Abruptly she changed the topic; she seemed very proud of herself.

Just like that, we started chatting. I learned that her mother and father were working in the city, so she and her brothers were living under her grandmother's care. Her parents must have gone back to the village just to give birth—one child a year, three in a row. Then they went right back to work. I didn't know where they were employed, but I knew it definitely wasn't somewhere they could use the FastForward. The monthly fee of that thing was not low. Its consumers were mainly urban, white-collar workers and middle-class folks—the so-called elites and those striving to become elites. There were also people such as delivery cyclists who received their FastForward doses from their employers, stored directly in their helmets. They could only use it during work hours, and were strictly prohibited from private use.

This girl was only here because she'd won a scholarship opportunity to come to the city and participate in an exchange program. She was studying at the city's best elementary school for the semester. If she passed her final exams, then she could stay on to finish elementary school. This program was intended to give children from impoverished areas an opportunity to better their prospects through education. Her teacher had snuck her out while her grandmother was in the fields, otherwise her family would never have let her go. Who else would do the housework?

"I definitely want to stay here, otherwise when I go home Grandma will kill me," she told me. "And Teacher Liu went to all this trouble—she had to go to our house and apologize to Grandma."

"So do you like your new school?" I asked.

"Oh, yes! Here, the desks are big, the lights all work, and I'm so comfortable when I do my homework." Her eyes shone as she spoke.

"Do you like your new classmates?"

She blinked forward, cupped her hands around her lips, and leaned in close to whisper, "No."

"Why not?"

"They never settle down. They won't pay attention in class. They're always fidgeting like crazy, it makes it hard for me to pay attention."

I was surprised—she'd observed the same thing I had. I asked, "Is everyone like that?"

"Oh yes—and when they talk, they talk so fast. They won't even finish one sentence before they start another.

They're always gulping down their words. And the games they play are the same. All they want to do is see who's the fastest, but that's so boring! Every time I try to join in, they say I'm too slow. I'm not playing with them anymore."

"Do you have any friends here?"

"One or two. But they're in other classes. They're sort of like me. They came from the countryside. We talk and walk at pretty much the same speed, so we have more to say to each other. It feels like we're in a completely separate world from the city kids."

Her words gave me pause. In the past, wealth and capital were probably the main barriers separating two worlds, but today's barriers were made of time. It was very clear—this had everything to do with the influence of the FastForward. The differences were already evident between young children. Would their differences be exacerbated in the future? Would they cease to understand each others' languages and cultures? Even if they lived in the same physical space, would they still live in different dimensions of speed, without any communication between them?

Over the long process of biological evolution, different species had split across different dimensions of speed. Mayflies hatch and die in a single day. Cypress trees can live for thousands of years. As a species, humanity has already spent far too long living on the same time. Perhaps we were now witnessing the evolution of a new species. These children who had been affected by the FastForward were better adapted to the new, accelerated world. But what about those who had failed to accelerate? What paths were left to them?

◈

AFTER CHRONICLING THESE stories, my anxiety has eased a bit. No matter what happens, I've done my best. I was able to leave behind this written record. At the very least, this chronicle is a summation of my writing career.

Over the past dozen years or so, the world has changed dramatically. Because of the FastForward's popularity, the concentration of time radiation on Earth's environment has rapidly increased, accelerating the passage of time on an even larger scale. Those who actively embraced the acceleration technology stride ahead of time. They consume T-42, emit time radiation, create entropy, and keep sprinting at the fore. And as for those who refused acceleration technology—even if they stayed in place where they were, they were still passively carried forward, as if they were standing on a conveyor belt. The whole world's acceleration has become inevitable.

We all know what the end point of acceleration will look like: the heat death of the universe, the collapse of time. Everything will come to a halt. But there's nothing we can do to stop it coming. The accelerated ones think they have lots of time before doomsday arrives, which means there's lots they can do to prevent it. But all of their actions only speed up that day's arrival. For everyone in the slower dimensions, that day still approaches, and the only way to subjectively delay its arrival is to choose to join the others in speeding up.

Everyone I love has entered the accelerated world. I never saw them again; I lost them to another time. At times, I envy people like Mo Xin—at least she found a partner to slowly grow old with. I don't know if I have the courage to face doomsday alone. But I'm even less certain about whether I'm willing to give in and join the accelerated masses.

At the very least, it's not today. Not at this moment.

About our Contributors

Z. K. Abraham (she/her) is a writer and psychiatrist. She completed a Master's in Creative Writing with distinction from the University of Edinburgh. She has been published in *Clarkesworld, Fantasy Magazine, The Rumpus, Podcastle, Apparition Lit,* and more. She is represented by Carleen Geisler at ArtHouse Literary.

Ash Arya was born and raised in Delhi, India, where her love of fiction, mythology and history led her to pursue an MA in Literature. Now, she blends said love and education to create flawed characters navigating dilemmas—both ethical and emotional—in magical-but-imperfect worlds balanced on hope. As of now, her works have appeared in publications by Flame Tree Press and Tassavvur.

Sharang Biswas is a writer, artist, and award-winning game designer based in NYC. He has won IndieCade and IGDN awards for his games and has showcased interactive works at numerous galleries, museums, and festivals, including Pioneer Works in Brooklyn, the Institute of Contemporary Art in Philadelphia, and the Museum of the Moving Image in Queens. His writing has appeared in *Strange Horizons, Lightspeed, Fantasy, Baffling Magazine, Eurogamer, Dicebreaker, Unwinnable,* and more.

Nkone Chaka is a science fiction and fantasy writer from Lesotho. They hold a BA FA from the Michaelis School of Fine Art in Cape Town, and their work has appeared in *Fiyah Literary Magazine, Asimov's Science Fiction Magazine, Solarpunk Magazine,* among others. Despite not being a very good cook, a hearty meal and a long nap are among their favorite things to do on a weekend.

Eliza Chan is a Scottish-born speculative fiction author. Her Sunday Times bestselling debut novel *Fathomfolk* — inspired by mythology, East and Southeast Asian cities and diaspora feels — was published by Orbit in 2024. The sequel *Tideborn* will be published in 2025. Her short fiction has featured in *The Dark, Podcastle, Fantasy Magazine* and *The Best of British Fantasy.*

Kwame Sound Daniels is a black dyke poet and a traditional and fiber artist based out of Maryland. Xe are an Anaphora Arts Residency Fellow and an MFA candidate for Vermont College of Fine Arts. Xir first collection of poetry, *Light Spun,* was published in 2022 with Perennial Press. Xir second collection of poetry, *the pause and the breath,* was on Lambda Literary's Most Anticipated for January and came out in 2023 with Atmosphere Press. Kwame learns plant medicine, paints, and makes what can tentatively be called potions in xir spare time.

Maria Dong (she/her) is the author of *Liar, Dreamer, Thief* and *Psychopomp,* as well as a prolific writer of short fiction, articles, essays, and poetry. Her work is featured in dozens of publications, including *The Best American Science Fiction and Fantasy, Apex, Apparition, Augur, Fantasy, Fusion Fragment, Kaleidotrope, khōréō, Lightspeed,* and *Nightmare Magazine.* Maria lives in southwest Michigan in a centenarian saltbox house that is almost certainly haunted, watching K-dramas and drinking Bell's beer. She is represented by Amy Bishop at Trellis. She can also be reached via Bluesky @mariadongwrites.bsky.social or on her website, MariaDong.com.

Carson Faust is two-spirit and an enrolled member of the Edisto Natchez-Kusso Tribe of South Carolina. His debut novel, *When the Living Haunt the Dead,* is forthcoming.

Tessa Fisher is a post-doctoral researcher at the Steward Observatory at the University of Arizona, and possibly the world's only openly trans lesbian astrobiologist. A member of the Alien Earths NASA NExSS team, her research is largely focused on using advanced mathematics to develop better ways of detecting the presence of life and/or technology on exoplanets, based on their atmospheric composition. When she's not doing science, her hobbies include burlesque dancing, singing in the Phoenix Women's Chorus, yoga, and writing LGBTQ-positive science fiction and fantasy. Some of her short fiction has been published in *Fireside Magazine, Analog,* and *Baffling,* amongst other venues. She resides with her wife in Tempe, AZ, along with a fairly aloof bearded dragon.

S. M. Hallow is a speculative fiction author whose short stories have been nominated for the Pushcart Prize, Best of the Net, and Best Microfiction. Hallow's short stories have appeared in *Baffling Magazine, CatsCast, Seize the Press,* and *Taco Bell Quarterly,* among others. Hallow is represented by Laura Zats of Headwater Literary Management. Learn more at smhallow.com.

Ana Hurtado is a speculative fiction writer and a Clarion West 2022 alum. Her work has been published by *The Magazine of Fantasy & Science Fiction, Strange Horizons,* and *Uncanny Magazine,* among others. LeVar Burton read one of her stories for his podcast LeVar Burton Reads. You can find her via her website www.anahurtadowrites.com

Rebecca F. Kuang is the award-winning, #1 New York Times and #1 Sunday Times bestselling author of the Poppy War trilogy, *Babel: An Arcane History,* and *Yellowface.* She has an MPhil in Chinese Studies from Cambridge and an MSc in Contemporary Chinese Studies from Oxford; she is now pursuing a PhD in East Asian Languages and Literatures at Yale.

Sean Robinson lives in the Upper Valley of New Hampshire. You can find him on most social media @ Kesterian.

Tehnuka (www.tehnuka.dreamhosters.com) is an Eelam Tamil writer from Aotearoa New Zealand who calls on all of us to use our wonderful, unique minds and/or bodies in whatever way we can to refuse and resist the genocide of Palestinian people and the colonisation of Palestine. Resist with every breath and deed until Palestine is free—until we are all free.

Regina Kanyu Wang is a writer, researcher, and editor born in Shanghai and currently living in Oslo. She writes science fiction, nonfiction, and academic essays in both Chinese and English. She has been awarded multiple Chinese Nebula Awards and finalisted for Hugo and Locus Awards for her writing, editorial, or fannish works. She has published two story collections in Chinese, a novella in Italian, and a forthcoming story collection in German. Her stories can be found in *Clarkesworld*, *Galaxy's Edge*, and various anthologies like *Broken Stars*, *Sinopticon*, and *Best SF of the Year*. She has also co-edited *The Way Spring Arrives and Other Stories*, *New Voices in Chinese Science Fiction*, *The Routledge Handbook of The Wandering Earth*, the Chinese SF special issue of *Vector*, and the bilingual special issue of *Journey Planet* on Chinese Science Fiction and Space.

Story Acknowledgements

"Mama uat-ur" by Zebib K. Abraham originally appeared in *PodCastle*

"A Promise in Bronze" by Ash Arya originally appeared in *Lost Atlantis* (Flame Tree Press)

"The Birds I Pull" by Sharang Biswas originally appeared in *Tales & Feathers*

"Sentience" by Nkone Chaka originally appeared in *FIYAH*

"The Ng Yut Queen (The 五月 Queen)" by Eliza Chan originally appeared in *Worlds of Possibility*

"Baobab Lover" by Kwame Sound Daniels originally appeared in *Augur*

"Braid Me a Howling Tongue" by Maria Dong originally appeared in *Lightspeed*

"Eulogy for a Brother, Resurrected" by Carson Faust originally appeared in *Never Whistle at Night*

"Morning Star Blues" by Tessa Fisher originally appeared in *Rosalind's Siblings*

"Mandy and Lulu Welcome Walter" by S. M. Hallow originally appeared in *CatsCast*

"Parásito" by Ana Hurtado *Wilted Pages: An Anthology of Dark Academia*

"Three Nights in Orissa" by Sean Robinson originally appeared in *Prismatica*

"Please Mind the Poltergeist" by Tehnuka originally appeared in *Worlds of Possibility*

"A Record of Lost Time" by Regina Kanyu Wang (translated by Rebecca F. Kuang) originally appeared in *Lightspeed*

About the Editors

Darcie Little Badger is a Lipan Apache writer with a PhD in oceanography. Her critically acclaimed debut novel, *Elatsoe*, was featured in Time Magazine as one of the best 100 fantasy books of all time. *Elatsoe* also won the Locus award for Best First Novel and is a Nebula, Ignyte, and Lodestar finalist. Her second fantasy novel, *A Snake Falls to Earth*, received a Nebula Award, an Ignyte Award, and a Newbery Honor and is on the National Book Awards longlist. Darcie is married to a veterinarian named Taran.

Charles Payseur is an avid reader, writer, and reviewer of speculative fiction. His works have appeared in *The Best American Science Fiction and Fantasy*, *Lightspeed Magazine*, and *Beneath Ceaseless Skies*, among others, and many are included in his debut collection, *The Burning Day and Other Strange Stories* (Lethe Press 2021). He is the series editor of the Locus and Ignyte Award winning *We're Here: The Best Queer Speculative Fiction* (Neon Hemlock Press) and a multiple-time Hugo and Ignyte Award finalist for his work at Quick Sip Reviews. When not drunkenly discussing Goosebumps, X-Men comic books, and his cats on his Patreon (/quicksipreviews) and Twitter (@ClowderofTwo), he can probably found raising a beer with his husband, Matt, in their home in Eau Claire, Wisconsin.

About the Press

Neon Hemlock is a Washington, DC-based small press publishing speculative fiction, rad zines and queer chapbooks. Publishers Weekly once called us "the apex of queer speculative fiction publishing" and we're still beaming.

Learn more about us at neonhemlock.com.